Outstanding Praise for *Truly, Madly*

"Fun characters, sparkling prose, and a twisty plot add up to a great beginning for Valentine, Inc."
—*Publishers Weekly*

"Snappy and fresh—a delightful mix of intrigue and humor!"   —Jane Porter, author of *Mrs. Perfect* and *Easy on the Eyes*

"Lucy Valentine is as comic and romantic as her name implies, not to mention engaging, sexy, and smart. She has an otherworldly knack for finding lost objects, and will undoubtedly find her creator, Heather Webber, many new fans."   —Harley Jane Kozak, Agatha, Anthony and Macavity award-winning author of *A Date You Can't Refuse*

"With characters that sparkle like diamonds on the page, this is my new favorite Valentine! Heather Webber has created a bright new world, populated by quirky characters and brimming with non-stop action—I'm a fan!"
—Beth Harbison, *New York Times* bestselling author of *Shoe Addicts Anonymous* and *Hope in a Jar*

ST. MARTIN'S PAPERBACKS TITLES
BY HEATHER WEBBER

Truly, Madly

Deeply, Desperately

Deeply, Desperately

HEATHER WEBBER

St. Martin's Paperbacks

This is a work of fiction. All of the characters, organizations, and events portrayed in this novel are either products of the author's imagination or are used fictitiously.

DEEPLY, DESPERATELY

Copyright © 2010 by Heather Webber.
Excerpt from *Absolutely, Positively* copyright © 2010 by Heather Webber.

All rights reserved.

For information address St. Martin's Press, 175 Fifth Avenue, New York, NY 10010.

ISBN: 978-0-312-94614-2

Printed in the United States of America

St. Martin's Paperbacks edition / August 2010

St. Martin's Paperbacks are published by St. Martin's Press, 175 Fifth Avenue, New York, NY 10010.

10 9 8 7 6 5 4 3 2 1

To my family.

You've taught me what true love is all about.

Acknowledgments

My deep gratitude goes to Jacky Sach, who heard a proposal about a psychic matchmaker and thought it was a *great* idea; Jessica Faust, who made what could have been a difficult transition as easy as could be; Hope Dellon, whose amazing editing encourages me (and Lucy) to dream bigger; my St. Martin's family, including Laura Bourgeois, Anne Marie Tallberg, Matthew Shear, Ryann Gastwirth, Eileen Rothschild, Jennifer Enderlin (thank you, especially, for the titles), and everyone who had a hand in *Truly, Madly* and *Deeply, Desperately* going from manuscript to bookshelf; to my Massachusetts friends, who remind me of the little details when my memory falters; and to all the readers who have taken the time to tell me that You Love Lucy. Thank you all.

1

Justifiable homicide might be hard to prove, but my had-it-up-to-here brain was giving it a hearty stamp of approval as a reasonable defense.

Because if reporter Preston Bailey didn't stop peppering my client with annoying questions, I might have to strangle her.

And because that might be bad for business, I clasped my hands together to resist the urge. I looked across the conference table, trying to get Preston to shut up with a not-so-friendly glare.

She ignored it.

A month ago when the Lost Loves division of Valentine, Inc., my family's Boston-based matchmaking firm, was officially created, my office had undergone a subtle transformation. I opted to add a cherrywood conference table, downsizing my desk to a small corner unit. I liked the new look, which was usually all warm and cozy, but right now it felt more like a potential crime scene.

"And what's your favorite brand of underwear, Leo?" Preston was saying. Long blond hair had been piled atop her head in a messy knot, strands spiking out every which way. It was an edgy look Preston pulled off well, but would look like bedhead on me.

My client, Leo Epperson, who was eighty-three years old, glanced helplessly at me.

"Really?" I asked Preston. "Really? Underwear?"

"What?" Her razor-cut blond bangs puffed upward on a drawn-out sigh. "Lucy, everyone knows that your brand of underwear says a lot about your personality." She eyed me, narrowing her blue gaze. "I bet you're a Fruit of the Loom girl. Granny panties. Cotton. Maybe polyester. No. Definitely cotton."

Leo's sagging cheeks colored.

Justifiable. Homicide.

I shifted in my seat, suddenly uncomfortable in my—hah!—Victoria's Secret cotton undies. "I think Leo and I should have some time alone."

Preston's face paled. "What? No way. I need all the information I can get. Remember, Lucy, your father agreed to these articles. And so did Leo." She smiled at him, warm, friendly, and sincere.

I had to admit the smile did a lot to soften her angular features, dull the irritation of her presence. Preston worked as a reporter for the *South Shore Beacon,* a small newspaper with a low (and dropping) circulation. We'd met a month ago under some not-so-great circumstances and somehow—my (traitorous) father had a hand in it—she had talked me into doing an article on my role at Lost Loves.

My role being the finder of lost loves. As in, Lucy Valentine, Lost Love Locater. I liked the sound of it.

Sometimes good old-fashioned legwork was all it took to track a lost love. And other times . . . Other times I had to rely on my psychic ability, a gift that allowed me to find lost objects—and lost objects only.

That hadn't always been the case. Once upon a time I'd had the ability to see auras—like my father, world-renowned matchmaker Oscar Valentine, and all bloodline Valentines. It was a gift supposedly bestowed upon our family by Cupid himself centuries ago, but at fourteen my power to read auras had been zapped out of me by an electrical surge during a thunderstorm and my gift of finding lost objects had been zapped in.

For years I believed myself the black sheep of my family (which was saying something) because the success of my family's matchmaking business, Valentine, Inc., relied on pairing lovers by secretly matching the colors surrounding them. Feeling like a familial failure, I disavowed my trust fund and spent years jumping from one dead-end job to another until I realized that finding lost objects could be instrumental in finding long-lost loves . . .

Like Leo Epperson's lost love, a woman named Joanne Winston.

"I'm staying," Preston stated, obviously taking my silence as an unspoken dismissal.

If only it were that easy to get rid of her.

"All right," I said. "But no more questions."

She arched a thin eyebrow. "But—"

"No." Frankly, she was lucky I'd let her in the building. We didn't have a good history. And it hadn't gotten any better after she talked me into locating her long-lost boyfriend, only to tell me, once I found him, she had no interest in rekindling that particular relationship. She'd simply wanted to document the search for an article for the *Beacon*. The reunion might have been a bust, but the article had been a brilliant success, and because of it Preston and my father had agreed to extend the article into a series of pieces.

The publicity had been great—the phone at Valentine, Inc., had been ringing off the hook with potential clients. The downside was that Preston was around. A lot.

"Fine," she said, slumping back in her chair. She left her digital recorder running on the table.

"Is it still okay with you?" I asked Leo. "I know you agreed to have Preston chronicle the search for Joanne, but it's not too late to back out."

Please back out, please back out.

"No, no. She's fine."

"Thank you," Preston said, giving me a glare. She then turned to him and smiled, a hundred watts of pure charm.

Leo winked at her, but not in an icky Anna Nicole Smith/J. Howard Marshall kind of way. More like a co-conspirator, we're-in-this-together, leave-no-man-behind kind of way.

This meeting was going downhill fast.

Leo rubbed a gnarled arthritic finger on the tabletop. "Have you had any luck, Lucy? In finding Joanne?"

"A little bit," I said.

"Is that like being a little bit pregnant?" Preston asked, a grin pulling on her smug lips.

"I thought you were going to be quiet."

Preston addressed Leo. "Did I agree to be quiet?"

His face brightened at her attention. "Not that I recall, though you did agree to no more questions."

I gave her a so-there look.

She wouldn't let up. "You're not pregnant, are you, by any chance? That would be a great headline. A scoop like that could take me places."

Justifiable, my brain hummed.

"No," I squeezed out. But the word "pregnant" hung askew in my thoughts, reminding me of my grand-mother Dovie, who was on a quest to see me with child as soon as possible. Her motivations were purely selfish—she wanted a great-grandbaby.

"Pregnant" also reminded me of Sean Donahue, the sexy PI who was also now my business partner in the Lost Loves venture. Chemistry sizzled between us, but he was recovering from the breakup of a long-term relationship, and I had commitment issues stemming from Cupid's Curse, an ancient hex placed on my family that prevented any Valentine from finding his own perfect match.

It didn't bode well for my future with Sean.

So we were taking things slowly. Painfully so.

I didn't want to think about it, so I checked my watch. I was meeting Marisol, one of my two best friends, in a half hour for some sort of secret rendez-vous she wouldn't tell me anything about. "Be there or be square," she'd said. How could I possibly resist?

"Leo, you remember Sean Donahue, our in-house investigator?"

He nodded.

"Sean tracked Joanne to a residence in Lakeland, Florida," I said, trying to ignore that Preston was even in the room. "She lived there until three years ago, but from there she's disappeared."

Small and wiry, Leo was all of five five and weighed a hundred fifty pounds at most. Still sprightly, his face normally glowed with good health but was now wrinkled in concern.

Leo had come to me after hearing about Lost Loves through a friend of a friend who'd been matched by my father. Sean and I had been on the case for just over a week.

Leo had met Joanne Thomasino, now Joanne Winston, right after high school at a Cape Cod beach. They'd flirted, he asked her out, she agreed. Not six months later, at the end of 1943, Leo was on his way to the South Pacific to fight in World War II. Joanne promised to always wait for him.

His leg bounced. "You think she's dead, Ms. Valentine?"

"I honestly don't know, Leo. There's no death certificate. But there hasn't been any activity on her credit reports, either."

"Wouldn't that be rich," he said, flinging his hands in the air. "All this time she thought I was dead and now she might be."

"Oh, that's a good quote!" Preston leaned forward to check her recorder. "Can you say that again? Just in case?"

"Preston," I warned.

She released an exasperated sigh and pulled a notebook from her bag on the floor. " '. . . dead and now she might be,' " she murmured while she wrote. She waved her pencil. "Go on, go on."

It all spilled out. How Leo had been taken prisoner overseas, marched to a POW camp. Along the way, many of his buddies had been killed, dumped into a mass grave. Leo feared he eventually might be killed as well, and his body possibly never found. He didn't want his family to always wonder what had happened to him, so he'd taken his dog tags off and thrown them into the grave with his fallen comrades.

He sat in a POW camp for four years, well after the war ended, before finally being released. But the damage to his personal life had already been done. Two years before, the mass grave had been uncovered and his family had received a notice of his death. When he (surprise!) returned to the States, his family informed him that Joanne had married another after mourning her beloved Leo.

That other turned out to be Charles Winston. With him she had had one son, David. When Leo found out, he'd been devastated. It took time, but Leo eventually settled down. However, he never forgot about Joanne, especially after his wife passed away fifteen years ago. He'd been looking for Joanne since.

"What now?" he asked.

The sadness in his eyes tore at me. "We tried all the conventional methods. Now we try a little bit of the supernatural."

He nodded, leaning forward. "How does that work?"

"Oh, it's something," Preston interjected, leaning forward. "Have to admit, I thought it all hocus-pocus at first, but Lucy here is the real deal. You're in good hands."

I scanned her face, looking for any sign of sarcasm

beneath the unexpected compliments. Surprised, I found none. Well. Hmmph. Color me shocked. "Thank you," I murmured.

She tipped her head in acknowledgment.

I said to Leo, "All I'll do is hold your hand while you think of something you may have given Joanne."

"That's it?"

My abilities didn't come without rules. I could only locate inanimate objects. Not humans or pets. And I could only get a reading from the object's true owner. However, there were exceptions to my rules. Most notably, gift giving, when objects had two owners. In this case, I hoped it would lead Leo straight to Joanne.

"That's it. The trouble is, if she didn't keep whatever you gave her, then we're back to square one. Can you think of something?"

His eyes lit, sparkling. "My class ring. Gave it to her on our one-month dating anniversary. She cried."

Preston scribbled away. I tried to swallow over a sudden lump wedged against my windpipe. "Okay, let's try."

I reached out my hand. Tentatively, he laid his palm against mine. Images swirled as the room tilted. After a minute, I pulled away, fighting waves of dizziness.

"Does she have it?" Preston asked.

Leo's eyes widened with hope.

I shook my head. "I don't think so. I saw it in a store. Not a pawnshop, but more like an antiques shop."

He barked out a laugh. "Antique it is."

Preston laughed, a tinkly musical sound that didn't seem to fit her personality.

I smiled. "It's mixed in with a jar of buttons."

"So a dead end," he said.

I didn't like that term. "Anything else you gave her?"

He closed his eyes, thinking. "I don't know. I didn't have much back then. And Jo and I, well, we had to keep our relationship quiet for the most part because my parents didn't take a liking to her."

"Ooh," Preston mumbled, jotting notes.

"Why's that?" I asked, still trying to pretend she wasn't there.

"She was Catholic," he said, smiling. "They were stubborn about that sort of thing."

"That's so wrong." Preston shook her head. "People should have been more open-minded."

"We snuck around mostly." Amusement brightened his eyes. "Had ourselves our share of fun."

"You devil you," Preston said, poking him in the ribs with her elbow.

He loved the attention, blushing to the roots of his white hair.

I bit the inside of my cheek, wondering at the type of love that would last over sixty years. Amazing. I had to find her. Had. To. "Did you give her any clothes? Pictures? Books?"

He slumped in the chair. "I don't think there's anything else."

"There has to be!" Preston urged.

Looked like Ms. Professional Reporter had become emotionally involved in this article of hers.

"I'm sorry, Leo. We'll keep trying on our end. There has to be a trail somewhere."

"Surely you're not giving up," Preston said to me.

My phone vibrated in my pocket, an incoming text message. "No. I'll contact the antiques store about the jar of buttons."

Slowly, Leo stood and held out his hand. "Thanks, Ms. Valentine."

I didn't offer mine. "If you don't mind . . ."

He laughed. "Guess you had enough for today, eh?"

I was still a little dizzy from his reading. It always took a few minutes to shake off the lingering effects of a vision. "A little. But please call me if you think of anything else."

"Yeah," Preston said. "Call her."

He smiled, squinted at us. "You two aren't related, are you?"

We both snorted.

"Us?" I said. "No. What makes you think so?"

True enough, we were both blondes, though mine was more of a natural honey and hers was straight-from-the-bottle platinum, but that's where the similarities ended. I was five inches taller than her five foot three and probably a good forty pounds heavier, as I didn't think she weighed more than a hundred pounds. Her eyes were an inquisitive blue, mine were smoky amber. She had Kewpie-doll lips, while mine were wider, plumper. I had a long nose, a heart-shaped face, eyes that turned slightly downward. Her nose was up-turned, her face a perfect oval, and her eyes were just a hairsbreadth too close together.

"Just something," he said.

"Only child," I added, just for further clarification.

Preston shot a look at me I couldn't quite interpret, then quickly dropped her gaze to the ground.

Odd. Very, very odd. Where were her jaunty remarks? Her ribbing? It was unlike her not to take a stab at teasing me.

"Maybe it's just 'cause you squabble like siblings," Leo finally said.

Okay, the squabble thing I could see.

Leo crossed to the door, stopped, and looked back at us, a serious spark in his eye. His hands twisted nervously. "I loved my wife, Ms. Valentine, I really did. But my heart never let go of Joanne. I'm not getting any younger. If she's able and willing, I'd like my last days to be spent with her."

Throat tight and unable to say anything, I nodded.

Preston reached for her notebook, scribbled away as Leo turned left into the reception area at the end of the hall. My phone buzzed again.

"You gonna get that or do you like the vibration?" Preston tucked her notebook and pen into her bag. She hauled it onto her shoulder.

"You're very charming," I told her. I pulled out my phone, checked the message. It was from Marisol. RECON 1 PM. DONT BE LATE.

I was due to meet her downstairs in fifteen minutes, which didn't give me any time to run upstairs to SD Investigations to tell Sean about my meeting with Leo.

Preston blatantly read over my shoulder. I quickly cleared the screen.

"Recon, huh? Reconnaissance? Sounds exciting."

"Good-bye, Preston."

"Maybe I should come along? Is it for a client?"

"Good-bye, Preston."

My phone vibrated in my hand, an incoming call. I checked the ID screen—Aiden Holliday, a Massachusetts State Police detective lieutenant. Through him I'd become a police consultant helping to solve missing person cases—mostly cold cases but some current ones as well. Was there a new case?

Or did his call have something to do with the strange letters I'd been receiving?

I'd have to keep wondering. A conversation with Aiden wasn't something I wanted to have in front of Preston. I let the call go through to voice mail.

"Not going to answer?" she asked. "Rather rude of you."

"Good-bye, Preston."

She leaned against the doorjamb, smiling. "C'mon, you can tell me."

"What?" I asked, biting back a sigh.

"Fruit of the Loom, right?"

She must have seen the murderous look in my eyes because she quickly said, "I'm going, I'm going." Halfway down the hall, she looked back, over her shoulder. "But I'll be back."

I didn't need the reminder.

2

Thirty minutes later, I was reconnoitering with Marisol. I glanced around nervously as we tiptoed down the spacious corridor that linked four nearly identical loft-style condos. No one seemed to be around on a Wednesday afternoon, but we couldn't be too careful.

We didn't want any witnesses.

"'Twas two weeks before Christmas and all through the house—"

"Will you stop it?" I asked, my whisper harsh. "Someone will hear you."

9×6 is 54.

In times of stress, I turned to solving simple math problems in my head. For some reason it soothed my troubled mind like nothing else.

Marisol Valerius stopped short, and I bumped into her. Glancing up at me, she said, "Where's your holiday spirit?"

"You shouldn't be so giddy. I'm pretty sure breaking and entering is a felony."

"Lucy, Lucy," she tsked. Her brown eyes danced as she slid a key into the lock of unit 4A, twisting the knob and pushing open the door. "It's not breaking and entering if we have a key, now is it?"

"I'm pretty sure it is."

"Spoilsport."

"One of us has to be reasonable here." I quickly closed the door behind us while she disabled the beeping alarm, punching in the code we both knew by heart.

"You didn't have to come along." Her sleek black bob shone as she swung her head from side to side, taking in the living room.

I'd known her since we were three, had been best friends with her since the age of five. There was nothing I wouldn't do for her. "As if I had a choice."

"You could have stayed downstairs in the lobby."

"If Em finds out . . ." I said.

"She'll thank us."

After Marisol picked me up at the corner of Beacon and Charles, she dropped the bombshell: she was on a hunt for irrefutable evidence that Joseph Betancourt was a "cheating, slimy scuzball who needed to be exposed before the wedding."

Joseph, aka the cheating, slimy scuzball, was due to marry our best friend Emerson Baumbach on Valentine's Day.

"Look, just look," Marisol said in disgust.

Everything was neat, tidy. Hard not to be with the minimalist style. There was a streamlined L-shaped couch, a sculptured coffee table, two chrome chairs. Dark hardwood covered the floors. The fixtures were black and chrome. On the wall was a hideous piece of art I'd never seen before: all red squares, silver rectangles, oblong purples, and yellow circles with dots in the center. I squinted. Those circles looked a lot like breasts. And those oblongs . . . My eyes widened.

"What?" I pulled my gaze from the suggestive painting. Aside from exhibiting some seriously bad taste in art, the place was immaculate.

"It's two weeks till Christmas and there's not a Ho Ho Ho to be seen."

I opened my mouth. Marisol spun my way, a finger jabbing the air. "Don't even."

I blinked innocently. "What?"

"Make a comment about my love life."

She knew me too well. "I'd never!"

And she was right—there wasn't a single sign of Christmas. Cheery, I mused sardonically, thinking of my cottage, which looked as though Christmas had exploded inside. It was my favorite time of year.

"You would so."

"How *is* Butch these days?" I asked, following her into the sparkling kitchen, which was smothered in black granite and stainless steel. Butch was her latest boyfriend, a match made in a roundabout way by my grandmother, Dovie.

"He's fine."

"Uh-oh."

"The fact that he looks like Matt Damon is really the only thing he has going for him. We don't really have anything in common." Marisol closed one drawer, opened another. "Maybe I should make an appointment with your dad."

My father's matchmaking had a 98 percent success

rate. It was all in the auras. Every person carried with them an aura that is invisible to most people, but not to Valentines. And though we loved to play up the Cupid theory, truth was, the ability to read auras is a type of ESP—just like my ability to find lost objects.

But our clients didn't know about the auras. Neither did Marisol or Em. I could hardly imagine how they'd react. They were still getting used to the idea of me being psychic, something they'd learned only recently. And I couldn't tell them about my father's secret—the family had decided long ago never to tell anyone for fear of being labeled a fraud. Only a select few outsiders, like my father's longtime valet and family friend Raphael, knew. The Valentines simply wanted to make matches and . . . make a lot of money. It wasn't by luck that my father, the King of Love, was one of the richest men in the country. He loved being a minor celebrity, though a recent brush with the dark side of media attention had dampened his enthusiasm a bit.

"Are you really ready to settle down?" I couldn't see her married or with kids. Never mind owning a minivan, a complete set of Calphalon, or one of those enormous jungle gyms that could house a small family under its rock wall.

She opened kitchen drawers, shuffled through takeout menus. "Who said anything about settling? What's wrong with just having a companion? Shacking up, maybe?"

I should have known. Marisol was marriagephobic.

"Nothing, I suppose. But people do like to get married. Settle down." Softly, I added, "People like Em."

And me, though I didn't say it. I was fighting against Cupid's Curse as it was—making finding true love virtually impossible. There was certainly no need to tempt the fates as well. As of right now Sean and I were happy and taking it day by day. Did I want more? Absolutely. But I also knew better. Not a single Valentine marriage had ever survived Cupid's Curse—not even my parents', though they pretended otherwise in an effort to keep the public from finding out that the King of Love himself couldn't keep a marriage together.

Marisol pulled a notepad from the drawer. "No one would be more thrilled than me to see Em settled down and happy. But *he* isn't the man for her."

"He" being Joseph. Marisol never referred to him by name, simply because she had never—ever—liked him.

"I mean, look around," she continued. "There aren't even any Christmas cards out. Where's the tree? You know how Em likes a big tree."

They certainly had the ceiling height. Twelve, fourteen feet. "Maybe they haven't gotten around to getting one yet."

Marisol rolled her eyes. "When are *you* going to come around?"

"I'm thinking never. Joseph seems like a perfectly . . . fine man." He was no Sean Donahue, but I kept that to myself. "Em is happy. We should just tiptoe right back out that door and—"

"Em doesn't know happy. And I can't believe you're as blinded by him as she is."

I laid a hand on her arm. "But how do you know he's not good enough? Em's never said a bad word about him."

"Look, Lucy, do you ever just get a vibe? A feeling? Down deep?"

"Do you remember who you're talking to?"

"Okay, then. You should know. There's something just off. I can feel it." She held up the notepad. "There's a phone number indented." She found a pencil in one of the drawers and started coloring over the numbers—a trick straight out of a *Magnum, PI* rerun.

She was utterly and completely convinced that Joseph was up to no good. I could either walk away from all this, dismissing her gut feeling, or I could trust her—just like I asked people who didn't entirely understand my abilities to trust me.

Put like that, I really didn't have a choice in the matter. "Can you read the number?"

Pulling out her cell phone, she nodded and punched in the seven digits. She put the phone on speaker so I could hear.

A female voice said, "Spar, reservations."

Marisol didn't miss a beat. "Sorry, wrong number." She hung up and looked at me. "See?"

She did have a point. Spar was an ultratrendy bar in the Back Bay and known as one of the biggest meat markets around for up-and-comers. I didn't point out that Joseph probably took clients there—as an executive banker, he was out to impress potential business partners and a trip to Spar would be just the thing for a certain clientele.

"He's probably been out living it up while Em was working twenty-hour shifts at the hospital."

"But what about now?" I asked. Em had quit her job as a pediatric intern and was planning on going back to school for an early-education degree. "Em doesn't start classes until January. She's home all the time now."

Marisol strode into Em and Joseph's bedroom. I stopped at the door. There was no way I was going in. I looked around. Minimalist in there too, with only a bed and two nightstands. On Em's, there were two picture frames. One held a black-and-white engagement photo of her and Joseph, looking all demure and sophisticated. The other was a picture of Em, Marisol, and me, about seven years old, sitting on a beach blanket having just eaten red, white, and blue Popsicles. Our arms were linked so tight it looked as if we were never planning on letting go of each other. We were all grinning ear to ear, teeth missing, our lips smeared in red and blue. We hadn't a care in the world at that point, not really.

And now here Marisol and I were, breaking and entering Em's home. Something like this could cause a serious ripple in our friendship with Em—if she ever found out.

She could never find out.

"Sure, but she's so wrapped up in planning the wedding— Aha!"

Marisol came out of the bathroom, carrying a box of Trojans in the air like a trophy.

"I think we should go," I said, peeking over my shoulder. I was quite sure GUILTY was stamped all over my face.

"Hidden behind a stack of washcloths in his vanity."

I closed my eyes, counted to ten.

"Em's been on the pill since she was sixteen," Marisol pointed out.

I cracked open an eyelid. I'd forgotten. "Maybe they're old."

Marisol checked the expiration date. "Nope. New."

I hadn't even known condoms had an expiration date. I should probably learn things like that if I wanted to take my relationship with Sean to the next level. "Okay, so what now?"

"Now," she said, a wicked gleam in her eye, "we get serious."

As if breaking and entering and poking through your best friend's private life wasn't serious. Slightly afraid of the answer, I asked, "What do you have in mind?"

"Oh, you'll see, but I'm going to need your help."

3

Taking a deep breath, I raised the collar of my wool peacoat against the bitterly cold December gusts blowing through the streets of downtown Boston. Marisol had dropped me off at the corner, and I trudged, head down, against the cold, toward the Valentine, Inc., office.

The three-story brick building, sandwiched between similar brick buildings on touristy Beacon Street, had been owned by my family for years and years. The Porcupine, a small restaurant leased by Maggie Constantine, occupied the first floor; Valentine, Inc., the second; and the third floor was leased to Sam Donahue, Sean's brother. In the past, their private investigation company, SD Investigations, had provided discounted services to Valentine, Inc., in exchange for a break in the rent, and now Lost Loves was one of SD Investigation's biggest clients.

Beacon Street was crowded for three o'clock on a Wednesday afternoon. I noticed the shopping bags in people's gloved hands and winced. I'd been working so much I hadn't bought many Christmas presents yet.

I glanced in the windows of the Porcupine and

wasn't the least bit surprised to see Raphael inside manning the cash register. He'd recently begun to date Maggie, the Porcupine's feisty owner—a match nearly five years in the making. By the color of their auras, my father had known they were destined for each other but had bided his time until they figured it out for themselves.

Technically Raphael still worked as my father's right-hand man, but lately he'd been spending more and more time at the Porcupine, helping Maggie with day-to-day operations.

I pushed open the door, breathed in delicious scents of sautéing garlic and onion.

Raphael beamed when he saw me. "Uva! You're a sight for these old eyes." He came around the counter and wrapped me in a hug. Raphael gave the best hugs—and had been giving them to me since I was three years old.

After my parents secretly separated twenty-five years ago, my father had moved to his penthouse in Boston and hired Raphael to take care of his life . . . and me. Dad liked to swoop in to lavish me with love and praise, or lecture about impudence and attitude, but hated all the in-between. When I was little, board games bored him. Homework drove him to the liquor cabinet. And any talk of proms, boyfriends, makeup, or school events had him running for the door. He left that all to Raphael—who hadn't minded a bit.

"Hardly old, Pasa," I said, using my special nickname for him.

Raphael was on the shorter side of five ten, with crinkled olive skin, dark eyes, and salt-and-pepper hair, more pepper than salt. Recently he'd started grow-ing a mustache and beard, and I couldn't get over the change. I wasn't a fan of the look, but Maggie loved it.

My opinion lost out in that battle.

"Mmm-hmm. You wouldn't be biased, Uva?"

He'd been calling me "Uva," Spanish for grape, since the day he chaperoned one of my school field trips when I was five years old. I'd thrown a tantrum on the deck of the *Mayflower II* and turned as purple as a Concord grape. Not long after I began calling him "Pasa," Spanish for raisin.

Raphael had been part of my life for as long as I could remember. There were photos of us together making Play-Doh cookies when I was three, of him waving to me as I stepped on the school bus my first day of kindergarten (my mother was a firm believer in public education, much to my father's dismay), at my sixth grade, eighth grade, and high school gradu-ations. As best I could recall, he'd never missed an important event in my life. Not a single one.

I loved him more than I could ever express.

I sat at the lunch counter. "Hardly."

"Coffee?"

"I'd die for coffee." I couldn't feel my fingers. If this weather kept up, it was going to be the coldest winter on record.

He slid a mug over to me. "Leave the dying to us old folks."

"You're not old." I sipped at the coffee. Heaven.

"Sixty-one next birthday."

"I'll be sure to get an over-the-hill card."

He wrung a dishtowel.

I set my mug down. "You're not serious? Didn't you know sixty is the new forty?"

"Then what's forty? The new twenty? Either way, I'm still twenty years older than Maggie."

"Sixteen."

"Close enough."

"Is this about the beard?" I asked.

He glanced over his shoulder. "Don't you hate it?"

"More than anything."

He laughed. "Me too. Me too."

"So shave."

"But Maggie likes it."

I read between the lines. Maggie liked it, and he liked Maggie . . . "She liked you just fine without it."

"It does cover the wrinkles."

I stood up. "That's it. I'm leaving. You're not old. Or wrinkled. Or old."

"Come for dinner tonight?" he asked. "Your father just called and said he has last-minute plans. I have a whole pot of cacciatore simmering."

I scrunched my nose. "I'm supposed to be meeting Em and Marisol."

"Bring them."

"You sure?"

"Nothing would make me happier."

Or them. They loved Raphael almost as much as I did.

"Okay." I leaned across the counter and kissed his furry cheek. "Weren't you always the one telling me to never change who I was for someone else?"

He snapped the towel at me. "Get out of here, you. Throwing my words back at me."

I blew him a kiss as I opened the door, braced against the cold. I slid my key card through the lock of the nondescript door that opened into the stairwell leading to the upper floors. Beautiful cherrywood stairs shone in the late afternoon light filtering through the decorative windows overlooking the Public Garden. I didn't so much as pause at the second-floor landing, but headed straight up to the third floor to see Sean.

The reception desk was empty, as it usually was. Rumor was Sean and his brother Sam couldn't keep a receptionist on staff. Sam blamed their last full-timer, Rosalinda, a tiny wisp of a woman who apparently had ties to Santería. Word was that when she was fired for a little embezzlement, she placed a curse on whoever took over her job. All six women after her had quit for one reason or another.

As I knew a thing or two about curses, I hadn't laughed when Sean and Sam told me about it, but suggested they look into asking Rosalinda's forgiveness.

I think they thought I was kidding.

The scent of a Yankee candle filled the air, something strongly laced with berry. A hint of coffee tainted the smell, beckoning me to the coffeepot in the small utility kitchen off the hallway beyond the empty reception area.

For some reason I felt at home up here with the burnt-orange walls, thick area rugs, and masculine paintings. Maybe because I sensed Sean in the space. Though he spent a lot of time in my office now, this felt like his territory.

My hands full with a mug and my tote bag, I

stopped at the hallway console, looked into the mirror hanging on the wall. My hair, blond and unruly, fell well below my shoulders. I smoothed it down, hoping to control the waves. No luck. Unless I used a flatiron, my hair would always have a mind of its own. I plucked an eyelash off my cheek, wished on it.

When I opened my eyes, Sean was standing behind me. My heart did a little thumpity, thump, thump.

"What did you wish for?" he asked.

"Can't tell."

"Very secretive of you, Ms. Valentine."

It was a thing between us, using salutations with each other. For some reason I found it extremely sexy. But then again, everything about Sean was extremely sexy.

"Some things should be very closely guarded."

He crossed his arms over his chest. His black hair had grown out a bit, the short spikes I was used to now curling softly at the ends. "And exactly how am I going to get you to let your guard down?"

"There may be ways."

I took in his once-broken nose, his high cheekbones, his superhero jaw, his lips. I dropped my gaze. He wore charcoal-gray pants, black boots, black belt, a blue button-down shirt, the top two buttons open, the sleeves rolled. Under the collar, I could barely see the scar from his heart surgery.

He tapped his chin. "Chocolate?"

I crunched up my nose.

"Alcohol? Maybe some spiked eggnog?"

My mouth was impossibly dry. "Are you suggesting you get me drunk? And then what, Mr. Donahue?"

He smiled wickedly. His eyes promised things my libido had only dreamed of. My heart nearly stopped right there.

Very slowly, he said, "Some things should be very closely guarded." He boxed me against the console table. Our hearts raced against each other.

With the tip of his finger, he nudged my chin upward.

Sighing, I looked into his eyes.

A stunning pearly gray, they were filled with lust. I nearly crumbled.

I didn't know how much longer I could hold out. And right now, this very minute, I was having trouble remembering why I wanted to take things so slowly.

Lifting my lips to his, I flinched when something vibrated against my hip.

And right then I remembered why I'd wanted to take things slowly.

Cupid's Curse.

And it was at work.

"Is that you or me?" I asked, drawing back.

He mumbled under his breath about timing, and said, "Me." He pulled his BlackBerry from his pocket, checked the screen. Some of the color drained from his face as his eyebrows snapped into a concerned V shape.

"What is it?" I asked.

"Nothing." He tucked the phone back into his pocket without answering.

"Something."

He cupped my face, leaned in and kissed me until my toes curled inside my boots. I'd always thought that just a phrase—had never believed toes could curl. How wrong I'd been. And it made me wonder how else my body would react if it had his full and undivided attention.

I grew warm. Very warm.

Slowly, he pulled away.

"Good try, Mr. Donahue, but I'm not so easily distracted."

"No?"

We had an undeniable connection. His caresses, his skin on mine, even if we were simply sitting shoulder to shoulder, created a whirlpool of desire, pulling me closer to him, making me fall that much harder, when I knew better. It didn't help that his was the only hand I touched where I saw visions of things other than lost objects. When I touched him, I saw visions of us together in the future. Usually sexy in nature.

Those visions had always come true, but I'd yet to have one where I saw us having twenty-four hours of the best sex ever.

Unfortunately.

I was holding out serious hope that it was only a matter of time, when Sean said, "Then I guess I'll just have to try harder."

I was about to make a saucy comment about not needing it to be any harder, when he swooped in for a kiss that had me wriggling out of my coat, trying to undo the buttons on his shirt, and completely forgetting any definition of SLOW my brain might have stored away.

Sean's hand slid up under the hem of my sweater,

his fingers glancing over my stomach and cupping my breast.

Hot. Seriously hot in here.

I unwrapped my scarf, started peeling Sean's shirt down his arms.

His hand circled to my back and, with a flick, my bra was undone.

A voice in my head was screaming to stop, stop, stop, but it was quickly quieted by my libido shoving a rag in its mouth, duct-taping it for safe measure, and sticking the now muffled voice into a closet at the back of my head.

Finally. Maybe my wish would come true!

"Ahem."

The voice barely registered.

"Ahem!"

Sean slowly dragged his lips away from mine. We both turned.

Sam Donahue was leaning against the kitchen door frame, smirking. Funny, but he looked nothing like Sean with his light brown hair and dark blue eyes. The only thing they had in common was their height. Both stood just shy of six feet. "You've heard the phrase 'get a room'?"

Sean tugged down my sweater before turning his attention to his buttons. I picked up my coat from the floor and caught a glance of myself in the mirror. Beyond the fuss and muss of our almost-rendezvous, I couldn't help but notice my eyes. And the disappointment in them.

Sean said, "Aren't you supposed to be in court?"

"You wish," Sam answered.

I certainly did. Sam had no idea how much.

"Case was dismissed," he added, turning away. "I'll, ah, be in my office. Not that you two will need me."

As soon as he was out of earshot, Sean said, "So close."

I tried to keep the disappointment at bay. "Try, try again?"

He pushed a hand through his hair. "Doesn't it always feel like something's trying to keep us apart?"

"It's the Curse," I reminded him. I'd told him all about it after we started dating. He was one of the few who knew all the Valentine secrets.

"Honestly? I hadn't really believed you."

"And now?"

"I'm starting to believe."

"Welcome to my world." I reached around my back and fastened my bra. I swore I could hear that little voice in my head laughing in triumph.

"How was the meeting this morning?" he asked, tucking his shirt into his pants.

I bit back a sigh of longing when I spotted the trickle of hair leading from his belly button down below his waistband. "Good." I forced myself to look away. "Well, mostly. Preston *was* there." I filled him in. "The antiques shop where I saw the ring is in Falmouth. I'll make a trip down there tomorrow. You free?" Thursdays were usually quiet at both of our offices.

"I'll make some time."

I was suddenly thinking of all the quaint inns on

the Cape and how we could make a whole day—and night—out of the trip. Maybe a long weekend.

"Preston's not going, is she?" he asked, leading the way to his office.

"No." Hell no. My brow wrinkled.

"What?"

I sat in one of the two chairs in front of his pristine desk. "Something Preston said earlier is bothering me. Or didn't say, really." I told him all about Leo's comment about us being related, and Preston's strange reaction. "You don't think we look alike, do you?"

"No."

"I don't think so either." I wouldn't so much as consider the idea that we might be related somehow—too dangerous to my mental health. I needed to change the subject ASAP. "I need to borrow some toys."

He blinked, then a slow smile spread across his face. "What kind of toys?"

"Investi— Wait." My eyes widened. "What kind of toys are you talking about?"

"Oh, I don't know. Some things should be very closely guarded."

"Very, very secretive of you, Mr. Donahue."

"There are ways," he said, his voice husky, "of getting the information out of me."

The voice in my head had clearly busted out of the closet because it was screaming at me to get a grip. I cleared my throat. "I'll definitely keep that in mind. I'm in need of toys of the investigative variety. Cameras, video recorders, bugs, wires, night vision goggles. Those sorts of things."

"Toys?" He was offended.

"What would you call them?"

"Equipment."

"Ah. So noted. Can I borrow your equipment?"

"Why?"

"Marisol."

"That's all you're giving me?"

"That should explain it all." I glanced at my watch, reluctantly stood. "Can I pick up the *equipment* in the morning?"

"I'll see what I can find."

I didn't dare go around the desk and kiss him good-bye. I only had ten minutes before a meeting with a potential client.

And what I had in mind with Sean would take much longer than ten minutes.

As I headed back downstairs, I suddenly remembered the call he'd gotten and realized that maybe I was easily distracted after all.

4

"She's dead." Detective Lieutenant Aiden Holliday shoved an expandable file folder across my father's kitchen island. His usual Marine-like shorn blond hair had grown out into something resembling a Chia Pet. His blue eyes were bloodshot. Scraggly reddish-blond stubble covered his cheeks, his chin. He looked as though he hadn't had a decent night's sleep in a week.

The "she" in question was Sarah Loehman. "If this is a homicide case, then why come to me? I only work with missing persons." I released the elastic around the folder's clasp and peeked inside at the thick mass of papers.

Raphael was stirring a giant pot of cacciatore and pretending not to eavesdrop. I knew him better than that.

Marisol and Em were supposed to meet me here in twenty minutes for our once-weekly dinner. How Marisol and I were going to keep our mid-afternoon snooping from Em I didn't know. I just hoped I wouldn't accidentally blurt out something. Like the fact that Joseph had a box of condoms hidden behind the washcloths or a comment on the new sexual artwork. Those sorts of revelations could be a bit awkward to explain.

Raphael set a plate of steaming linguine smothered in cacciatore in front of Aiden, who glanced up. "But—"

"Don't bother to argue." I handed him a napkin. "Just say thanks."

I'd finally reached Aiden after meeting with my last client of the day. He had a case he wanted me to look at and, as he happened to be going to a Celtics game tonight, I asked him to meet me here before tip-off.

"Th-anks," Aiden said, still bewildered. He cautiously picked up a fork. Raphael nodded, silently urging him to dig in.

I took a second to admire the stunning view beyond the floor-to-ceiling living room windows. Under bright moonlight, Boston Harbor swayed, small crests crashing atop each other, bright white smudges in a sea of black. Along the opposite shore lights twinkled.

My father had moved to this penthouse in the exclusive Waterfront District when he and my mother separated, twenty-five years ago. It was as much a home-away-from-home to me as my mother's place in Cohasset.

Aiden said, "Aren't you eating, Lucy?"

"In a little bit. Go ahead without me."

"Wine?" Raphael asked, poised to pour into the long-stemmed glass that he'd just set on the counter.

Aiden said, "Thanks."

Obviously a fast learner.

"My pleasure." Raphael retrieved another glass, poured Pichon Lalande to the rim. He slid it in front of me.

He knew me well too.

"Technically the case is missing persons," Aiden clarified between bites, picking up our conversation. He pointed with his fork at the plate of cacciatore. "This is really good."

Raphael beamed with pride and turned to wipe down a counter.

I flipped through the papers in the file while Aiden ate. "Why technically?"

"Scott Loehman's a cop. He knows the ins and outs of law enforcement. He knows how to cover his tracks."

"Why don't you start from the beginning?" I asked, nursing my wine. A dull ache pulsated behind my right temple. It had been a long day.

He twirled his fork, dragging linguine through a river of sauce. "Sarah Loehman, age twenty-one, disappeared from her middle-class Rockland home on June twenty-second, two years ago. Her kids, one and three, were at a neighbor's house. When the kids were to be dropped off, no one was home."

I pulled a picture of Sarah from the file. Short dark hair framed her face. Brown eyes with long inky lashes dominated her features, and a pout pulled at the corners of her lips. She landed somewhere in between cute and beautiful. A smile could easily push her over to stunning.

I vaguely remembered the case—young missing

mothers tended to dominate the news. Throw in a cop as a husband, and the media sank their eyeteeth into the story. Her abandoned car had been found in a CVS parking lot, her purse inside, her wallet missing. Theories of robbery or carjacking abounded, but nothing ever came of them.

Essentially, she'd disappeared without a trace.

Her husband Scott had been named a person of interest in the disappearance, but due to a lack of evidence and no body, charges had never been filed.

"Is he still a cop?" I asked.

Aiden swirled his wine. "Yeah. Was put on paid leave when she disappeared but the department had to let him back on the streets eventually."

"Did he have an alibi for when she disappeared?"

"Said he was boating with some friends. Time frame is fuzzy. Nothing could ever be nailed down a hundred percent."

"How did Scott take the news that she'd disappeared?"

These questions were merely formalities. I didn't need background on the case; all I needed was to touch the palm of someone who'd given Sarah a gift that she might still have on her—or on her skeleton. However, I liked to know the history before I signed on.

"Big, fat crocodile tears, the cradle robber. She was only eighteen when they married."

"How old was he?"

"Twenty-four."

A plane descended into view, coming in for a landing at Logan. "You think he did it."

He didn't disagree. "There were whispers that the kids had been abused. A bruise here, a broken arm there. Nothing ever substantiated."

"And he currently has custody?"

"Like I said, nothing was proven. Nothing the courts could do, even though Sarah's mother fought for the kids." His lips twisted into a frown. "Scott's being careful now, the perfect dad."

"Raphael!" My father's voice preceded him down the stairs. "These damn cuff links. Oh," he said, stopping short. "I didn't know we already had company."

Oscar Valentine was nothing if not debonair, and tonight he fit the role to a T. Dark Armani suit, pristine white shirt, silk tie. Dark brown eyes, dark hair. Strong chin, chiseled cheeks, full lips. He was like something off a 1940s movie poster.

It wasn't too long ago that he'd had a heart attack, but tonight he showed no signs of lingering health problems. He looked smooth, suave, sophisticated. Like always.

He kissed my cheeks. Aiden rose and held out a hand. My father looked at him for a long moment while he shook. I knew that look. My father was making a match.

I held out my hand for the cuff links. Dad placed them in my palm. "When will the girls be arriving?" he asked.

"Five minutes."

"Girls?" Aiden asked.

I pushed the cuff link through the slit in my father's cuff. "Marisol and Em are coming for dinner."

"I didn't know." Aiden pushed away his empty plate.

I hadn't wanted to tell him. I knew how he felt about Em and had hoped he'd be gone before she arrived.

"Have you met the girls?" my father asked him, an arch to his left eyebrow.

"A few times," Aiden said. He'd turned a pale shade of red.

To take the pressure off, I asked my dad, "Where are you off to tonight all gussied up?"

"L'Espalier."

"Ooh, la, la. With Mum?" I already knew the answer, but I liked to watch him squirm once in a while.

He adjusted his tie. "Er, no."

"Anyone I know?"

His face darkened. "No. No one you know."

"You're being quite mysterious."

"And you're being nosy."

I flinched at his tone. It was unlike him to be so curt, so hard.

"I'm sorry," he said. "I'm just a little . . . stressed."

I wondered if "stressed" was a euphemism for something else, like, oh, randy. One didn't go to L'Espalier without romance on the mind. He had been behaving himself lately, ever since the media storm, but I imagined all that celibacy could cause a little stress.

I should know.

But . . . there was something in his face, a pinch that had me worried. "Are you feeling okay?"

"Fabulous," he said, the pinch gone just as fast as it had appeared.

"Did you at least get a private room?" I asked, recalling the field day the local papers had had after my father had a heart attack on a Marblehead beach—sans pants and with a woman who wasn't my mother. The King of Love having an affair? It trumped all other news. If the media had an inkling that he was back on the prowl . . . I didn't even want to see those headlines or how they might affect the family business. As far as the public knew, my parents were happily married, and though there were stories of infidelity, there were still those foolish enough not to believe them.

"Lucy Juliet."

His tone was lighter. More like I was used to.

He straightened the cuff of his jacket. "That's none of your business."

"I beg to differ."

"Impertinence. You get that from your mother."

"Of course I do."

According to my father, all my bad qualities came from my mother.

Raphael chuckled.

My father scowled at him.

It only made Raphael laugh harder. "Refill?" he asked me.

I nodded and he poured.

"Have you seen my billfold, Raphael?" my father asked.

"No, but I'll help look." Raphael set the wine bottle in front of me (I loved that man) and followed my father upstairs.

Aiden leaned in. "Why didn't he just ask you where it was?"

"He doesn't like to abuse my powers more than necessary."

"What's necessary?"

"Oh, more than a dozen times a week. He's already at his limit." I took a sip of wine. "I'll help him if I have to."

Aiden waited a beat, then said, "So, Sarah . . . ?"

I knew immediately what he was referring to. He had a one-track mind when it came to work.

"I'll do a reading."

"Great. I'll get in touch with Sarah's mother. Have her call you. She said something about giving Sarah an ankle bracelet. You can probably get a vibe from that."

I couldn't help but smile. His belief in my abilities had come a long way. Miles.

"I'll do what I can."

"I appreciate it. I should go or I'll miss the national anthem."

I knew he wasn't in a hurry to hear the national anthem. He was in a hurry to get out of here before Em arrived. There was no mistaking the crush he had on her—or how crushed he'd been to learn of her engagement.

"Before you go . . ." I began.

He pulled on a fleece coat. "What's on your mind?"

"The letters?"

The muscles in his face hardened. "Nothing yet, Lucy. Waiting on the crime lab. Did you get another one?"

I shook my head. "Do you think the threats are real?"

"No telling, Lucy. Just be careful, okay? The guy is going to slip up sooner or later."

I nodded, but Aiden's reassurance brought me little comfort. Staying busy would help. And now that I had Sarah Loehman's case along with Leo's . . . maybe I could forget about the letters altogether.

"I'm going to keep this file, okay?" I flipped through the paperwork on Sarah Loehman and tried not to think about a potential stalker.

"It's yours."

I jumped at a knock on the front door. Marisol sailed in. "Oh my God. Wine. Good stuff too. I love Raphael."

Em stood near the marble console table, frozen as if her feet had been cemented to the floor. Her gaze had landed squarely on Aiden.

Aiden stared at her with wide blue eyes.

It didn't take a psychic to see how he felt.

"I, ah, was just leaving," he said.

"You don't have to go." Em set down her handbag and hung her coat on the rack.

Marisol elbowed me, eyebrows raised and waggling. I could practically read her mind about how Aiden could be a great tool in getting rid of Joseph.

No way. Uh-uh. That was much too risky.

Color rose along Em's neck. She raised her hand to her throat as if trying to keep the heat in check. There was no missing the giant rock on her ring finger.

Aiden stammered. "S-sorry, but I can't stay. I have, ah, the national anthem . . ." He glanced around like a caged animal. "Tell Raphael I said thanks."

He made his escape before any of us could get a word out.

"That was interesting," Marisol said, taking his vacated stool after grabbing a wine glass.

"What was?" Em slid onto the stool on my other side.

"Come on, you'd have to be blind not to see it."

"See what?" Em said, finding great interest in the tines of a fork.

"The way he looked at you! I want a guy to look at me like that."

"You're seeing things," she said.

Marisol gaped at me. "Lucy, tell her."

Em tipped her head, waiting. The three of us had been friends for so long, there was little we didn't share with each other, including our love lives. But this . . . this flirtation between Em and Aiden . . . it wasn't something I wanted to delve into. I was already feeling guilty for breaking and entering into her private life. "I didn't see anything." I sipped my wine.

"Lucy!" Marisol cried, her dark bob swaying. "How could you?"

"How's Butch?" Em asked Marisol, blatantly trying to turn the tables.

Butch, Marisol's latest boyfriend, also happened to be Aiden's roommate. I could imagine the phone call he'd be getting tonight. Would Marisol be able to rope him into her plans?

Undoubtedly. She had that effect on men.

"All right," Marisol said.

"Just all right?" Em asked.

I kept silent, already having had this conversation today. I poured myself another glass of wine and filled a glass for Em too.

"Why don't you break up with him?" Em asked.

"He looks just like Matt Damon!"

I laughed. Marisol cracked a smile. Em shook her head.

"I know I ought to end it," Marisol whined, "but Christmas is coming up. I hate being alone at Christmas."

No one liked being alone during the holidays, and with Valentine's Day fast approaching, my father would be working long hours to match lovers. This was one of the busiest times of the year for Valentine, Inc.

I knew I'd spent far too many holidays alone. This year would be different. I had Sean. And maybe, finally, our relationship would move out of slow motion and creep into something less torturous.

"It's no reason to stay with someone," Em lectured, her red hair tamed into a ponytail that snaked over one shoulder.

"And what is?" Marisol countered. "Comfort and familiarity? Like you and Joseph?"

I gaped, shocked. Not because she'd asked the question, but because she'd actually said his name.

Em sputtered. "What are you trying to say, Marisol?"

Marisol pushed her glass back and forth across the quartz countertop. Soft wrinkles burrowed on her forehead, her expression serious. Softly, she said, "Have you gotten your Christmas tree yet?"

I refilled all our wine glasses and looked around for another bottle. It was going to be that kind of night.

"Not yet," Em admitted.

"Why not?" Marisol pressed.

"Joseph's been working long hours."

Marisol raised her eyebrows.

"And not just him," Em added. "I've been working hard on the wedding now that my mother isn't talking to me."

Em's mother had been outraged when her daughter gave up her M.D. to teach five-year-olds, which, according to her, was "beneath a Baumbach."

"They're saying they won't pay for the wedding"—Em sipped her wine—"and are threatening to cut me off altogether."

Marisol gasped. "They can't do that."

"They can," Em said. "I've had to contact almost all the vendors and cancel. It's like starting all over again. My budget is shot."

I felt the color drain from my face. Em's wedding was an elaborate affair her mother had orchestrated. The price tag had been well over half a million dollars.

"What's Joseph say about all this?" I asked.

"He's not too happy about the money."

"That's because he's cheap," Marisol said, sniffing the air. "I'm starving."

"He's not cheap," Em countered. "He's . . . frugal."

Marisol squawked like a chicken, "Cheap, cheap, cheap."

I stood, wobbled a little—I should cut back on the wine—and gathered three plates from the cabinet.

Em glanced at me, desperation tingeing the blue in her eyes. "Is there more wine?"

I grabbed a bottle from the rack, used Raphael's fancy corkscrew, and poured.

Secretly, I had to agree with Marisol. I was under the suspicion that the minimalist design in Em and Joseph's condo had nothing to do with style and everything to do with dollar signs.

I pictured him finding out that he had to foot the bill for his wedding *and* help pay for Em to go back to school while she was bringing in no income . . .

My smile fizzled.

Considering how cheap he was, he must really love her. A pang of guilt swept through me.

Shit. What had I gotten myself into, agreeing to Marisol's crazy plan?

Em sighed. "I really do want a Christmas tree. I found the sweetest angel topper at the Christmas Tree Shop in Pembroke."

Marisol jumped up. "Then we should go get one."

"Now?" I asked, scooping pasta.

"Right now," Marisol said, checking the thin gold watch on her wrist. "I'm working the graveyard tonight."

Marisol, a vet, volunteered hours at a local animal hospital downtown at night and worked during the day at a vet clinic in Quincy. I suspected it wouldn't be long before she had her own office.

Em's eyes brightened. "Really?"

I put the plate down, glanced at Marisol, and couldn't say no when I saw the softness in her eyes. "Okay, I'm in."

Em let out a little happy squeal. It was the most animated I'd seen her in a while. Maybe Marisol was right. Em *wasn't* happy with Joseph.

Em slid off her stool. "I'm going to run to the washroom—be right back."

As soon as the door to the guest bath clicked closed, Marisol said, "Did you get the stuff?"

"Tomorrow morning."

She rubbed her hands together. "I can't wait."

"Look, I don't think—"

My objection was interrupted by the sound of feet on the stairs. My father and Raphael were discussing facial hair.

I tried not to groan.

"Good evening, Marisol," Dad said, kissing her cheek.

Marisol let out a wolf whistle.

My father soaked it in, even did a little twirl for her.

Em emerged from the bathroom, still beaming. "I'm going to get a Christmas tree."

Dad kissed her cheek. "How lovely."

"You look spiffy," she said, fussing with his lapels.

He looked over her head at me with an expression that clearly asked how much we'd had to drink.

I held up two fingers to signal just a little.

Then his gaze narrowed on the empty wine bottle.

That's what I got for not recycling.

"A fancy date with Judie?" Em asked, slipping on her coat.

"Um, er, no," my father answered Em.

"No?"

"No."

"Back to reality?" she asked him.

I couldn't help the smile. He and Mum had been faking it all over town these last few weeks, trying to keep up the image of a happily married couple. Last I heard, they were both ready to strangle each other.

Dad looked at me. "She's impertinent too."

"Does *she* get it from Mum?"

"Of course."

"You're going *now*?" Raphael asked us.

"A tree must be got," Marisol said to Raphael, kissing his cheeks. "No time to waste."

"Rain check?" I asked him, my head spinning a bit as I tried to keep up with the conversations.

"I'll hold you to it, Uva."

I wrapped my scarf around my neck as Raphael held open the door for us. Em and Marisol were giggling as they called for the elevator.

"Lucy?" my father said. "A moment?"

I stepped back inside and had another pang of guilt as I saw Raphael ladling cacciatore into Tupperware. "Something wrong?"

"Depends."

"On?"

"Em? She's due to be married soon, correct?"

Dad had yet to meet the elusive Joseph. "Not if Marisol has her way."

"Ah. She still doesn't care for him?"

I shook my head.

He retrieved a long coat and a silk scarf from the closet. "Well, Lucy, she may be on to something."

"Why do you say that?"

"Your friend Aiden?" He looped the white scarf around his neck, making him look even more dashing.

"Yeah?" Woozy, I leaned against the door frame.

"And Em?"

I was desperately trying to follow along. "Yeah?"

"Their auras are a perfect match."

5

It was late. By the time Em, Marisol, and I bought a tree and dragged it back to Em's place to decorate, I'd missed the last commuter train out of the city and had to take a very long, very expensive taxi ride to the train station in Cohasset. I'd had to scrape ice from my windshield in the parking lot, but thankfully home was only a few minutes away.

My brand-new GPS unit glowed in the darkness of the car, its soft light comforting even though I didn't need the system right now—I knew these roads like the back of my hand. However, I foresaw a lot of traveling with Lost Loves, and the GPS would come in handy once business took off.

I carefully navigated the narrow lanes leading to Aerie, Dovie's cliffside estate. Bare branches hovered over two copper mailboxes standing side by side along a small half-moon dirt turnoff just before Aerie's drive. I checked my rearview mirror to make sure I hadn't been followed (all clear), pulled up to the second box, reached in and scooped out a stack of mail.

Setting the pile on the passenger seat, I cut the wheel sharply, turning between two stacked stone columns. To my right, a wooden sign that read AERIE in elegant script glowed from a hidden up-light. Graceful garden lanterns lined the sides of the lane, guiding me up the sloped, twisting gravel driveway. Around a bend, Dovie's house suddenly appeared as if by magic, a sprawling classic century-old New England estate, complete with weathered shingles, gorgeous slate roof, juts, jogs, angles, and utter elegance. It was decked out in sedate white Christmas lights, twinkling happily.

Forgoing her three-car garage, I veered to the right, off the main drive. A crushed shell lane led down to home sweet home.

The one-bedroom guest cottage, shingle style in design, was almost all windows, mostly arched. A narrow wraparound front porch with wooden archways curved around the foundation. Throw in the antique front door, stone steps, and attic dormer, and charm oozed from its rafters.

Colorful Christmas lights dripped from the edges of the eaves, wrapped the columns on the front porch, and adorned the dormers, door frame, and windows.

A brisk, icy breeze blew off the ocean, swept across the yard. A fieldstone path led to the porch, flanked on each side by a short boxwood hedge. In the warmer months, flowering annuals would color the way to my door. I turned up my collar, slipped the key in the lock, and turned the dead bolt.

The circles on the alarm keypad blinked a bright red, blending well with the whole Christmas theme. I punched in my code as my cautious gaze swept the open layout, bouncing like a racquetball from the small Christmas tree near the fireplace, into the kitchen, over the breakfast bar into the tiny dining room, and beyond into my bedroom. Other than the fact that I'd forgotten to make my bed that morning, everything seemed just right.

No intruders. No stalkers. No fanatic looking to snuff out the "Devil's Handmaiden."

I set the mail on the table next to the door, reluctant to go through it. The first letter addressed to the "Devil's Handmaiden" had arrived two weeks ago. It had spewed about my sins, harping on the First Commandment, and how being psychic was akin to being evil. A new letter arrived every couple of days, each one more intense than the last. And more threatening. I'd stopped opening them after the fifth; now I simply passed the envelopes on to Aiden.

I dumped the rest of my things on the floor next to the door, slipped off my boots. Grendel, a Maine coon cat, sauntered out of my bedroom on his three legs, meowing pathetically, pawing the hem of my trousers. He hated being left alone. And he hardly counted Odysseus, my one-eyed hamster, as company. Both had come to me via Marisol and the animal hospital where she volunteered.

My heart tripped. I didn't even know what to do about the whole Em situation. I rather wished my father hadn't told me she and Aiden were a perfect match. It was too big a secret to keep, though I knew I had to. The fact that the two were destined to be together did help lessen my guilt about helping Marisol— somewhat. If only I could get rid of the feeling that someone was going to be very hurt . . .

Scooping up a weighty Grendel, I whispered sweet nothings to appease him. The cottage had originally been built as an artist's studio, then later converted by Dovie into a guesthouse. During the renovation she'd kept all the original custom-made windows. Six of those lined the eastern side of the house, stretching from the living room all the way into my bedroom at the rear of the house, letting in abundant sunlight and offering stunning views of the ocean.

Until recently, the wall of windows had been my favorite part of the cottage. I never had a desire to cover them, even at night when they became black holes. Darkness had never bothered me until the Handmaiden letters started arriving.

I'd had drapes installed around the same time as the alarm system. Thankfully Dovie knew an interior designer who managed to blend the shabby-chic décor of my cottage with simple treatments that offered me privacy without overwhelming me with fabric.

I drew in a deep breath, inhaling the scent of the Charlie Brown tree in the corner. The live balsam fir was the runt of the litter on the lot this year with its four-and-a-half-foot height, sparse branches, tilting stance. After Christmas the sad little tree would have a chance to grow into a strong mature fir, mixed in with those from Christmases past on Dovie's acreage.

It was a lovely little tree. Really. Just . . . a bit . . . crooked.

From the fridge, I pulled a slice of white American. As soon as Grendel heard the crinkling of the cellophane wrapper, he hopped down, circled excitedly. I broke the cheese into quarters, dropping one on the floor for him. He pounced and dragged it around the corner into the dining area to feast in privacy under the rickety plastic table. I'd yet to save enough to buy my dream table, so the folding card table had to suffice for now. A tablecloth hid its many flaws.

I tossed another quarter of cheese over the breakfast bar into the dining room. Grendel attacked with a loud thump. As I checked my voice mail I found myself worrying about my father.

I couldn't erase that pinched look on his face from my thoughts. Though he tried to hide it, something was truly bothering him. What was going on? I needed to talk to him, look him in the eye to get some answers. Stress wasn't good for his heart.

For now, I didn't want to think about it anymore. I picked up the phone, dialed Sean.

Cupid's Curse wasn't the only reason I wanted to take things slowly with sexy Sean Donahue. Truthfully, I was scared. Terrified that no matter how much I cared for him, in the end my heart would be broken. But he was so hard to resist with those milky gray eyes, that heavenly body, kisses that melted, and a heart in need of healing. Literally.

A defibrillator had been implanted last year after he almost died from undiagnosed cardiomyopathy. Due to health concerns, he'd had to resign his job as a firefighter and eventually took Sam's offer to join his PI firm as an investigator.

These days we worked almost solely together, investigating not only Lost Love cases but missing person cases for the police as well.

It was getting harder and harder to keep my hands off him.

Our chemistry was pure magic, but I knew the outcome of any potential serious relationship we'd have. Doom. Crushing dark doom.

But not having him in a serious committed relationship with me was almost as painful as not having him at all. Dating him casually was a wonderful torture, one I loved *and* hated.

Sometimes being a Valentine just plain sucked.

After four rings a woman picked up. Stunned, I leaned against the counter. "May I speak to Sean, please?"

"You have the wrong number," she said sharply and hung up on me.

I hit the redial button, watched the numbers fill in on the screen.

It had *not* been the wrong number.

My call went immediately to voice mail. I left a quick message for Sean to call me back.

Absently, I nibbled one of Grendel's remaining cheese squares, trying not to get worked up and jealous.

So what, a woman answered Sean's cell phone, claiming it wasn't his.

Big deal.

No problem.

We weren't in a committed relationship.

I looked down. Grendel's last corner of cheese had

been squished into the tiniest cheese ball known to man.

I dropped it in the garbage disposal and poured a cup of veterinarian-approved kitty kibble into his bowl as he looked on.

His tail shot into the air as he prowled around my feet, staring at me accusingly. I'd veered from our norm. He was missing two cheese squares and wasn't happy about it.

And I had to admit I wasn't happy about a woman answering Sean's damn phone.

"You're supposed to be on a diet anyway," I said to him. "Take it up with Marisol."

He gave me a look that promised revenge.

I ignored it (probably a mistake) and grabbed a grape from the bunch on the granite countertop. I dropped it in Odysseus' cage on the bureau in my bedroom. He was nowhere to be seen, but I heard scratching from beneath his shavings. I made kissy noises, but he didn't surface. I gave up.

In the living room I turned on the gas-burning fireplace, gathered up the mail, and sank into the coziest chair ever made. It was a deep club chair that rocked *and* swiveled. Using the hearth as my footstool, I put my feet up. Crackling orange flames danced, warming my toes.

The stack of mail was larger than usual, with an assortment of Christmas cards mixed into the usual delivery. I pulled the cards aside, leaving me with a pile of mail from strangers, most wanting my help, some wanting me to know what happens to sinners.

Inevitably, I separated my fan mail (as I'd come to

call it for lack of a better term) into four piles: Crackpot, Consider, Can't Help You, and Copy (before I gave the original to the police). I was continuously torn between wanting to help everyone and wanting to protect my sanity. Some of the letters were simply heartbreaking. If I worked every case I'd need antidepressants. The flip side of that was the guilt. What if I could help these families find their loved one, find closure?

It was wrenching.

Grendel pouted near his food dish as I opened the first letter. It went into the "Can't Help" pile, as it was a request for me to connect a woman with her dead husband. Sorry. I didn't do séances.

There were three missing children requests in a row. Desperate parents who'd heard about the little boy I'd found. Unfortunately, most cases of missing children didn't turn out with happy endings, but I knew after working with the police that most people, though hopeful to have their loved ones returned home, were searching for closure. The first case I worked on was to help locate teenager Jamie Gallagher who had been missing for months. When I was able to find her remains, her mother told me that it was the first time she'd slept the whole night through since Jamie had been gone.

I set the letters in the Consider pile.

The next letter had familiar handwriting. My heart froze in fear. Carefully, I put the envelope into a plastic bag. Tomorrow, I'd give it to Aiden.

The handle on my front door rattled, and I nearly jumped clear out of my skin.

"It's me, LucyD!" Dovie called out, using her and my mother's pet nickname for me. The *D* stood for "diamonds." As in "Lucy in the Sky with . . ." My mother had been a huge Beatles fan and Dovie simply loved diamonds.

I dumped the rest of the mail onto the coffee table and opened the door for my grandmother.

"I can't get used to you locking that thing," she said, rushing past me waving a binder, a whirl of energy.

I dropped back into my chair.

Seeing Dovie this late at night wasn't the least bit surprising. She tended to spend more time here than at her own home. I put up with her intrusions into my life because I loved my cottage, its view of the ocean, and her—most of the time. More now that she'd let up on trying to matchmake me. She was convinced Sean and I would be walking down the aisle any minute now. A notion we played into for my sake, because before Sean came along, she was intent on matching me with every eligible (and some not so much) bachelor on the South Shore. It was nice not coming home to strange men invited to dinner by Dovie in hopes I'd fall madly in love and promptly produce a dozen babies.

I eyed the Handmaiden letter. The envelope itself looked innocuous enough. It was the message inside that had me locking my doors and windows for the first time in my life. No one other than Aiden knew of the threats I'd been receiving. The only thing that would come out of telling anyone else was a stifling overprotectiveness. It was better they didn't know.

And that included Sean. He'd probably want to move in.

And while that didn't sound like a horrible idea to me, I wanted him to move in for the right reasons, not to be my private bodyguard.

Hmm. I let that idea sit for a minute before I shook myself out of the fantasy. Dovie sat on the sofa, her long legs stretched out. She wore a silk pajama-and-robe set complete with fancy marabou-feathered heels. She'd been a burlesque dancer when she met my grandfather and still had a dancer's physique nearly sixty years later. Her eyes glowed, and I was happy to see it. This was normally the worst time of the year for her. Not only was it when she first met my grandpa Henry, but also the month when their secret divorce was finalized a year later. That was back in the 1940s, before things like secret divorces were splashed across tabloids, world-round.

I eyed the binder. "What brings you down here?"

Her long white hair had been pulled into a beautiful knot at the base of her neck. "Party stuff. Guest list, food. Thought I'd have you take a look, a second pair of eyes. RSVPs are rolling in."

Dovie's famous Five Days before Christmas Bash was next Saturday night, ten days away.

With my toe I nudged the Handmaiden letter under the stack of mail. "Tea?" I asked, heading for the kitchen.

"Lovely!"

Grendel leaped onto the couch, blatantly bathing Dovie with his affection, trying to make me jealous.

Too late—that particular sentiment had already been claimed for the night.

I glanced at my grandmother over the curved granite breakfast bar separating the kitchen from the open living and dining rooms. I set two mugs on the counter, trying not to think about Sean.

"I'm still not sure why your father insisted on inviting that reporter to the party," she said, skimming the guest list with her finger.

Reporter? "Preston?"

"Who else?"

I nearly dropped the kettle I was filling.

I came around the counter. "Dad didn't say why?"

"No."

I peeked at her binder as if it would offer insight. Sure enough, right there in Dovie's green ink, read, "Preston Bailey and Cutter McCutchan."

"Who's Cutter McCutchan? Do you know him?"

"Not personally," she said. "I believe he's the son of . . ." She squinted as if it would help her recall her many acquaintances. "Do you remember?" she finally asked me.

I shook my head. The name wasn't the least bit familiar.

"Lovely woman. Tall, striking looks. Fair skin, dark hair, red lips, looked like Snow White. She owned that ceramics gallery in town . . . Your parents invested in it. You know how they feel about the arts."

I knew my mother adored the arts. As a private music teacher, she often supported other mediums. My father, on the other hand, simply liked to appear to support the arts. It helped his image.

"It'll come to me."

"They're on the same invite? Are they dating?" I asked, wondering why this man had been linked to Preston's invitation. It wasn't the way invitations were normally sent. It should have read "Preston Bailey and Guest."

Preston hadn't mentioned a new boyfriend, which surprised me. She was the type to brag.

"Your father was specific about the wording. I assumed a relationship," Dovie said. "But of course I don't know for certain."

"And you didn't ask him why?" The kettle whistled. I dropped two teabags into the mugs and filled the cups with steaming water. I brought them into the living room.

"I do not ask many questions of Oscar, Lucy. He asked, I complied."

Strange.

Dovie snapped her fingers. "Sabrina! Sabrina Mc-Cutchan. Lovely. Just lovely. Her son is Oliver, he goes by Cutter. He's an artiste," she said in a fancy tone.

"You just now remembered all this?"

"My mind is a mystery."

I laughed. "That it is."

"Hush now." She sipped her tea. "Look over the list. Tell me if I've forgotten anyone. There's still time to send out invitations."

Dovie never partied lightly. My gaze slid over the list of over two hundred names, skidding to a stop on Sean's.

Who is she? Will he bring her to the party?

Would he have kissed me the way he did this afternoon if he was seeing someone else? I doubted it, but with the Curse at work, anything was possible.

She rose. "Keep the list overnight for a look-see. I should be going, it's getting late and maybe you have company coming?"

"Sean and I don't have that kind of relationship." Much to my dismay.

"I know. And it's getting old. I'm getting old. Too old to enjoy my great-grandbabies should you *ever* have any."

"You're forgetting the Curse . . ."

"I've been thinking."

"Dangerous."

She shook her finger at me. "I'm wondering if you're crying Curse every time you get close to someone out of fear."

"Of course I am. I've seen what happens to the relationships in this family."

"But you've never been a victim of the Curse, LucyD. Perhaps you wouldn't even be afflicted. Maybe that lightning strike zapped it out of you? Have you ever thought of that? Hmm? Hmm?"

I hadn't.

"I didn't think so," she went on. "It's time you gave commitment a chance. Maybe there's hope for you yet. And hope I'll get those great-grandbabies before I die."

"Have you been talking to Raphael?"

"Raphael?"

"Never mind," I murmured, the words "commitment" and "hope" dancing in my head like sugar plums.

The possibility that there might be a chance with Sean excited and frightened me at the same time. It was something to think about. But who was that woman who'd answered his phone?

6

The next morning pain radiated through my head, lobbing between my temples. It was an ache that had started last night after Dovie left and hadn't subsided. I partly blamed it on all the wine I'd drunk and partly on that phone call to Sean.

He hadn't called me back.

I didn't want to think about it. It didn't bode well for my mental health.

Neither did thinking about Preston Bailey. Why had my father insisted on inviting her to Dovie's party? And who was Cutter McCutchan? It was strange he had ties to my family. Too coincidental to ignore.

I sipped at my coffee, hoping the aspirin I took would kick in before I hit the road. I was meeting Sean at the office and then heading to the antiques shop in Falmouth to see about Leo's class ring. Any lead at this point was a good lead.

My cell phone rang a peppy canned version of "Deck the Halls." It hurt my head. Why couldn't I have picked a more sedate, hangover-friendly tune? Like "Christmas Canon" by the Trans-Siberian Or-chestra? Now, there was a song I could get behind right now. Or not. Because unfortunately, it was a version of Pachelbel's *Canon*, a classic wedding processional. Which reminded me of Sean. Which hurt my head even more.

The phone went into a second chorus. I didn't recognize the number. Wincing, I said, "This is Lucy."

Grendel strode into the room looking like a poofy fur ball, eyed his food dish, and glared my way.

"Ms. Valentine, this is Faye Dodd, Sarah Loehman's mother. Aiden Holliday gave me your number. Thank you for agreeing to talk to me."

I was suddenly very awake. "I'm sorry for all you've been through."

A deep exhale came across the line. "It's been rough."

I sprinkled some kibble into Grendel's bowl. He stuck his fluffy tail in the air and walked off, his limp barely noticeable.

"I'm going to be honest," Faye said. "I don't know if I believe in psychics. But I'm desperate."

"I understand." Many people didn't know what to believe, what not. Often it took proving my abilities to someone before they accepted what they could not understand. Even then, there were still skeptics who would rather believe any absurd notion than see what was plainly in front of their eyes.

"We'll have to meet." I sank into my favorite chair and swiveled in time to see my mother's Land Rover coming down the lane. "I can only do readings through palms."

"Can we meet soon?" she asked hesitantly.

"Tonight?"

We set a time to meet here this evening and hung up. I quickly made sure the Handmaiden letter was tucked away in my tote bag and opened the front door. In the distance, I spotted Dovie headed down the hill from her house.

I really needed that aspirin to kick in soon.

"Hi, Mum." I kissed her cheek, let her squish me. There was nothing quite like my mother's embrace, all warm, soft, and . . . home. And she always seemed to hug for dear life, as though she hadn't seen me in months. "What are you doing here?"

"Came to pick up Dovie and saw you were still home. Thought I'd pop in and say hi since I haven't seen you in a while."

"Two days?"

"Interminable."

I smiled, closed the door to keep the cold from seeping in.

My mother tipped her head as she stared at my Christmas tree.

"It's not you. It has a crooked trunk. Watch your neck or you'll get a crick. Coffee?"

"My God above, I'd love some. Could it be colder?" She drew herself up onto a counter stool. She hid her generous curves beneath a beautifully knitted shawl, clasped at the shoulder with an emerald brooch. A pair of trouser-style jeans skimmed her ankles, and cozy suede boots rested on the stool's foot bar. "I hear a storm is coming. A doozy."

I smiled as I poured. No one loved a good storm like my mother. The (disturbing) enthusiasm of the local forecasters had nothing on her.

I'd just set my mother's mug in front of her when a thud came from my front door. I rushed over to open it.

"Damn it all to hell!" Dovie exclaimed, rubbing her shoulder. "I hate that lock."

I had hastily acquired the habit of locking my front door. In the last two weeks, Dovie had yet to adjust.

I blew across my coffee mug. "If you'd knock first . . ."

"Where's your sympathy for an old lady?"

I laughed. "You're not old."

"You're forgiven." Dovie shivered as she shook off the cold. "Do I hear that coffee calling my name?" She cupped her ear. "Why, yes I do. Dovie, it's saying. Come drink me. I'm here to chase the chill out of your aging, great-grandchildrenless bones."

"Subtle," Mum said, grinning. Her round cheeks were aglow, her slightly down-turned eyes bright. Highlights glowed throughout her blond pixie cut.

Dovie parked herself on the stool next to Mum's. "Subtlety was never my strong suit."

"No kidding," I said.

"Sassy," Dovie accused.

Mum shrugged. "She gets that from me."

"As if." Dovie snorted. "That trait came straight from these aging, great-grandchild—"

"I get it," I said, cutting her off. "I'll see what I can do about having triplets, okay?"

"Soon?"

I rolled my eyes.

Grendel looked up from his perch atop the fridge, yawned widely, nestled his head back into the underside of his belly, and curled his tail next to his head so he was in the tightest ball possible.

Morning had dawned gray and damp. Beyond the bluffs, the ocean rose and fell, whitecaps breaking the monotony of the solid blue.

Dovie eyed me. "You look like shit."

I gasped. "Such language from an old woman!"

"You said I wasn't old. You're un-forgiven."

Mum gave me a not-so-sly once-over. "You do look a little rundown."

"Like shit," Dovie repeated.

"All right!" I cried, making a note to dab on a little more concealer. "Not that I don't love this little impromptu get-together, but I need to go to work."

"Oh, and we should be going too," Dovie said, downing her coffee in three gulps. She looked like a chic lumberjack with her black turtleneck, cable-knit sweater, and flannel pants. Yes, somehow she made flannel pants look fabulous. Her white hair hung in a sleek twisted ponytail down her back.

I was afraid to ask but couldn't help myself. "Where are you two off to?"

Dovie's eyes glittered with mischief. "There's a rally downtown."

Mum and Dovie had become instant best friends when they met almost thirty years ago at an antibusing protest. They shared poor backgrounds, an affinity for picketing (but not necessarily for the causes), and a similar history with Valentine men. Their friendship drove my father nuts, which was an added perk in Mum's and Dovie's eyes.

"What kind of rally?" I asked. "A war protest?"

"No, no," Mum said. "That's next week. Today is the annual tree protest."

"Ah." She didn't need to explain. Every year the city of Boston received a cut Christmas tree from Nova Scotia, a thank-you for helping the province in the aftermath of an explosion way back in 1914. The enormous tree was set up on Boston Common, decorated and lit. And every year a small group of protesters picketed the gift tree, asking instead that a live tree be used, all in the name of a greener earth.

I hadn't come by my Christmas-tree requirements by accident.

"Care to join us?" Dovie asked, slipping off her stool.

"I'll pass this year," I said through a yawn. My head hurt less, though knowing I had to face Sean in an hour had turned my stomach. *Who is she?*

My mother patted my cheek. "Wise choice."

"Just don't get arrested," I said as they headed for Mum's car.

Their laughter carried on the wind.

That didn't bode well for my mental health either.

My preferred mode of transportation to work was the commuter ferry. I disembarked at Rowes Wharf, not far from the New England Aquarium. I hurried, head down, toward the Boston Harbor Hotel. I spotted Raphael waiting to pick me up, a rare treat he bestowed on especially cold mornings.

When he saw me coming, he slid out of the driver's seat, smooth as silk, and walked toward me, giving me a hug and kisses on both cheeks.

"Quick escape last night," he said as we settled into the heated leather seats.

I bit back a contented sigh. The temperature outside was hovering around eighteen degrees with a wind chill that knocked it down another ten.

"Marisol thinks Em is unhappy."

"What do you think?"

I recalled what my father had said, about Em and Aiden being a match. It was hard to miss the chemistry between the two, but I didn't know what to do about this new knowledge. "I don't know. I think she's comfortable. And there's not anything wrong with that except . . ."

"Except?"

I glanced at him. "We know Joseph isn't her true love. I can't say anything without giving away Dad's secret."

"It's of my belief that what is meant to be is meant to be. Aiden and Emerson have met. They know. They *feel*. What they choose to do about it is a different matter—and their decision."

"You met Maggie at least a dozen times before realizing you were her soul mate."

"I"—he looked at me—"am stubborn."

I laughed. The radio was set to WEEI, the local sports talk radio. There was a heated conversation about the Patriots' quarterback and his off-the-field relationships.

I nibbled the corner of my lip. "What if Aiden and Em's decision could be helped along?"

We slowed to a stop at a red light. "Helped how?"

I hedged.

"Uva?"

"With, let's say, with a little investigative work. As in investigating whether a certain someone due to be married soon might be dabbling on the side."

With a sly smile, he said, "Emerson? I'm shocked."

He teased with good reason. Em was the most straitlaced, monogamous person I knew. It had to be killing her to have feelings for Aiden.

"Marisol and I are going to follow Joseph."

He let out a low whistle. "Very dangerous."

I had a feeling he'd say that. "I know."

Because if we found anything, how were we going to explain to Em? And if we didn't say anything, how could we let her marry a slimeball?

Either way, I knew there was no stopping Marisol. I was along for the ride, whether I liked it or not.

We turned from Essex onto Charles. Walkers looked frozen stiff as they marched along, briefcases in hand.

"Is Dad already at work?" I asked, wanting to talk to him as soon as I arrived.

Raphael shook his head as the car inched along in traffic. "Took the morning off."

"Oh?" That was unusual, especially this time of year. "Late night?"

"Quite."

I rubbed a finger along the console. "Do you know who he went out with?"

"Uh-uh-uh, Uva. My lips are sealed."

I sighed. Though Raphael loved me like a daughter, his first loyalty was to my father.

"I'm just asking because he seemed a little stressed

out last night. As far as you know, everything is okay with him, right?"

"As far as I know."

"And you'd know."

"Uva."

"I'm just worried."

"Nothing to worry about."

Only I *was* worried. Worried about Dad's stress levels, his health, and why he'd added Preston to Dovie's guest list. It didn't make sense.

The car crept along. I turned down the radio. "Can I ask you a question?"

"Always."

I shifted in my seat, looked at him. "Do you know anyone named Oliver McCutchan? Cutter?"

I shocked him—I could tell by the way he snapped his head to look at me.

In a blink, gone was the surprise, replaced by his usual tranquil mask. "The artist?"

"That would be him. Why did you look so taken aback?"

Smoothly, he said, "I didn't know you knew him. He paints fine art. Usually portraits of famous sports figures. His most recent works include Red Sox players."

Ah. Raphael wasn't one to follow the art scene, but he knew the Red Sox in and out. "I don't know him. I know *of* him. Have you ever met him?"

"No."

"Has my father?"

"Why all the questions, Uva?"

I explained about the invitation.

"I see."

"And Dad was the one who asked they both be invited."

"I see."

"I thought you might know why since you know everything about Dad."

"I wouldn't go that far."

"Well?"

"What?"

"Do you know why Dad invited them?"

He turned up the radio. "Sorry."

When he didn't say anything more, I suspected he was holding back.

He double-parked along Beacon. "Will you need a ride back to the wharf later today?"

"I think Sean is bringing me home."

"If you need me, call."

I leaned over the console, gave him a kiss on his furry cheek. "I will. And if you think of anything you may have *forgotten*"—I stressed the word—"then call me."

Inside the Porcupine, Maggie was straightening tablecloths as I walked by. She looked up and I waved. From experience I knew Raphael would find a parking spot, then double back to share a cup of coffee with Maggie and help her around the restaurant.

How long before it became a full-time job? How long before he walked away from my father for Maggie?

I couldn't imagine that day would come.

And didn't know what I'd do if it did.

7

I dragged myself up the stairs to Sean's office. Better just to get the questions over with and get on with the day. There was probably a perfectly reasonable explanation as to why a woman was answering Sean's phone. Perfectly. Reasonable.

"Hello," a young man said as I walked into SD Investigations. "Do you have an appointment?"

He sat behind an antique table that doubled as a desk. His black-and-white Pumas stretched out far beyond the wonderful turned legs of the table, his jeans torn in the latest teen style. The hood of a UMASS sweatshirt covered his head, the strings pulled tight around his jaw.

The table was an original from the early nineteenth century. Dovie had a similar one at Aerie and I coveted that as much as I did this one—found by the interior designer Sam had hired to spiff up the place. But Federal-style tables simply weren't in my meager budget.

There were some days, like today, when I questioned why I ignored my trust fund.

"Do you have an appointment?" the young man

asked again. A worn, dog-eared Dennis Lehane novel lay facedown on the desk. He loosened the strings around his face, pushed his hood back an inch or two. Thick hair tumbled forward onto his forehead.

The hood, I noted, wasn't a fashion statement. It was self-preservation. The room was freezing, and the feeble warmth of a humming space heater lacked the power to fight off the chill in the air.

"Why is it so cold?" I asked.

A voice came from my left. "The freaking furnace is on the blink." Sam wore a thick corduroy barn coat. "It's being worked on right now. I'm thinking about taking the rest of the day off, just to defrost."

Defrosting sounded good. I was suddenly missing the seat warmers in my father's car.

"I see you've met Andrew." Sam nodded to the new receptionist.

"Not quite. I'm Lucy Valentine. I work downstairs. Sean and I . . . work together."

"Closely," Sam added, completely straight-faced.

The boy's eyebrows shot up, disappearing behind drooping tawny bangs.

I threw Sam an outraged look. I supposed this was payback for steaming up his hallway yesterday.

"It's nice to meet you, Andrew," I said. "I hope, ah, that I'll be seeing you again."

He shot a look at Sam, who was giving me his own outraged look.

"Is Sean in?" I asked.

Sam said, "Um, yeah, I think so. With a"—he coughed—"client. Coffee? You look like you need some coffee."

Coffee sounded amazing. My toes had gone numb. I followed Sam to the kitchen.

"Does Andrew know about the curse?" I asked as Sam pulled a mug from the cabinet.

Sam glanced nervously over his shoulder. "There's no such thing, Lucy."

"Oh, is that right? Should we start the pool now to see how long he lasts?"

Sam rolled his eyes. "Sean and I already did."

I laughed. "I'll take two hours."

"Generous," he said sarcastically, looking again over his shoulder. "I'll, um, be right back. You know where everything is, right?"

"Sam?"

"Yeah?"

"Why are you acting so strangely?"

"Strange? Me? No." He laughed. "Must be the cold air. Not enough oxygen getting to my brain."

I stared at him. He stared back.

"Right," he said. "Be back in a minute."

I poured coffee to the rim of my mug, enjoyed the warmth as it slid down my throat as I took my first sip.

The mirror in the hallway beckoned. I looked like something dragged in the ferry's undertow. My hair was a mess, windblown and frizzy. Nothing much I could do about it. Giving up, I turned . . . and found a woman staring at me with hard eyes. She was beautiful with an olive complexion, high cheekbones, and shimmering dark hair. Before I could say hello, she rushed forward, bumped into me, and kept on going. Coffee dripped down my hand, soaked into my trousers, puddled around my feet, leached into the thick throw rug.

"Cara!" Sean yelled, flying around the corner.

One look at me and he drew up short, nearly knocking into me too.

Sam stood behind him. "I'm going to, ah, see about the furnace." He edged around us and hurried away.

I blinked. Cara? Cara Franklin? Sean's ex-fiancée Cara?

"Shit," Sean mumbled.

I couldn't find my voice. I hadn't known he'd been speaking with her, let alone seeing her.

He brushed past me, turning into the kitchen. A roll of paper towels in hand, he tore a few off, handed them to me. He knelt down, dabbed at my leg. My calf smoldered beneath his touch.

20−4 is . . .

"Do you need to go after her?" I finally said.

16.

He tapped my foot so I'd lift it. Carefully, he slid a paper towel over my boot. "The dry cleaner should be able to get the coffee out of your pants. Send me the bill." He sponged the carpet.

"Do you need to go after her?" I repeated. I didn't know much about Cara other than her name, she was a nurse, and she'd been unable to deal with Sean's health troubles. And now I knew she was absolutely beautiful.

I could have done without that knowledge.

Whoever said knowledge was power had to have been crazy. Denial . . . now that was a sentiment I could get behind.

"No." Paper towels dripped as he stood. He carried them into the kitchen. He came back out, dragging a hand over his face. "This isn't how I wanted this to go."

My voice cracked as I asked, "Wanted what? Wait. You were with her last night, weren't you? I called. She answered."

"She showed up on Sam's doorstep last night, sobbing."

Sean and his dog Thoreau had been staying with Sam since moving out of the place he'd shared with Cara last month.

Stressed, I jumped right into division problems, which said a lot, because I hated division.

24/4 is 6.

"Lucy?"

I tried to breathe. "Are you going back to her?"

"What? No."

My stomach was starting to ache. "Then why was she here?"

"Come into my office."

I tried to move, but my feet wouldn't budge. It took the searing heat of Sean's hand at the small of my back to get me moving.

"Lucy?"

"Yeah?" I sank into a chair.

"Look at me."

I really didn't want to. "No, thank you."

"Please?"

I looked. His eyes, those alluring, sexy milky-gray eyes, held such tenderness that my breath caught.

"Sorry about the coffee," he said, his breath sweet against my lips.

"Why was she here?" My voice hardly shook at all, but it was a good thing I was sitting because my knees would have probably buckled.

My mind, bracing for something disastrous, started reeling with everything but thoughts of Sean. Of my Christmas list, of Preston and the mysterious Cutter, of my stressed-out father, of what Raphael didn't tell me, of Leo, of Aiden and Em, of Sarah Loehman, and of needing to tell Aiden about the latest Handmaiden letter.

Sean pulled me out of my seat and into a tight embrace. My skin sizzled. I nuzzled my face into the crook of his neck and drank in the scent of him. The soap, the cologne, coffee.

Finally my mind ran out of distractions and I had to repeat my question. "Why was she here?"

He pulled back, cupped my face with his hands, and kept looking at me with that same tenderness. His hands slid down to my shoulders, slipping down my arms. He took my hands in his.

A wave of dizziness nearly knocked me over. Visions came in snippets, a piece here, a piece there. Christmas lights glowing on bare skin, his mouth on my thigh . . .

I yanked my hands away. I couldn't take such sweet torture right now. "Why, Sean?"

"She needs me right now."

So much for Cupid's Curse having been zapped right out of me.

I drew in a breath and sank back into my chair. "What's that mean?"

"She's sick. Maybe." He shook his head, raked his

hand through his hair, sending floppy spikes upward.

"Maybe?"

He sat on the edge of his desk. "She called yesterday—when we were in the hallway."

Ah. So it had been her number that had caused his frown.

"The doctors need to run tests. Spinal taps and MRIs and all kinds of things. She doesn't really have anyone else, Lucy, to be with her right now. And she shouldn't have to do this alone."

"No family?" I hated the pettiness in my voice, but it couldn't be helped.

"No siblings. Her dad left when she was little and her mom remarried and is in Arizona. Cara doesn't want to bother her until she finds out what's wrong."

Cara, however, didn't mind bothering Sean.

Pettiness was ugly. I closed my eyes and tried to find a little compassion. "What's wrong with her?"

"Don't know for sure. Some dizziness, some numbness in her hand, some tingling in her leg. She fainted the other day."

I supposed I should thank my lucky stars that she wasn't pregnant. After all, she and Sean only broke it off six weeks ago. Though, according to him, they hadn't had a physical relationship for months before that.

I wanted to believe him, so I did. I was a Valentine. I was allowed.

"This doesn't change us," he said.

Something rattled and clanged. A burst of heat shot through the radiator. I guessed the furnace was fixed. "Okay."

"It doesn't."

I flashed to that image I'd just had of us. Our naked bodies, his lips on my thigh . . . It was destined to come true (*when* was another issue), so maybe he was right.

"It's just," he began.

"What?" I prompted.

"She sat by me when I went through all my testing. Never left my bedside."

She'd also resented him for it. According to Sean, she hadn't been able to deal with the scope of his illness, with his life changing so drastically. As soon as Sean was out of danger, she opted out of the relationship.

He'd almost died, and still lived with the possibility on a day-to-day basis. If not for the defibrillator implanted in his chest, he could go at any minute. She didn't want to deal with it.

At the thought of losing him, chills swept down my spine and the ache in my stomach intensified. This was where Cara and I differed the most. She ran while I wanted to hold on for dear life.

"It's the least I can do for her," he said. "Then I can cut all ties. No looking back."

I wanted to hate his loyalty, his empathy, but I couldn't. In truth, it made him all that more attractive. "Sean?"

"Yeah?"

"What if they find something seriously wrong? Are you going to be able to walk away?"

Essentially, do to her what she'd done to him? Her rejection had hurt him, and I couldn't see him walking away—if only to prove that he was, in fact, the better person.

I glanced into his eyes. The tenderness had turned to anguish.

My stomach churned.

"Yes," he said.

I wanted to believe him, but I didn't. I was a Valentine. It was my birthright.

"She has a spinal tap scheduled at noon. I told her I'd be there."

"But Falmouth is at least a ninety-min—oh." I stood. "That's okay. I can go it alone."

"Lucy, this won't be for long."

"No, no. It's all right. Really." I was lying through my teeth. But at this point I just wanted to leave.

"You're lying through your teeth, Ms. Valentine."

Oh, just twist that knife a little bit more. My name on his lips was too sexy to endure.

"But I promise I'll make it up to you," he said, pulling me into an embrace.

"Oh?" I asked, slightly (okay, highly) intrigued.

He let me go and picked up a duffel bag on the floor. "All the toys you asked for. And there may be one or two I left at home. To show you in private. Sometime. Perhaps soon?"

A blush climbed my neck, settled into my cheeks. I was definitely intrigued, though I couldn't keep that little knot of doom and gloom from sitting heavily in my stomach.

I took the duffel from him and headed for the door. "Perhaps."

"Dinner tonight?" he asked.

"My place, eight?"

"I'll be there."

"I'll hold you to that."

He grinned. "I hope that's not the only thing you'll be holding."

"Mr. Donahue! I'm shocked." And giddy, but I didn't mention that. I had my pride, after all.

His laugh followed me down the hall. In the reception area, I found Andrew doubled over, writhing in pain.

I rushed over to him. "Andrew! What's wrong?"

"Don't. Know. My stomach. Hurting." He gasped for breath as sweat beaded along his hairline. "Sam's taking me. To the hospital."

Sam rushed through the door, saying, "I'm double-parked, can you make it downstairs?"

Andrew nodded and hunchbacked his way to the door. Sam helped him down the steps, a sturdy arm around his shoulders.

I was about to say something about the office pool, but Sam looked back at me with a grim expression. "Not one word, Lucy Valentine. Not one word."

8

The door leading into Valentine, Inc., tended to stick. I gave it a good shove. As it opened, two heads turned my way.

"You look like death," Suzannah Ruggieri said. "Are you okay?"

Tall and curvy, she had the look of a model, right down to incredible cheekbones and amazing blue eyes. Her hair was pulled back today, held in place with a chopstick. She'd worked for Valentine, Inc., for years and was such a trusted employee that she even knew about the auras.

"Yeah," Preston said, frowning. "Food poisoning?"

"No," I snapped, determined to look into other brands of concealer. "I'm fine. What are you two looking at?"

Both stood by the windows overlooking Beacon Street and the Public Garden. "Looks like some sort of protest is about to start on the Common," Suz said.

I ran over to the window. The Public Garden stretched far and wide, bathed in the beauty of the Christmas season, with lights and garlands and wreaths. I looked to the left, toward the Common. A large group had gathered. I squinted. No sign of Dovie or Mum. Yet.

"Do you know what's going on?" Suz asked me.

"Nope." I shook my head emphatically. "Not a clue."

"What was going on with Sam?" Suz turned to me. "Saw him double-parked out front."

"The new receptionist needed to go to the hospital," I said.

Suz made the sign of the cross.

"What receptionist?" Preston asked. "What was wrong?"

I could see why she'd become a reporter. She was nosy. "SD Investigations' receptionist."

Suz said in a reverential whisper, "Sixth this month."

"Sixth?" Preston's blue eyes widened. "What's going on?"

"A curse," Suz said.

Preston laughed. "As if."

She had no idea.

Preston's attention returned to the window. "Maybe I should go down and see if there's a story there in the crowd." She craned her neck to get a better look at the commotion.

"No!" I cleared my throat. "It's just that . . ."

They both stared.

"It's just . . . What are you doing here anyway?"

A fire flickered in the fireplace, warming the chilly room. The heat must have been off in here too. I dropped into one of the russet-colored love seats, set the heavy duffel bag at my feet. I couldn't wait to go through it.

Preston wouldn't leave her post by the window. "I

was supposed to meet with Oscar, but apparently he's not coming in."

"I've had to cancel all Oscar's morning appointments." Suz sat in her desk chair, crossed her legs at the ankle. "Do you think Sam's new receptionist will be back?"

"You two are crazy," Preston said. "There's no such thing as curses."

Suz rolled her eyes. She knew all about Cupid's Curse too. It was hard to keep secrets when she was such an integral part of our lives.

"Why were you meeting with my dad?"

Preston flipped her hair. "About the articles. Look! The protesters are on the move. I'm going down."

"Wait!" I jumped up. I did not want to see Mum and Dovie on the front page of the *Beacon*. Sure, they were somewhat well known for their protest-loving natures (six arrests between them), but the family's run with bad press couldn't go on.

"What?" Preston asked. "Do you want me to help with your makeup? Because I can."

I might have to take her up on that offer. "Actually—" What the hell was I doing? "I'm going to Falmouth today. I'm going to see about Leo's class ring. Thought you might want to tag along. You know, for the article."

I felt queasy.

Her eyes narrowed in suspicion. "*You* want *me* to come along?"

Really queasy. "Sure?"

Suz's jaw dropped.

"All right."

"Okay," I croaked. "Just give me a few minutes. Suz, can you see about getting one of SD's cars for me to borrow?"

"Sure."

"I can drive," Preston said.

Shit. I was going to be sick. "All right. Sounds good. A few minutes," I said, lifting the duffel.

"What have you got there, Lucy?" Suz asked.

"This? Nothing." I shrugged, shook my head, and sidled to the arch that led to the back hallway.

In my office, I dropped the duffel bag, picked up the phone. Marisol answered on the first ring.

"The eagle has landed," I said.

"Now you're getting into the spirit. I don't have to work tonight, so we're going to pick up his trail as soon as *he* leaves work. Where do you want to meet?"

"Uh," I said.

"Don't tell me!"

"I can't tonight. I'm meeting with a police client." I didn't mention my dinner with Sean. Marisol might not find that a valid excuse. But to me, there wasn't one more compelling. I was trying my best not to dissolve into a jealous hag, but it wasn't easy. "Sorry."

"You better be free tomorrow. Friday nights are prime prowling nights."

I didn't ask how she knew. I knew how she knew.

"I will be. Promise."

She heaved a sigh.

"I have everything you need. I'll leave it with Suz, okay?"

"Okay. I can swing by on my lunch break."

"You'll call me if you find out anything, right?"

"Possibly."

"Marisol!"

"Bye, Lucy." She hung up.

It would be just like her to leave me hanging. Well, I wasn't canceling my date with Sean, so there was no use stewing about it.

The coffee was drying on my black pants and thankfully the stains didn't show. I didn't have time to run home and change, so this outfit was going to have to do.

My cell phone rang. I checked the readout, answered immediately. "I was going to call you later," I said. "I need to stop by."

"Not a friendly visit, I suppose," Aiden said.

I turned on my computer. A quiet hum filled the air. "Another letter."

I heard him inhale. "You didn't open it, right?"

"No. Put it into a plastic bag like you told me."

"Good. That's the second one this week."

I figured he was talking more to himself than to me, so I didn't confirm. We made plans for me to stop by the DA's office where his detective unit was stationed on my way home from work.

"I heard you're meeting with Sarah Loehman's mother tonight."

I sat in my desk chair, swiveled. My window overlooked the alley behind the building. Great view of the Dumpsters and the brick building directly across, but little else.

"At five."

"Did she tell you about the ankle bracelet?"

A pigeon landed on the roof of the building across the alley. "No, but it's a good lead."

"We need one. We don't have enough circumstantial evidence to pursue a case against the husband. We need a body, Lucy."

The background noise of his office carried through the line. Raised voices, blips and bleeps of computers, filing cabinets. Silently I reviewed the circumstantial evidence. The hints of abuse, Scott Loehman unable to prove where he was that day, rumors of an unhappy marriage.

Aiden went on. "Loehman disputes all allegations from Sarah's mother that he was too controlling. He says Sarah didn't like her family, and that she no longer had anything in common with her old friends once she settled down into family life and they didn't."

"Could that be true?"

"Doubtful. All abusers know how to double-talk." The phone jostled. "I gotta go, Lucy. See you this afternoon?"

The letter was tucked in my tote bag. "Yeah. And Aiden?"

"Something else?" he asked.

I was about to say something about Em, something gooey and sappy and melodramatic like "Don't give up hope," but I couldn't do it. Finally I said, "Do you believe in love at first sight?"

There was a long silence. "Have you been drinking, Lucy? A little early, isn't it? See you later."

I hung up, stared at the pigeon. It suddenly spooked and flew away.

I checked my e-mails, powered down the computer, and gathered up my tote bag. In the reception area, Suz was telling Preston all about the curse put on SD's receptionists. Preston was taking notes.

Great. Although I supposed it was better than having her nose pressed to the window.

"Suz, Marisol is going to be stopping by later to pick up the duffel bag in my office."

"Okay," she said.

Preston shoved her pencil behind her ear. "Marisol Valerius? Your best friend."

Uneasiness settled in my chest. "How do you know Marisol?"

She laughed, that tinkling, pleasing sound that didn't match her personality. "Lucy, your Fruit of the Looms would be all in a twist if you had any idea how much I know about your family."

9

"How long have your parents been married?"

A cowbell jangled as I pulled open the front door of Falmouth's Ye Olde Antique Shoppe. The town center bustled with activity. A jovial Santa had a tent set up on the green, and shoppers were out in full force, bundled against the cold.

"I thought you knew everything about my life?"

"Are you always so literal?" Preston asked.

"Are you always so annoying?"

"Yes," she said, cracking a smile.

The ride down here hadn't been too terrible. Actually (though I'd never admit this aloud), I'd had fun. We'd sung the whole _Mamma Mia!_ soundtrack at the top of our lungs. Seemed Preston and I were both Broadway-musical fans.

Genetic? I wondered, stealing a glance at her. Really, I couldn't see any resemblance. Not to me—or my father.

"Thirty years?" Preston guessed.

Fidgety, I unbuttoned my coat. This was dangerous territory.

"Twenty-nine years."

Despite their separation, my parents remained friends, sometimes lovers, and were great, if not a bit odd, parents. Right after Dad moved out, Mum threw herself into a home renovation, converting the carriage house into a music studio, and began offering music lessons. It kept her occupied during those years when she was trying to adjust to living without Dad. And eventually music had grown into her true love.

Trying to coax warmth, I rubbed my hands together as I entered the shop. We'd had to park in a lot down the block near the marina, and the stiff wind blowing off Nantucket Sound sliced the air temperature in half. At least.

My phone rang, a welcome distraction. I answered before the second verse of "Deck the Halls."

"How's it going?" Sean asked.

"Preston and I just got here."

"Preston?"

"Long story."

He laughed.

I lowered my voice. "Not funny."

Preston motioned that she was going to browse around. Two other customers roamed the shop, lifting, inspecting, tsking. I breathed deep. There was nothing like the scent of an antiques shop, that mix of old dust and history.

"Is the test done already?" I asked.

"Not yet. We're still waiting. I should probably go and see Andrew. I think he's still in the emergency room."

It wasn't funny, but I couldn't help the smile. "What's wrong with him?"

"Looks like his appendix."

Ouch. "Poor kid. Who won the pool?"

I heard the reluctance as he said, "You did."

"Are you ready to apologize to Rosalinda?"

"This has to be a coincidence, Lucy."

"Right."

He coughed. "Maybe I should look up her up, just in case."

I smiled. "I knew you'd come around. Oh!"

"What?"

My feet cemented to the floor in front of a small burl-elm and fruitwood dining table, magnificently crafted, early nineteenth century. I skimmed my hand over the dimpled surface of the table, worn by time. An inlay of acorn and oak leaf circled the outside. The finish was original and generous waxing had brought out the wood's natural glow.

"Lucy?"

"It's gorgeous," I breathed.

"What is? Me?"

"That goes without saying."

"I like to hear you say it."

"Are you flirting with me, Mr. Donahue?"

"Who, me? Never. That would be inappropriate in a hospital waiting room, Ms. Valentine. Don't you think?"

"And you're never inappropriate."

He laughed.

"Actually, I was talking about a table. A gorgeous table. Here in the store. It's the most beautiful thing ever."

"I'd disagree."

Suddenly warm and gushy, I smiled like a fool. "I better go."

"We're still on for tonight?"

"You tell me."

"Thoreau and I will be there."

"Grendel will be beside himself." He had a thing for Sean's Yorkie. No one pretended to understand it.

I slipped my phone back into my bag and found Preston standing under a large oil portrait of a weathered seafarer. It was a lovely piece, but dust and dirt had muddied the surface, dulling its beauty. Someone could do a lot with it.

"Sean?" she asked.

"How'd you know?"

"The oopy-goopy look on your face while you were talking."

"It could have been from the table," I said, wandering back to it, drawn like a moth to flame.

An old woman, stick thin, appeared next to me as I crouched down to eye the detail on the table's edge.

"You have an excellent eye. It's an Austrian piece," she said, her voice warbling, as some voices did as they aged.

"It's lovely. Truly lovely." I'd been looking forever for the perfect table for my small dining room. This one appeared to have been custom made for me. I flipped the dangling price tag, and tried not to suck in a deep breath. Three thousand dollars. "But a little beyond my budget."

Creased eyes took me in. Wrinkles, like rings on a tree, lined her face. Short curly white hair hinted that this woman, eighty if a day, had decided to live life to its fullest. She wore a black track suit, sneakers, and a fifties-era apron around her waist. "How far?"

"Unfortunately, miles. But it is lovely."

Preston snorted. "Budget? You?"

"Guess you don't know me as well as you think."

Confusion swept across her face as the cowbell rang as the other customers headed back into the cold.

"Are you looking for something in particular?" the old woman asked.

It pained me, but I forced myself away from the table. "Buttons."

"You were right about miles," she said with a small crackly laugh. "Over here."

Preston and I followed. The woman had a long stride for being such a petite little thing. "Can I ask a question?"

"Indeed!"

"How do you collect your inventory?" I picked up a jar of buttons, poked around them. Preston's eyes were wide as they watched my fingers sort.

"Estate sales, auctions, consignments, off-the-street sales."

"Would you happen to remember where you would have gotten a jar like this?" I picked up the Mason jar that held Leo Epperson's ring hidden among the many buttons.

She flipped the tag tied round the mouth of the jar. "Estate sale."

"Do you happen to know whose?" Preston asked, jumping in.

I glared.

She ignored it.

"For provenance?" the woman asked.

I shoved the jar of buttons into Preston's hands to occupy her. "Something like that."

She pulled a leather-bound log from behind the counter. Her blinding white eyebrows rose. "That lot came in eighteen months ago. The David Winston estate."

Preston gasped and nearly dropped the buttons. Her amazed gaze met mine for a second before she said, "Sorry, too much caffeine this morning."

My adrenaline surged. David Winston was the name of Joanne's son. Somehow Leo's ring had ended up in a jar of buttons sold at his estate sale.

Though it was terrible Joanne had lost her son, it might help me find her. All I needed to do was search for David's obituary in the newspaper archives at the local library to see if she was listed as a survivor, and if so, if a current location (at that time) had been printed.

The door opened, letting in four chattering shoppers, talking loudly about Christmas presents and what to buy for whom.

Christmas.

It was less than two weeks away, and I'd barely made a dent in my shopping. My family was nearly impossible to buy for because they already owned everything their hearts desired. And Sean. I had no idea what to get him. A bottle of cologne wouldn't cut it.

"Thank you," I told the woman. "We're just going to take a look around."

"We are?" Preston asked, clutching the jar of buttons as we wandered deep into the shop. It was irresistible, filled stem to stern with pottery, books, linens, furniture, and everything in between.

"Take your time," she called after us.

"What did you mean earlier?" Preston asked. "About a budget?"

There was really no use keeping it secret. "I gave up my trust fund when I turned eighteen."

"You did what? Are you crazy?"

"A little."

"Why?"

I couldn't explain to her how I didn't feel worthy of the money because of my inability to read auras. "Young. Prideful. I wanted to make it on my own."

"And now that you're working for daddy dearest?"

Dad would have a fit at the nickname. "The fund is still there waiting for me."

"And what, exactly, are you waiting for?"

Letting my finger glide along the spines on a bookshelf, I absently checked titles. "Something important."

"I don't know. That table looked pretty important to you."

I felt a stab of longing. So stupid to want an object so much, but I couldn't deny the pull. "Not that kind of important."

"You're crazy."

"So you've said."

"It bears repeating."

I smiled as I continued to skim titles.

Preston pulled a Laura Ingalls Wilder title from the shelf, ran a loving hand over its cover. "I grew up reading these stories."

"You? Really?"

"No, I was thumbing through Joan Didion since first grade. Of course I read the Little House books, who didn't?" She placed it back on the shelf, a wistful look in her eye. "My mom used to read to me every night."

"Was it just you and your mom?" I asked, trying to piece together her early years.

"And Nana for a while."

Sounded familiar. "Did you always live on the South Shore?"

"Scituate, all my life."

Scituate bordered Cohasset. It was possible my father could have run into her mother at one point or another. "What did your mom do?"

"Why the twenty questions?"

"Curious."

"She was a librarian."

"Was?"

Preston continued to browse. "She died when I was seventeen."

"I'm sorry," I said. I couldn't imagine not having Mum in my life.

"Life goes on." Preston moved over to the next bookshelf.

It was obvious she didn't want to talk about it, but I was dying to rule out any chance that we might actually be related. I just didn't know how to ask that question. I pretended to study book spines. I suddenly froze. Gently, I took the novel off the shelf, dusted the torn cloth cover.

"What's that?" Preston leaned in.

"A second edition of Henry David Thoreau's *Cape Cod*." It had been published in 1864 and was currently in sad repair, with a cracked binding, water marks, and tears, but as soon as I spotted it, I had to have it.

This was it. Sean's present.

"It looks older." She wrinkled her nose. "And it smells."

Peeking through one eye as though that would lessen the shock, I checked the price.

Nine hundred dollars. A bit high, considering the condition.

"Nine hundred!" Preston snorted. "As if!"

As I pulled my lower lip into my mouth and contemplated whether I could afford the book, my gaze landed on a Regency-era tortoiseshell, ivory, and mother-of-pearl tea caddy with four tiny copper ball feet, all intact. It fairly cried Dovie's name. Magnetized, I walked over to it. Grasping the white metal knob, I opened the chest, tried to imagine who'd been using it for the past two hundred years.

Holding my breath, I checked the tag. Three hundred dollars.

If I didn't eat for the next three months . . .

"What are you doing?" Preston asked.

"Christmas shopping."

She laughed. "I thought we were here about the ring." Shaking the jar of buttons, she added, "We should probably check the local library for an obituary for David Winston."

"My thoughts, too, but look at this caddy."

"It is pretty," she admitted, running her finger

across the top. "My nana had one just like it. Well, a knockoff."

I heard sadness in her tone. "Do you have any shopping you want to do?"

"Nah. Not really."

"Are you done shopping already?"

She turned away, suddenly interested in a porcelain vase. "It's just that I don't really have anyone to buy for. Oh, stop."

"What?"

"Looking at me that way. I don't need your sympathy."

This was my chance to pry a bit, but somehow it felt wrong. Still, I couldn't help myself. "No other family?"

"All dead. My dad when I was two, Mom when I was seventeen, Nana when I was twenty. And I was an only child."

"I'm sorry."

"There's that sympathy again. It's all right." She shrugged. "I'm doing okay for myself. Sure, I get a little lonely sometimes, but work fills the void. You're really lucky, you know."

"Why's that?"

"Your family loves you. As crazy and messed up as they are—and they are—they really love you."

She was right. About all of it. Yet it made me wonder. Just how much did she know about my family? Had she learned about Cupid's Curse? My grandmother's secret divorce? Did she have proof my parents were married in name only? Did she know about the auras?

"I always wanted brothers and sisters," she said. "Did you?"

I couldn't bring myself to look at her. Was she hinting? Trying to warn me? "I, ah . . . never really thought about," I lied. I'd always wanted a sibling. Someone to laugh with, play with, share the burden of my heritage with.

The subject was making me really uncomfortable, so I picked up the tea caddy and said, "How long do you think I'd last eating peanut butter and jelly?"

"Not long, I'm guessing."

Over the top of her head, I caught sight of a wooden flute, standing upright, leaning against a shelf as if waiting for someone to come by and pick it up.

"Oh God. What now?" she asked.

I edged past her, gently lifted the flute. Made of boxwood and ivory, it had to be early nineteenth century. I checked for a mark and located "Astor & Co., London." As a collector of antique instruments, my mum would be in heaven to find this under the tree Christmas morning.

"Budget, remember?" Preston goaded.

"And to think for a second there I was liking you."

"It was bound not to last."

Smiling, I checked the tag. Six hundred. A steal. An absolute steal.

I played mental banker. The book, the flute, the caddy, the buttons.

"That's a lot of PB and J," Preston said as if reading my mind.

In my head I kept hearing, *trust fund, trust fund, trust fund.*

It would be so easy to dip into it.

Why shouldn't I? It was mine, after all. Maybe it was time to grow up and accept the fact that I came from money. It was nothing to be ashamed of.

But why, then, did it make my stomach ache?

Making up my mind, I headed to the register before I spotted anything else.

Preston whistled low. "You must have good credit."

A smile played on the old woman's thin lips. "Oh, my."

I placed my haul on the countertop. "Thirteen hundred for it all, including the buttons." The thirty-five-dollar jar of buttons.

Her gaze sharpened as she took in each item. "Including the buttons?" she asked, her eyes dancing. "Seventeen."

"Fourteen."

"Sixteen."

I faltered. Sixteen hundred!

"Fifteen?" Preston offered. To me she said, "You would have regretted walking away."

"Sold." The old woman beamed. "Cash or credit?"

I handed over a credit card. Undoubtedly I would be paying for these gifts for years to come at a ruthless eighteen percent interest rate.

I needed the Lost Loves venture to succeed. Emotionally, because I had a lot invested in the company. For years I'd longed to be part of the family business, and now that I was, I didn't want to fail. And financially, because the longer it took for me to be successful, proving myself worthy of the money earned by generations of Valentines putting their psychic abilities to good use, the longer my trust fund would sit, untouched.

"The library?" Preston asked after we dropped the goods in my trunk.

Snowflakes started falling as I checked my watch. I still had enough time before my meeting with Faye Dodd. "The library."

As we headed back toward the center of the square, I could have sworn I heard Preston humming *Mamma Mia!*'s "Money, Money, Money."

And damn if I didn't find myself enjoying it.

10

Three hours later, Preston had dropped me at the shipyard to pick up my car. I drove to the district attorney's office and left the latest Handmaiden letter for Aiden on his desk since he wasn't in. I spent the rest of the drive home with one eye on the road and one on my rearview mirror.

I was doing my best to not only be careful and aware of my surroundings, but not totally freak out as well. I wanted to live normally, as I did before the letters arrived. It would be too easy to sink into fear and paranoia.

Preston and I hadn't learned much at the library, but we had discovered the name of the lawyer who handled David Winston's estate. Unfortunately he hadn't been in his office when we called.

It was closing in on five o'clock by the time I walked in my door. Faye Dodd was due here in fifteen minutes.

I checked my messages as I walked around the cottage pulling drapes. I glanced around for Grendel. He finally emerged from the windowsill in my bedroom where he liked to watch the seagulls. I popped open a can of tuna and dished half of it into his bowl.

He pounced with a fervor he usually reserved for Thoreau.

There was one message, from Raphael. I called him back.

"Uva, you don't happen to know anything about this electric razor that was delivered here today?"

"Why would I know anything about that?" I tried for outrage but couldn't keep the humor out of my voice.

"Mmm-hmmm."

"Don't get started with your mmm-hmming. Is Dad at home? I need to talk to him."

"Out for the night."

It was early to be starting the weekend. He must really have it bad for his latest paramour. "With his new lady friend?"

"Uva . . ."

"Fine, fine."

"Nothing's wrong, is there?" he asked.

Only if you didn't count that Preston Bailey, roving reporter, might be my sister. "I just wanted to check on him."

"I'll tell him you called. You can always try his cell."

I knew from experience he never answered it while gallivanting, but I could give it a try. I raised myself onto the counter. Grendel had finished dinner and hopped atop the fridge, his favorite napping spot. "It's just that I'm worried. Something is going on with him."

"Is there?"

"Don't give me that. You know him better than anyone."

"Mmm. Yes. I suppose so."

"Come on, you have to tell me."

"It's not for me to be involved."

"But you know what's going on with him."

"It's not for me to say, Uva."

"Secrets can only hurt at this point, no?"

"The truth, also, can hurt."

The truth? About what? "But—"

"His secrets are not mine to tell, Lucy. Please don't press. I must go."

"Pasa—"

He hung up.

Well, fine. I looked up at Grendel and made kissy noises. He didn't so much as twitch an ear.

"Fine," I said again, hopping off the counter. I went in to see Odysseus, but he was buried under shavings, sleeping, the pine rising and falling with each breath he took.

I was just about to call Marisol to vent and maybe ask about getting a nontemperamental dog, but the doorbell rang.

Faye Dodd was older than I expected. Late fifties, with brown hair streaked with gray and haunted green eyes.

I took her suede coat as she came in and offered tea.

"No, thank you," she said, wringing her hands.

"Sit, please."

She did, smoothing her brown tweed tulip skirt as

she did so. A soft creamy sweater softened the hard lines of her face, but couldn't disguise the pain etched in her features. Crossing her feet at the ankles, she rocked ever so slightly.

Curious, Grendel hopped from the top of the fridge to the counter to the floor. He hobbled in to the living room, meowing pathetically. He wasn't above playing the sympathy card for affection.

"What a beautiful cat. What happened to him?" She rubbed her fingertips together and Grendel went to investigate.

"I adopted him through an animal hospital in town. The doctor thought he might have been hit by a car. They had to amputate his leg to save his life."

"The poor thing," she said, scratching his ears. Grendel purred loudly, rubbing his face against her stockings. He looked slyly at me out of the corner of his eye.

See if he got *any* cheese tonight.

"Sarah always loved cats. The fluffier the better. She would love yours." A small smile faded into a frown. "Scott never liked them." Her eyes flashed, dark and bright, and full of hatred.

She seemed to want to take the reading slowly. I'd learned over the past few readings just to let everything unfold naturally. Sometimes readings were quick. Sometimes people needed time to adjust to the situation.

Looking around, Faye said, "This a beautiful place."

"Thank you."

Her gaze landed on my Christmas tree, and she

tipped her head at the same angle as the tree. "Is that going to fall over?"

"Hopefully not, unless Grendel climbs it. It's the trunk that's crooked."

"Grendel? What an unusual name."

"It's from *Beowulf*," I said, understanding her need for small talk. "He was quite a hunter."

"Is yours a hunter?"

"Genetically, yes. But my Grendel only likes to hunt Cheerios and cheese squares and, when he's really desperate, kitty kibble."

She smiled. "You're not like I imagined."

"No?"

"It's silly. I pictured more of the boardwalk fortune-teller. Yet you have no crystal ball or turban."

"Every medium is different," I said.

"But you're so . . ."

I raised an eyebrow.

"Normal. Glamorous even. You could model."

I fidgeted. "Thank you."

"Sarah wanted to model. Petite catalogues."

The Christmas lights twinkled, and the electric candles in the windows glowed behind the drapes. "Why didn't she?"

"She met Scott when she was eighteen. He was twenty-four. Within a year they were married and had a baby on the way. She never had the chance." Faye drew in a deep breath. "Do you think you can find her?"

"I don't know. But I can try. You gave her an ankle bracelet?"

"For her sixteenth birthday. It was a—" She broke off.

"It's okay," I said. "You don't have to tell me what it is."

"I just don't want—"

"To influence me. I know. It's okay that you don't trust me. It really is."

"It sounds harsh."

Grendel, never tired of affection, leaped onto the arm of the chair. "It's human," I said. "You can push him away."

"He's just fine."

"Are you ready?" I asked.

She nodded.

I rose and sat on the edge of the coffee table, in front of her. I held out my hand. "Think of that anklet."

Worry creased her forehead as she slipped her hand into mine.

I closed my eyes as visions flashed like colorful lightning. The images took me north, into New Hampshire, to a high school in Portsmouth. Inside a crowded gym, past a basketball game, to a cheerleader on the sidelines. Blond, blue-eyed. Glitter eye shadow. Small stud earrings. Heavy chain of silver around her wrist with thick links, a fancy clasp and a dangling heart. It was engraved with an *S*. I recognized it immediately as a Tiffany piece.

I pulled my hand back, steadied myself. Vertigo washed over me. My stomach rolled with the dizziness, and when I blinked the lights in the room blurred together as if I'd been rubbing my eyes too hard.

"Are you okay?" Faye asked.

"I'm all right. It just takes a second . . ."

I drew in a deep breath, rose carefully and sat on the couch. When I regained my bearings, Grendel was on my lap, pushing his nose into my stomach.

I rubbed his head. "Did you . . ." Faye started.

"Did you say it was an anklet?"

"Yes," she said, sitting on the edge of her seat.

"I saw a bracelet, not an anklet."

She covered her mouth with her hand. "It was a bracelet, Lucy. But it didn't fit Sarah's wrist. So she always wore it around her ankle."

"That makes me feel better. I was worried I wasn't seeing the right thing."

"Can you describe it?"

"It was a Tiffany bracelet. A chunky silver piece with a dangling heart."

Her voice wavered. "Anyone could have one of those."

"It was engraved with an *S*."

Keening forward, she wrapped her arms around her stomach. "Oh God, oh God, oh God. Where is it?"

I swallowed hard over the lump in my throat. "All I can tell you is that a teenage girl has it."

"But where? But how? Sarah never took that piece off. Ever. It was her lucky charm."

"It will be looked into," I said. My agreement with the police was that Sean and I had free rein to investigate my visions, without interference. Previously I'd been put in the position of implicating an innocent man through my visions. I didn't want that to happen again. Until I had valid, relevant information, the state police would be kept in the dark.

"Did . . . did you see Sarah at all?" she asked.

"I'm sorry."

She steeled her shoulders, but her bottom lip quivered. "I made a lot of mistakes with her. Too many. I wish I could apologize, take back everything, and start new. I know that's not going to happen." Rising, she straightened her skirt. "I lost hope a long time ago that I'd ever see my daughter alive again. I just want to bring her home, bring Scott to justice, and make sure my grandchildren are safe. I'm putting my faith in you, Lucy. Please don't let me down."

11

"This has been the most boring two hours of my life. I wish you were here." Marisol's voice carried loud and clear through the phone.

"To be bored with you? No, thanks."

She groaned. "I'm cold. I'm hungry. I need to pee. This is no fun. This is supposed to be fun."

"What's he doing?"

"He went straight home from work. He's been inside since. Do you think he's up there with someone?"

"Other than Em?"

She growled. "Of course, other than Em."

"No."

"Really?"

"He's not that stupid."

"You may be right."

I sorted through the stack of mail delivered today. A few Christmas cards, one bill, some junk mail, and only one request, which went into the Can't Help file. Someone wanted to know if Elvis really was alive. I wished I had an Amused file. That letter would go in there.

No Handmaiden letter. Thank goodness.

"Maybe we're wrong about him," I said, making sure I used "we" and not "you" so she wouldn't get pissed off at me.

"We're not wrong."

"How long are you going to stay outside Em's place?"

"I don't know. I really have to pee. You know what we need? Someone on the inside."

"To let you use the bathroom?"

"No, though that's a good idea. Someone who can tell us things. Be a spy."

"Like?" We certainly couldn't ask Em.

"I have an idea." I heard her engine turn over. "I've got to go."

"Marisol? Marisol!" But she'd already hung up.

I didn't want to know. Did. Not. Want. To. Know.

I'd defrosted some leftover marinara Dovie had made. It simmered on the stovetop. Water had risen to a soft boil. I was just waiting for Sean to get here before I put the pasta in.

I dropped several Cheerios in Odysseus' cage and filled his water bottle. Grendel eyed me, hoping a wayward Cheerio would fall—or maybe that I'd leave the cage open and he could get rid of his competition once and for all. On the safe side, I dropped a Cheerio on the floor and he dragged it under the flimsy dining table.

I stared at it, picturing the table I'd seen at the antiques shop in its place. A girl could dream.

A knock sounded on the front door.

I checked my reflection in the mirror hanging above the mantel. Yes, I'd changed into a lovely wrap dress. Yes, I'd done my hair, working my natural waves into bouncy curls. And I'd shaved my legs to smooth perfection—the number-one mistake in any girl's handbook when *not* wanting to sleep with a man.

What this told me—well, that was easy to figure out.

I was ready to sleep with Sean.

And more than willing.

I tried not to think about Cara or what might be wrong with her or anything other than Sean undressing and having his wicked way with me.

I flipped the dead bolt, opened the door. Sean stood on the porch, the breeze ruffling his hair, his eyes on me. In one hand he held a poinsettia. In the other, a leash. Thoreau barked and leaped and tugged. Sean let go, and the Yorkshire rushed into the house to find Grendel.

The two were crazy for each other.

Sean stepped onto the threshold, said, "I've been looking forward to this all day," and kissed me.

If not for the shriek of the fire alarm, we might not have stopped. "The bread!" I ran into the kitchen, pulled the smoking Italian loaf from the oven.

Sean set the poinsettia on the counter, grabbed a dishtowel, and fanned the alarm until it silenced. "Raphael warned me about your cooking."

"He did not!" I said, dumping the charred bread in the sink.

"He did." He glanced at me. "You look adorable all dressed up and in bare feet."

Adorable?

"What's wrong?" he asked.

"Adorable? I didn't spend half an hour doing my hair to look adorable."

"Okay, then," Sean said, coming up behind me. "How about good enough to eat?"

Hard. To. Think. Especially with him nuzzling my neck that way, nipping at the sensitive skin at my nape. And oooh. His hand slid down my rib cage, grazing my breast.

The bread wasn't the only thing smoking hot.

I turned in his arms to face him. "Better."

Unbuttoning his shirt, one slow button at a time, I reached in, skimmed my hands over his chest, over his scar. My fingertips glanced over his nipples and he sucked in a breath.

"You like that?" I asked.

"Love that."

Behind me I heard the splash and gurgle of the boiling water as I tugged on the hem of his shirt. I desperately tried not to think. Just to be. To let it all go and trust that everything would work out. Leaning on my tiptoes, I kissed him, pulling gently on his bottom lip while my hands roamed.

Everything I felt for him came out in that kiss. The love I couldn't share, the hopes I didn't dare hold on to. All the things I couldn't say, all the things I dreamed of one day.

He held me close, letting me explore. His kiss

went from tender and sweet to heady and passionate. It was getting seriously hot in the kitchen. Really hot.

Really, really hot.

The fire alarm shrieked again.

Flames shot out from the bottom of the pasta pot. The water had boiled over and the oil had caught fire. "Oh no!"

Sean quickly put the pot in the sink, and turned off the gas, but the flaming oil danced.

"Baking soda?" he asked.

I opened a cabinet and grabbed a box of Arm & Hammer's finest. It seemed an odd choice to me, but as a former firefighter I figured he'd know how to put out a grease fire. He sprinkled the baking soda over the flames and they immediately died down.

I checked the sauce. A burned layer coated the bottom of the pan. "I know when to give up. Takeout?"

"I'll call."

I frowned at the dishes in the sink. They could wait. Sean, much to my dismay, buttoned his shirt.

I supposed the moment had been ruined.

Probably Cupid's Curse at work. Or fate. Either one. And at this point, I hated them both.

I poured us both a glass of wine and took mine to the couch. Flames leaped at the gas logs, and Christmas carols played softly.

Thoreau and Grendel were already curled by the fire. "I'm jealous," I said, nodding to the pair.

Sean sat down next to me, curving my body against his. He kissed my temple. "You haven't had enough fire for one night?"

"Not near enough," I told him, loving the way his eyes darkened.

"I like the sound of that."

My cell phone rang. I dropped my head back against the couch.

"Not going to get it?"

"The only person I really want to talk to is my dad, and it's not likely to be him."

Sean swirled his wine. The color danced in the firelight. "What's going on with your dad?"

"Oh, you know, the usual. He has a new girlfriend, he might be Preston's father."

Sean choked on his wine. Coughing, he said, "You don't really think that, do you?"

"I don't know. She's asking strange questions. How long my parents have been married, if I ever wanted brothers and sisters. And then she was acting all strange when Leo made that comment about us being related."

"It does seem strange."

"It *is* strange. And I can't exactly ask Preston outright. Although she's pretending to be all friendly, she's a reporter at heart. She'd give just about anything for that kind of headline. Dad is the only one who has the answers."

The phone on the kitchen wall began to ring just as the doorbell sounded. Thoreau jumped up, yapping.

Grendel streaked to my bedroom.

I couldn't help but laugh.

"You get the phone," Sean said, "and I'll get the pizza."

I answered on the fourth ring.

It was my mother. And like I thought, the call wasn't good news.

After hanging up, I grabbed my coat. "We have to go."

Sean set the pizza on the coffee table. "Where?"

"That was my mum. She and Dovie are in jail."

12

Sunbeams stealthily slipped in between my drawn curtains, teasing me awake. I rolled to look at the clock. Almost eight A.M.

Grendel swatted my face with his paw. I rubbed his head.

I curled my arms around my pillow and a small part of me—okay, a big part of me—wished to stay in bed all day. Rest. Relax. Chill out.

Not worry about my father, or Sarah Loehman, or if my mother and grandmother would face serious jail time.

Coffee. I needed coffee.

I threw back my covers. Grendel wiggled out from beneath the pile and thumped to the floor, charging ahead of me into the kitchen. He gleefully ran figure eights around my feet until I popped open a can of cat food and plopped it into his bowl.

He attacked with vigor.

I washed my hands, set to grinding coffee beans.

My cell phone rang as the coffee perked. I frowned at the display, but knew I had to answer.

After requisite niceties, Faye Dodd said, "Anything, Lucy?"

I didn't want to tell her that I hadn't had a chance to follow up on my vision yet. "Nothing overtly useful," I said, pulling open the drapes in my bedroom. Sunlight exploded into the room. The ocean was still sleeping, calmly swaying in rhythm with the currents. The flurries that fell yesterday covered the grass in a thin white sheet. So much for a doozy of a storm. "But we're still looking into it."

Barring any complications from Cara, Sean and I were taking a trip to Portsmouth today.

Faye let out a loud sigh. "I'd been hoping . . ."

"Don't give up yet." I worried my lip as I opened the drapes in the living room. I spotted Dovie heading down my lane and unlocked the door. "However, I do want you to be prepared."

"For what?"

"If my current lead doesn't pan out, I might need to go see Scott."

"Why on earth would you need to involve him? He's brought nothing but misery onto this family. I don't want him to be any part of this."

Faye couldn't see past her loathing to the bigger picture. Sarah's anklet wasn't the only jewelry she wore daily. "I might be able to find Sarah's wedding band."

She gasped. I gave her a second to process.

Finally, she said, "And you can only get that reading from Scott."

"Exactly."

"I still don't like it."

"I know."

"What if he won't do the reading?" Faye asked suddenly.

It would say a lot about his guilt, in my opinion. "If I can get him thinking about wedding bands, I might still be able to get a reading if I touch his hand, even in passing, like a handshake."

"So you'll trick him."

"Yes."

"I like it."

Her hatred made me uneasy. "Tell me a little more about Scott. I've heard whispers that he may have been abusive, to Sarah and the children."

"He's . . ." Her voice shuddered. "Despicable. Stealing a young girl's innocence, controlling her, brainwashing her."

"How so?"

"After they married, Sarah would never come home."

Home. The word stuck in my head. After she married, Sarah's home would be with Scott, not her parents any longer. How much of Faye's anger toward Scott was justified, and how much was from a parent who resented the man who precipitated her daughter growing up and moving on?

"Poor Maddie had a broken arm at three years old and Jake had emergency surgery at a year old. All accidents, Sarah said. I didn't believe it for a minute."

Dovie burst through my door. She saw me on the phone and she helped herself to a cup of coffee and felicitous greetings from Grendel.

"Were social services ever involved?"

"I could never bring myself to call. I just kept trying to talk Sarah into leaving Scott. But she insisted on staying."

Her voice trailed off and I could practically follow her line of thinking. That staying with Scott had possibly gotten Sarah killed, leaving her children motherless, and her mother childless.

"I'll call if I find anything. I promise."

I snapped my phone closed. "The Sarah Loehman case."

"Ah," Dovie said, sipping on her coffee and opening the morning *Herald*. "The husband got away with murder, right?"

"Everyone seems to think so." I poured a mug of coffee and looked her over. "How's my favorite felon this morning?"

She looked none the worse for wear, considering. Her hair was twisted into a fancy knot, and she wore tailored jeans, a cashmere sweater, and leather loafers. Grendel was swatting at the tassels.

"Such sass from you. I'm just fine, thank you."

"And Mum?"

"Lovely as usual."

I sipped my coffee. "Glad to hear it. When's your arraignment?"

She flipped through the paper. "Monday morning."

"You know, eventually they're not going to let you off with a slap on the wrist and a fine."

"We did nothing wrong."

"Dovie."

"What? Human bodies are beautiful."

"You're lucky you and Mum didn't get arrested for

indecent exposure along with the disorderly conduct charge."

"We were hardly indecent. We had on underwear and bras."

Thank goodness for small favors. I wondered what Preston would have thought of my mother's and grandmother's underwear choice. Both had been wearing animal-print thongs when arrested.

"I don't know how you didn't get hypothermia."

"Adrenaline."

"Good to know."

She turned another page. "Sass."

"I get it from you, remember?"

"Not me. Your mother."

I smiled. "What are you looking for in there?"

"Coverage of the protest. Nothing. Not even a picture."

My gratitude for that was endless.

"Thanks for bailing us out. Again." Dovie slid her foot back and forth. Grendel leaped to and fro, chasing tassels.

"How about no more protests? At least until after Christmas?"

"Okay, though your mother has her heart set on the war protest next week."

"I'll talk to her."

"Just don't have your father do it. You know how she likes to be contrary where he's concerned," Dovie said, kicking off her shoes. Grendel pounced on them, trying to drag one away.

"I couldn't, even if I wanted to. He's incommunicado. He has a new girl toy."

"You'd think he would have learned his lesson with the incident on the beach."

"You'd think. I wish he'd call. I really need to talk to him."

"About?"

"Work stuff," I lied.

"He'll turn up. He always does." She turned another page. "Oh ho! Speak of the devil."

"Dad?" I asked.

"None other." She tapped the page. "Out last night at the symphony and not alone."

"Do you know her?" I asked. The woman stood in the background of the shot, but she was watching Dad intently. A casual reader might not have picked up that they were together.

"If my eyes don't deceive . . . that's Sabrina Mc-Cutchan."

"Strange to hear that name again so soon," I said.

Dovie snapped her fingers. "I wonder if your father is matchmaking. Pairing Cutter and Preston together."

Something shifted inside my chest. It felt remarkably like relief. The explanation made perfect sense. It was something my father, a diehard romantic, would love to pull off.

She gathered up her paper and kissed my cheek. "I'm off. I have a meeting with the caterer."

"Try and stay out of trouble. I'm not sure you have many get-out-of-jail-free cards left."

She blew a kiss. "Don't worry so much, LucyD!"

If only it were that easy.

13

Sunbeams spread out from the horizon, welcome fingers of light massaging warmth into the day. Sean and I were on our way to track down the cheerleader I'd seen during my reading with Faye Dodd.

It was closing in on two o'clock, and we'd just merged onto the Southeast Expressway, heading north toward I-95 and New Hampshire. Bumper-to-bumper traffic stretched far and wide, on both sides of the highway. No reason for it that I could see, but around here reasons weren't needed.

My long legs ached with the need to stretch. It felt as though we'd been in the car for days, not hours. I tugged off my boots and pulled my feet up onto the seat, tailor style.

Sean eyed me. "Doesn't that hurt? Sitting like that?"

I batted my eyelashes. "Have you been checking out my legs, Mr. Donahue?"

"Every chance I get."

One little sentence and the car filled with anticipation. And tension—both the good and bad kind.

We'd come so close to taking that next step, but it

seemed something was always lurking, ready to trip us up. It happened to be Mum and Dovie last night, but they weren't the only obstacles recently.

I felt compelled to ask, "How's Cara today?"

I desperately wished she would just go away. Except I knew Sean couldn't walk away until all her testing was done. The spinal tap she'd had done yesterday had been normal. An MRI of her brain was scheduled for Monday.

"Not so good. Her right foot is dragging. Her doctor wants to check her into the hospital tonight for observation. She's going to have some special scan done tomorrow."

I had no doubt Sean would be there with her for the test. "What do the doctors suspect?" I asked, trying to keep my mind off how much time he was spending with her.

"Could be something spinal, an infection, a tumor, multiple sclerosis, Parkinson's."

"Holy shit."

The corner of his mouth lifted in a little grin. He had a fondness for my swearing.

He glanced my way. "I thought about what you said. About walking away in the long run."

Thinking about losing him caused a pain so intense, I had to divert my thoughts.

I stared at the colorful rainbow artwork on the side of the old Boston Gas (now Keyspan) tank. When I was little, I used to try and find faces in the paint. Fred Flintstone. The dad from the Munsters. Rumor was Ho Chi Minh was painted into the blue stripe and if I stared hard enough I could see why.

Finally, I said, "And?"

"I can't walk away from her right now, but I did tell her it was time to call her mother."

"You did?"

"My place isn't with her anymore," he said, staring at the horizon. "But I can't leave her to face all this alone."

"Did she call?" I didn't want to get my hopes up.

"Her mother is flying in on Monday night."

"She is?" I fairly cried in glee.

He looked my way.

"I, ah, mean, that's great. It'll be nice for Cara to have some family around."

He tipped his head back and laughed. I once asked my father the color of Sean's aura. It was a charcoal gray with a hint of steely blue I could almost picture in my mind's eye if I stared at him long enough. I, of course, didn't know my aura color—none of the Valentines could see the auras of blood-related family members, part of Cupid's Curse. Were we a match? Were he and Cara? If they were, I could find out—all I had to do was ask my father to take a look at her.

I'd never ask him to. That was something I just never needed to know.

I socked him in the arm. "Why are you laughing?"

"You. I see right through your enthusiasm, Ms. Valentine."

"Can you blame me?"

"No," he said softly. "I can't."

North of the tunnel, traffic eased. Snowfall had been heavier up here. The road before us was a ribbon of gray twisting through a winter wonderland.

My phone rang. I'd changed the ring tone from "Deck the Halls" to "Winter Wonderland." Preston's name came up on my screen. Had she discovered something about Leo's lost love?

"Lucy Valentine!" she snapped when I answered.

"You sound like my mother."

"Well, isn't that a coincidence? I'm calling about your mother."

"Oh?" I asked, a knot forming in my stomach.

"Don't pretend you don't know what I'm talking about."

"Does your editor know you use double negatives?"

"Don't be evasive!"

Sean lifted an eyebrow—obviously he could hear both sides of the conversation. "Evasive?"

"I saw the picture this morning."

Of Dad and Sabrina? My heart double-clutched.

"Your mother and grandmother look lovely in their skivvies."

It took me a second to realize what she was saying. I coughed. "There's a picture?"

"In the *Globe*."

Dovie would be thrilled at the news. "Ah. Well. Their proclivity for protesting is well known."

There was silence.

"Preston?"

"Did you only invite me to Falmouth to keep me from investigating the protest?"

The hurt in her tone confused me. "Yes."

"I see."

"But," I said quickly, "I was glad you were there. In fact, I need to go back tomorrow and speak to that lawyer." Sean would be busy with Cara, and it would be nice to have company—even if it was Preston. "Do you want to come too?"

More silence.

"Preston?"

"I'm thinking about it. That Christmas tree protest could have been a real scoop for me, Lucy."

I refused to apologize. I just couldn't bring myself to do it. I'd been trying to protect my family. "I'll see you tomorrow?"

I heard the pout in her voice. "I suppose."

As I hung up, Sean said, "She is like a little sister."

I groaned and dialed my father as we crossed into New Hampshire, paid our tolls.

His voice boomed, "Oscar Valentine."

"Where have you been?" I asked.

"Who is this?"

"Not funny."

"I'm amused," he said.

"I was worried."

"Who's the parent here?"

I was wondering the same thing myself. "Look, I need to know."

"What do you need to know, Lucy?"

"Preston Bailey. Is she my sister?"

"Preston?" he barked in surprise. Then he started laughing.

"Dad."

More laughter.

"Dad."

More laughter.

"Dad!"

More laughter. I hung up, looked at Sean. "Guess that's a no."

"I'd say so."

"Good to know, but I'd still like to figure out what the link is between Cutter McCutchan and Preston."

"You could call your father back."

I tucked my cell into my purse. "No, thanks. How's Andrew doing, by the way? Is he back to work?"

"Not yet. The hospital kept him for observation, but couldn't find anything wrong—it wasn't his appendix after all. Now the doctors think it was a bout of pancreatitis. He expects to be back at work on Monday."

Poor kid. "When are you going to call Rosalinda?"

"Sam said he'd take care of it."

"Mmm-hmm."

"What? You don't think he will."

"He won't."

"Time will tell, right?" Sean said.

Time might tell, but I was going to have to do something about this, for Andrew's sake.

Soon.

The cheerleader's name was Shannon. Shannon O'Meara. Sixteen years old. A junior at Portsmouth High School.

It amazed me how much information was willingly imparted to strangers. Sean and I sat across from each other at a local McDonald's, waiting for Shannon to take a break from her shift.

In my vision she hadn't struck me as the type who'd

flip burgers as an after-school job, but it turned out that Shannon's single mom had been diagnosed with breast cancer last year and was struggling to pay the bills. Shannon had taken a part-time job to help out.

As I watched Shannon now, taking orders and dropping baskets of French fries into hot oil, it was easy to see the cheerleader in her. With her bright smile and easygoing manner, she stood out among the other workers.

I dipped a fry into a tiny paper cup filled with ketchup. Finding Shannon had been easy.

We tracked her to the high school that I'd seen in my vision. A quick glance at the sports photos hanging on the wall in the school's lobby and I was able to pick her out of the team cheerleading picture. Thankfully the school was still full of kids staying after for various extracurriculars. Sean asked a girl walking by if she knew the blond-haired blue-eyed cheerleader. Not only had we learned Shannon's name, but her life history as well.

Some kids didn't mind talking to strangers. And talking and talking.

A peek in the phone book gave us an address for Shannon. She lived in a rundown duplex in a neighborhood of other rundown houses, cracked sidewalks, potholed streets, and enormous chestnut trees.

The door was answered by Shannon's mother. Maggie O'Meara was impossibly young to have breast cancer, mid-thirties at best. She was medium height, slender build. Baggy jeans and a Portsmouth High School sweatshirt nearly swallowed her whole.

I forced myself not to stare. She was completely

bald, lacking any hair at all—eyebrows and lashes included.

Sean handed her a card, and I introduced us. "We're looking into the disappearance of a woman named Sarah Loehman."

Maggie leaned against her door, glanced at the card. "I don't understand. I don't know anyone by that name."

Sean said, "We have reason to believe that the silver heart bracelet your daughter Shannon wears once belonged to Sarah. She had it with her when she went missing."

Maggie's eyes widened. "Come on in."

Tired wooden floors creaked as she led us past a dusty dining room into the family room. A large picture window looked onto a marsh behind the house. Sean and I sat on a lumpy couch. Pictures brightened the room. Family portraits of two similar-looking blondes. Mom and daughter through time. At Disney World, at the beach, at Canobie Lake Park, at a picnic, at a school football game. There wasn't a sign of a father in Shannon's life, and Maggie wore no wedding band.

An old armchair with a drooping cushion sat near the window. Gently, Maggie lowered herself into it. "I knew something was up with that bracelet. It looked too expensive to be a knockoff, like Shannon told me."

"Do you know where she got it?" I asked.

Though she looked fragile, her voice was strong. "She got it about six months ago, right around her birthday. A present from the boyfriend she doesn't know I know about. She tells me he's just a buddy."

"I think I had a few of those," I said, smiling.

Maggie laughed. "Who hasn't? It's why I keep quiet. Let her think she's got a big secret. Jimmy's a good kid—I'm not too worried about him."

"Do you mind if we talk to her about the bracelet?" Sean asked.

Cornflower-blue eyes stood out against her pale face. Worry wrinkled her brow. "She's not in any trouble, is she?"

Sean shook his head. "We just want to talk to her."

I pulled a picture of Sarah Loehman out of my bag, walked it over to Maggie. "Do you recognize this woman at all?"

Thin fingers held the picture. Her gaze took in every nuance of the photo. "She looks vaguely familiar. I think I may have seen her on TV?"

"Maybe," I said. "Her disappearance was in the news for a long time."

"And you think Shannon has her bracelet?"

"It's a possibility," I said vaguely. "We'd really like to talk to Shannon and get more information. Is she home?"

"Working. Down the street. I'll give you directions." Maggie stiffly rose to her feet. She caught us watching her. "I'm okay. Better than most with my diagnosis. The worst part?" she said, leading us toward the door.

"What's that?" I asked.

"Shannon has to take care of me now. I've always prided myself on being a good mom. Providing for her, caring, nurturing. But I can't find a job where I can work from home, and no one wants to hire someone so sick."

Sean held open the screen door for me. "I'm sure Shannon understands."

"Oh, she does and she doesn't complain," she said softly. "But it's killing me."

I could only imagine.

"I'll call Shannon," she said. "Let her know you're stopping by."

Hence our trip to the Golden Arches.

I pushed my fries away as Shannon bounced up to the table, a tentative smile on her lips. I slid over. "Do you want to sit?"

"No, thanks. My mom said you wanted to talk to me?"

"It's about your bracelet," Sean said.

Her smiled vanished as she protectively slid her fingers over the metal. "What about it?"

"We need to know where you got it," I said gently.

"At the mall," she said quickly. "From Claire's."

I shook my head. "That's not the truth."

Her pale eyebrows dipped. "It is the truth."

"They don't sell Tiffany bracelets at the mall, Shannon," Sean said, kindness lacing his tone.

I glanced at him. He'd known immediately to take a gentle approach. And it paid off as Shannon, her blue eyes brimming with tears, pleaded with him. "You can't tell my mom. She'll make me give it back."

I didn't have the heart to tell her that she'd probably have to give it to the police. "Back where?"

"To Jimmy."

"Your boyfriend?" Sean ventured.

She nodded. "He's, like, the greatest. He bought this for me for my birthday."

"Why would your mom make you give it back?" I asked.

"Because she doesn't know I have a boyfriend. You can't tell her."

Little did she know. "I'll make you a deal. We won't tell your mom if you tell us how to get in touch with your boyfriend."

"Why?" she said, tipping her head. Her blond ponytail slashed the air.

Sean smiled reassuringly. "We need to ask him about the bracelet."

Shannon seemed lost in his compassionate eyes.

I couldn't blame her.

"What's wrong with the bracelet?" she asked. "It's not fake, is it?"

"No, it's not fake."

"Good. It's like my prized possession. My good-luck charm. I never take it off."

Shivers ran up my spine.

According to Faye Dodd, Sarah had felt the same way.

14

"I can't stay," Sean said as he pulled up in front of my cottage.

"I wouldn't have been here anyway," I said smugly, pushing open my door. The cold air stung my cheeks, stole my breath. I braced myself against the wind whipping off the water.

Sean came around the car. "Why not?"

"You first."

"You don't want to know."

Cara. Had to be. I arched an eyebrow. "You don't either."

He set his hands on his hips. A smile tugged his lips. "Is that how it's going to be?"

"Yep." I turned for the house.

Something hard hit me in the back. I spun and snow exploded in my face.

Sean's laughter carried as the remnants of a snowball dripped down my chest. "Is *that* how it's going to be?" I asked.

"Yep."

I gathered up snow, formed a ball, and went after him.

He dodged between trees, but I managed to hit his shoulder. He returned fire with a shot that missed me by an inch. I ran for the safety of the arbor.

I quickly made five snowballs, my back pressed against the lattice. Slowly, I rose up, peering around a shrub.

A snowball zoomed by my ear. "Close!" I yelled, laughing. "But a miss."

"Are you taunting me, Ms. Valentine?"

"Absolutely." I aimed toward the area where his voice came, hitting nothing but a tree trunk. "All's fair in love and war, right?"

Carefully, I edged around the corner of the porch, looking for a flash of movement. Nothing. I inched slowly forward, armed to the teeth with icy ammunition.

An attack came from my right side. I turned to fire, but before I could raise my arm, Sean was there, tackling me to the ground, laughing—a sound that resonated deep within my heart, banging this way and that, loosening inhibitions. "Right," he said.

He lay on top of me and for a minute I couldn't breathe just from the sheer pleasure. Slowly, he rose up, bracing his knees on either side of me.

I smiled up at him. "You throw pretty good for a boy."

His eyes shone with happiness. I was pretty much a goner, my sappy self falling that much harder.

"I like when you look at me like that," he said, lowering himself to his elbows.

"Like what?"

His eyes flickered to hot, desire darkening his gray irises. "Like the way I'm looking at you now."

"Oh." I reached up, brushed snow out of his hair, and let my hand linger on the nape of his neck. His skin burned under my touch. "I like that too."

He lowered his head and kissed me. I barely noticed the cold, the snow. All I felt was heat, blistering its way along my skin, teasing places that ached to be teased.

More. I wanted more. I wanted it all. Everything. The heat, the ache, the release. I wanted him, his heart, his love . . .

A shudder rippled through me. Was I asking too much?

Sean gathered me in his arms. "Cold?"

I brushed his jaw with kisses. "With you around? Never, Mr. Donahue."

It was then that we heard the crash from inside the house.

Spar was too trendy for its own good, a modern-day supper club. It was all sleek and black, hot and sexy. The bar was a square in the middle of the room and, in its center, a boxing ring was set up, but there was no one sparring and I had to wonder if it was just decoration.

A jazz band was playing, a brassy backdrop to hundreds of voices raised in conversation over appetizers and cocktails. Marisol and I were at a back table, hidden behind two menus. It was rumored the food here wasn't all that good, but no one came here hungry for food.

All around women slinked by in minidresses clinging to toned bodies, necklines plunging low enough to see belly buttons. Men wore form-fitting pants, expensive shirts, designer cologne, and lascivious looks.

"I feel kind of dirty," I said.

"In a good way?" Marisol asked.

"Is there a good way?"

"Of course."

I rolled my eyes and wished I were somewhere else. Maybe with Sean. In bed. Naked. Moaning. Okay. Maybe there *was* a good way.

The crash had scared me half to death. In my mind, the sender of the Handmaiden had finally come for me.

Turned out, Grendel had knocked over a vase.

It was hard to blame Grendel for ruining a perfectly wonderful moment between Sean and me when I knew what was really behind the ruckus: Cupid's Curse. There had to be a way to break that damn curse. Had to.

"You look as good as I feel," Marisol said, watching me closely.

I knew how I looked, so she must have felt like shit. "What's wrong with you?"

"Butch broke up with me."

"What? Why?"

"Said he was sick of me talking about Em and Aiden all the time. He said he thought I was using him for his looks."

Even though it was all true I said, "His loss."

"I know, right?"

"Right."

She snuffled. I patted her hand.

Morosely, she said, "I think I'm done with men for a while."

I gave her two days. Three, maybe. "They're jerks," I said, feeling she needed some empathy.

"I know. I'm not sure what I ever saw in Butch."

He looked like Matt Damon was what, but I kept that to myself. I glanced around and slunk down in my seat. "Joseph is here."

"He is?" She turned and craned her neck.

"At the bar, far side, near the door."

Marisol moved her menu to cover her blatant staring. "He's alone."

And dressed like all the other men in the place. A woman slid up to him, but he held up his hand, waving her off.

I glanced at Marisol. "How'd you even know he'd be here tonight?"

"Remember I told you about getting someone on the inside? Well, I made buddy-buddy with the hostess. She takes reservations, so she knows when Joseph is coming in. She promised to call me whenever he calls."

"In exchange for?"

"She has three cats. I promised free care for a year. Look, look!"

Joseph was on the move. He shook the hand of a younger man, a slick twenty-something, and signaled the hostess. She led the two to a table on the other side of the restaurant.

The man with Joseph had a briefcase with him. He set it on the table and pulled out papers.

"Work?" Marisol gasped. "On a Friday night?"

"Maybe we should go," I said. It was pretty late, and I needed some sleep if I had to deal with Preston tomorrow.

"No, no. We can't. He's got to be doing more than working. Remember those condoms?"

"I'd rather not."

"Lucy!"

"Fine."

I ordered wine. If I was going to get through this night, I needed alcohol.

Marisol ordered a Cosmo, but changed her mind as soon as the server walked away. She hurried after him to change her order and didn't come back. First it was the bartender flirting with her. Then a man offered to buy her a drink. Soon, she was seated on a stool and lapping up the attention.

She never so much as looked back at me.

I glanced over at Joseph. He was still doing his business deal. I dropped a twenty on the table, gathered up my purse. I stopped by the bar on the way out to say good-bye to Marisol.

I don't even know if she heard me.

By the time I arrived home, it was well past my bedtime. I plugged in my crooked Christmas tree, grabbed my cordless phone, and plopped down on the couch. Grendel leaped up, looking for love and affection. I was happy to oblige by rubbing under his chin.

I dialed into my voice mail and had two messages. The first was from Dovie. "LucyD, did you see the picture in the *Globe*? The *Globe*!" She squealed. "I have to say I look damn good for going on sixty years old."

I smiled. She was almost seventy-five and none too happy about it. Seemed every birthday she took another year off her age.

The other message was from Raphael. "Uva," he said, "I don't suppose you know anything about the delivery of a case of titanium razor blades, do you?" He was laughing as he hung up.

It was a nice sound to fall asleep to.

15

I slept in.

Sometime in the middle of the night I'd moved from the couch to my bed. I had vague memories of upsetting dreams. If I tried hard enough, I might remember the details. I didn't try hard.

Grendel sensed me awake and crept up the bed, meowing loudly, voicing his displeasure at the lateness of his breakfast.

I threw off the covers, shivered at the chill in the air, and padded into the kitchen. I picked a can of cat food from the pantry and scooped it into Grendel's bowl. His nose twitched at me.

"You're welcome."

His tail rose and fell as he ate. I turned up the thermostat and pulled open the drapes. Muted, shady light filled the room. Outside, the snow around the cottage was tamped down and for a second I panicked, thinking someone had been lurking outside, but then I remembered the snowball fight. And smiled.

The ocean was calm. Too calm. Maybe Mum was right—there might be a doozy of a storm in the forecast after all. I went about brewing a pot of coffee, unable to shake my dreams. One of them must have involved Em because she was on my mind. I picked up my phone, called her. She answered on the third ring, and she didn't sound right.

"What's wrong?" I asked.

"It's nothing."

"It sounds like something."

"I don't know."

"Em."

"Joseph lied to me. He told me he was working late at the office last night, so I packed a picnic and brought it over to him. The office was locked up tight."

"But—"

"When I asked him about it, he said he decided to have dinner with his parents and stayed a while to visit."

I snapped my mouth closed. I'd been about to tell Em about Spar when she dropped that bombshell.

"Why didn't he just call me to let me know? And why didn't he invite me to come with him? Why did he lie?"

"I—I don't know." Joseph had clearly been doing business last night at Spar. Why not tell Em?

"He says I'm making too big a deal about it. Am I?"

I hedged. "I think you need to trust your instincts, Em."

"I just don't like arguing with him." She sighed.

"I'm sure everything will be okay," I lied. Sometimes lying wasn't wrong. Like now. Like when it would hurt my best friend to know that she was marrying a sleazy scuzball who had no compunction about lying to her. Marisol was definitely right about him—he was up to no good. We needed to find some solid evidence against him.

"I hope so. I have a fitting this afternoon, and I don't want to be mad at him when I try on my wedding dress."

The coffeepot gurgled. I poured a cup, sipped. I couldn't come up with anything else to placate her. The truth was, I didn't like Joseph. I'd been willing to overlook that fact if Em was happy. She didn't seem happy anymore.

Em filled the silence. "Did you hear about Marisol and Butch?"

"She filled me in last night."

"She's been asking a lot of questions about Aiden. Do you know why? Is she interested in him?"

Em tried to sound casual, but I saw right through her nosy façade, and it gave me hope. I decided to string her along. "Not sure."

"Oh. Well, I was just curious."

"I'm curious too," I said, sipping. The furnace rattled as heat emanated from the radiator. I wasn't sure where Marisol was going with the whole Aiden part of her plan, but I knew she had Em's best interests at heart.

"I mean," Em said, "she and Butch just broke up."

"I know."

"She should, you know, take some time for herself. Not jump into anything else so soon."

"Marisol said as much herself last night." Right

before she'd sauntered to the bar, surrounded herself with men, and flirted the night away.

Em let out a breath of relief. "That's good. I worry about her."

"Me too," I said honestly. But mostly I worried about Em hating us if she found out what we were up to.

Preston and I were lost.

I'd let her drive, and she didn't have a cool GPS system. We'd been circling Falmouth for the past half hour.

"I think we should go left up here," she said, peering at street signs from beneath edgy blond bangs. Big sunglasses covered most of her face, but the corners of her eyes crinkled as she squinted.

"We went that way already," I pointed out.

"We did?"

"Yes."

We turned right. We'd gone this way too.

"We need to ask directions," I said.

"We'll find it. How hard can it be?"

I stared at her.

"What? We've only been circling for a few minutes."

"More like thirty."

"Are you always so argumentative?" she asked.

"Are you?"

"Yes."

I smiled.

"It's kind of my job," she clarified.

"I thought your job was asking questions."

"Sometimes there's arguing involved."

I checked for our turn, an innocuous-sounding "Ocean Point Road." So far, no luck. "How long have you been a reporter, anyway?"

"I started working at the *Beacon* seven years ago, starting when I was sixteen, answering phones. At seventeen I was beat reporting. I work hard."

"Never said you didn't."

"You have a look," she said.

"What kind of look?"

"Disdainful."

I lifted a shoulder in a half shrug. "Can't say I always agree with what you write."

"The truth?"

"Sometimes your truth comes in shades of gray."

"What's true isn't always black-and-white."

"It's always black-and-white," I said. "That's why it's true."

"You're wrong."

"Is this where the arguing thing comes in?"

She smiled. "Pretty much. Are you working with the police right now?" she asked, sneaking a look my way.

"Why?"

"Just because."

"That sounds like a shade of gray."

"C'mon, Lucy, you owe me a story. I'm never going to get hired by one of the bigger papers unless I keep writing big stories."

She'd written a really big story—on me—not too long ago, and it hadn't gotten her very far. "Whatever happened to the *Herald*? I thought you were guaranteed a job there."

"It fell through."

"Why?"

"Black-and-white?"

"Yes."

"They wouldn't hire me because I don't have a journalism degree. Most papers require one now. But if I can only show them that I can write great stories . . . Big stories . . ."

"Why not get the degree?"

She slowed around a sharp bend. "It feels like taking a step back."

"But wouldn't it really be like taking a step forward?"

"Who are you, my older sister?"

Nope. Not if my father's reaction was any indication. I thanked my lucky stars for that. "Just seems like common sense."

She shrugged. "I prefer to do things my own way."

I frowned as we drove past another street that looked familiar. "We should get directions."

"We've been through this."

I groaned while we crept along looking for a street that I now doubted existed. Falmouth wasn't all that big. "Have you talked to my father lately?"

"Not really. He's been on the down low."

I didn't mention the new girlfriend. "I think he may be trying to match you."

Her head jerked up. "Me? What makes you think so?"

"Do you know someone named Cutter Mc-Cutchan?" I asked.

She looked straight ahead. "No."

"Well, his name was on your invitation to Dovie's party. Didn't you see it?"

"Didn't notice."

"I think my father is up to something. A little matchmaking maybe."

"It's the first I've heard of it," she said tightly.

"Does that upset you?"

She laughed. It wasn't tinkly at all. "No. Why would it?"

"I don't know. You tell me."

"It's just that I'm not really looking for a guy right now. I'm focused on my job. Aha!" she shouted as she swerved sharply onto Ocean Point Road. The sign for the gravel lane was nearly hidden behind an old maple tree. We must have driven past the entrance six or seven times already.

Preston pulled up in front of the only house on the street. Reaching over her seat, she hauled an enormous purse onto her lap and quickly hopped out of the car. I watched her go for a second, wondering why I had the feeling she was running from something.

16

John McGill, Esquire, might have had the best office location in all of Falmouth. He worked from home, a lonely beach house on a spindly point that jutted into Nantucket Sound. The stunning home, all glass and straight lines, was lifted off the ground by twelve-foot stilts. Ample protection from tidal surges.

Strong waves lashed against the shore, crashing in harmony. I pulled my hands through my windswept hair, trying futilely to tame it.

"I went into the wrong business," Preston said, staring in awe.

The house was a masterpiece, no doubt designed by some famous architect. We walked the stone path to the door. The Cape hadn't received any snowfall, but frost crunched under our feet.

"You could buy a house like this with your trust fund," Preston said.

"I like my place."

"It's kind of small, don't you think?"

"No."

"And isn't it weird living so close to your grand-mother?"

"No."

She took off her sunglasses and gave me a disbelieving glare. "I don't get you."

The feeling was mutual. I knocked on a thick wood door, taking in my surroundings. The day had dawned dark and gloomy and hadn't changed much as morning seeped into afternoon. Martha's Vineyard was but a speck in the distance, shrouded in mist.

John McGill had handled David Winston's estate after his death and would hopefully point me in Joanne's direction. I'd called ahead and Mr. McGill was kind enough to see me and Preston, though I doubted he often took appointments on Saturdays.

The door opened with a great whoosh, and a woman came out. She wore a nicely tailored suit, carried a briefcase, and said, "Thank you for your time."

Or maybe he was such a workaholic, weekends were just more billable hours.

The older gentleman standing in the doorway replied with, "Thank you for coming. I'll get back to you."

He wore a spandex biking outfit of screaming yellow and subtle black. An aerodynamic helmet was nestled in the crook of his arm. "Mr. McGill?" I asked.

Smiling, he bowed. "At your service."

Immediately, I was charmed. Preston too. She flashed him her hundred-megawatt smile.

"I hope we haven't caught you at a bad time?"

Smoothing back thick white hair, he said, "Is there ever a bad time when beautiful women are at your door? Come in, young ladies, my bike ride can wait. I don't suppose you're here about the job?"

I shook my head, and we followed him through a vestibule into a small office. "I called earlier. I'm Lucy Valentine and this is Preston Bailey. Thank you for agreeing to meet with us on such short notice."

"Happy to help." He eyed a pile of notepads on his desk, his longhand nearly impossible to read.

"I don't suppose either of you transcribe?"

"Not anymore," I said, grateful.

Preston glanced at me.

"I went to paralegal school for a while," I explained.

"You did?" she asked, eyebrows raised.

"Among other things." I wanted to tease her again about not knowing my life as well as she thought, but now wasn't the time.

"More's the pity," John McGill boomed. "I can't find the right fit. I just need someone to type up my notes. I hate these newfangled computers. But enough about that."

I tried not to let my gaze drop below his chest. The spandex left little to the imagination. "Have you been riding long?"

"Twenty years. I had a heart attack at fifty and made some changes. Now remind me of your name again, young lady," he said to me.

I sat in a worn leather chair. "It's Lucy Valentine, but I'm becoming partial to 'young lady.'"

He laughed and sat in a massive swivel chair behind his desk. The wall behind him housed floor-to-ceiling windows, but the inside wall was crammed with overflowing bookshelves. "Young lady it is, then. And you?" he asked Preston.

She introduced herself and pulled out a business card.

"The *Beacon*?" he said, squinting at the small text. "Never heard of it."

Preston groaned and sank back in her chair.

"We're here about Joanne Winston," I said. "You handled David's estate when he passed. I'm hoping you might have some information about his mother."

He steepled his fingers. "I was the Winston family attorney for years. What do you wish to know?"

"Anything, everything. Is she even alive?"

"I've not heard otherwise, and I think I would. News as such would travel quickly in this town. Charles and Joanne were mainstays, you see. Lived here for nigh on forty years, but moved on to Florida over a decade ago to take advantage of year-round warmer climes in hopes the various ailments plaguing Charles would benefit from the change. Unfortunately he died not long after the move. Joanne decided to remain in Florida, an address in . . ." He squinted one eye closed. "Lakeland. We had several conversations after David died, but nothing lately."

Sean had tracked Joanne to the Lakeland address. From there she had disappeared.

"Did she remarry after Charles died?"

"Not that I know. May I ask why you're looking for her?"

"Just trying to help someone track down an old friend."

"I see, I see. Have you tried contacting her daughter?"

I frowned. "Her daughter? I thought she and Charles only had one child. David."

"True, but Joanne had a little girl when she met Charles." He did the eye squint again. "Lea is her name. Her father died in World War II. Charles wanted to adopt Lea, but Joanne was adamant that Lea always carry her father's name."

Chills danced down my spine, swept up my arms, raising bumps along the way.

Preston found her voice first. "Do you happen to remember Lea's last name?"

More squinting. "Everly? Everson?"

"Epperson?" I asked.

He snapped his fingers. "Yes, that's it. Do you know her?"

"No," I said. "But I know her father."

Once we were back in the car, I called Leo. His home phone rang and rang with no answer and no voice mail.

"This is big," Preston said. "Bigger than big. Enormous. This could launch my career."

I frowned at her.

"What now?"

"This isn't about you. It's about Leo. He has a daughter."

"I know!" she squealed. "And it's going to make me famous."

I rolled my eyes.

"I think I'll turn down the *Herald* when they offer me a job. Hold out for something better. The *Globe*, the *New York Times*."

Leo had a daughter. My chest was feeling all funny, tight and swollen. I couldn't wait to tell him, to see the look in his eyes. Yet, I couldn't help wondering . . . Had his family known about Lea and kept the baby a secret because they hadn't liked Joanne? My instincts said yes, but I knew there was no way to learn the truth. My chest tightened, ached, at the sadness of it all.

I tried dialing Leo again. No answer.

Snowflakes floated from the clouds, swirling and twirling in a beautiful wintry dance. Temperatures hovered just below freezing, and according to the forecast on the radio, three to six inches of snow was predicted by morning.

Preston took a sharp turn and her handbag tipped over. I bent down to scoop up the contents that had spilled across my feet as she droned on about a career writing human interest stories.

I shoved a journal, her digital recorder, a checkbook ($193.28 balance), and her wallet back into her bag along with various receipts and notes. A glossy flyer caught my attention.

"I hadn't thought about human interest, not really," she said, speeding up to merge. "I always thought I'd be a little more hardcore, but human interest suits me just fine. I have a flair for it, if I do say so myself."

I couldn't pull my gaze from the flyer. Local artist Cutter McCutchan was holding a showing tomorrow night at a gallery on Newbury Street. The date and time were circled and Preston had written "Get copy of guest list."

I quickly shoved the paper in her bag. Preston had lied to me. She knew exactly who Cutter was, yet she'd denied it. Why?

Just ask her, I told myself. But I couldn't bring myself to do so. Something warned that if I did, it would open up something I wasn't prepared to deal with.

"Your father has contacts at the *Globe,* right?" she asked. "Didn't he match the editor with his wife?"

"My father knows a lot of people," I said numbly as thoughts of justifiable homicide once again flitted through my head.

"What's wrong with you?" she asked. "Is this about Leo? Of course I'm happy for him. He's going to be over the moon."

I was saved from answering by the sound of my phone singing. It was Marisol. I would normally let it go to voice mail, but I was in no mood to pick up my conversation with Preston. "Hi," I said.

"We need bait," she said.

"Bait?"

"For tonight. I just got a call from Desiree, the hostess at Spar? *He* has reservations tonight. Probably going to show up again with his spiffy business buddy, so we need some bait."

Preston slid her sunglasses on top of her head and glanced at me. She could obviously hear every word. I had to be careful what I said. "And where, exactly, are we going to get some?"

"Damned if I know. I thought you could find someone. Do *I* have to do *everything*?"

"Do *I* need to remind you whose idea this was?"

"Don't get all pissy on me. We're in this for the greater good."

Wipers slashed at the falling snowflakes. A headache was building behind my right eye. "Maybe he's going with Em. Did you think of that?"

"He's not. I'm meeting her in an hour for her fitting, then we're going to dinner and a movie."

"Then how are you going to be at Spar?" I asked.

"I'm not. You are."

"Marisol . . ."

"Lucy. Just find someone and be there. Eight o'clock."

She hung up on me.

"I'll do it," Preston said.

I shoved the phone in my bag. Sean and I had made plans to spend some time alone. I really didn't want to cancel, yet I couldn't back out on Marisol. Bringing him with me wasn't such a good idea. He was rather noticeable. Even in a place like Spar he'd stand out. And I really didn't like the idea of women in slinky dresses making passes at him. If anyone was going to be making a pass, it would be me. Though on second thought, me in a slinky dress with Sean glued to my side didn't sound like a bad idea.

"You don't even know what it is," I said.

"Sure I do. You need a decoy. That's what they're called."

"Who's called?"

"Women who entrap unsuspecting men, usually married men."

" 'Entrap' is a strong word."

"That isn't very black-and-white."

"Thanks for the offer, but no thanks." I needed to find someone I could trust. Like a hooker from a Craigslist ad or someone.

"Why not? And who are you staking out? Not Sean?"

"No!"

"The guy Marisol is dating?"

I glanced at her, suspicion in my eyes.

"I told you, I know a lot about your life."

I wasn't liking it one bit.

"Wait," she said, snapping her fingers. "The guy Em is engaged to. That makes sense, since Marisol is spending the evening with her."

"Does your brain ever shut off?"

"No. Do you want my help or not?" she asked.

I supposed hiring a hooker probably wasn't a good idea, whether she was more trustworthy than Preston or not. And now that she'd figured out what I was up to, there was no point in keeping her at bay. Dovie always liked to say, Keep your friends close, your enemies closer. I knew exactly where Preston stood in those categories.

"Okay," I said. "But no writing about it!"

"Off the record, I promise. On one condition."

"What?"

"You tell me about the missing person case you're working on. You owe me, Lucy Valentine, after squeezing me out of that protest story. I'm trying to build a portfolio, you know."

"Fine," I said through clenched teeth. "But you keep my name out of it."

"Agreed. Who is it?"

"Sarah Loehman."

"Holy mother of God. Have you found her body yet?"

"Not yet."

But I hoped it was only a matter of time.

17

I'd just walked in my door when the phone rang. It was Sean, and I'd decided that bringing him along tonight was better than canceling. I set the mail on the kitchen counter. No Handmaiden letter. I was thankful for the reprieve.

"I'm not going to be able to make it tonight, Lucy."

I took a deep breath. "Why not?"

"I'm back at the hospital."

"Oh my God! What's wrong? Are you all right?"

"It's not me, Lucy," he said in the barest of whispers.

I felt foolish. Of course it was Cara. Not his heart. Mine could settle down now, thankyouverymuch. "Cara?"

"Yeah. She fainted after I brought her home earlier, hit her head. I don't know how long I'll be here, but the doc thinks she'll be released soon."

"But then she probably can't be left alone."

"No."

I bit my lip.

"You understand?"

How could I not? "Pefectly," I said.

I snapped my phone closed, stared blurry-eyed through the living room windows. Snowflakes melted against the glass, leaving behind a polka-dotted screen.

I took a second to tend to Grendel's separation anxiety by rubbing his ears. After he settled down, I gave him his highly anticipated piece of cheese.

Looping around the living room, I turned on all the lights, added water to my tree.

Let it go. Let it go.

I couldn't control what was happening to Cara, or Sean's need to be there with her. I didn't doubt that he cared for me—maybe even loved me—but I also knew that at one point Cara had meant a lot to him too.

I slumped in my favorite chair and rocked. Grendel jumped onto my lap, started kneading my stomach. I rubbed the underside of his chin as his purrs filled the room with happiness.

I tried Leo again without any luck. I dislodged Grendel, fired up my laptop. I did a quick Google search on Lea Epperson. I didn't find anything helpful. I lacked the PI search engines Sean had access to. And I couldn't very well call him at the hospital.

But . . .

One-handed I flipped open my phone, dialed.

"Sam here," Sam Donahue answered brusquely.

"It's Lucy." Silence stretched a smidge too long. "I'm not calling about Sean, don't worry."

"Then you know where he is."

"It's not a secret."

"I wasn't sure . . . It's weird, Lucy. That's all."

"I know, but enough about that. I know it's Saturday and I know it's late, but I need a favor." I filled him in on Lea Epperson.

Girls squealed in the background. His daughters. My heart broke that Leo never knew his own little girl.

"I'll get right on it," Sam said.

"Thanks."

"And Lucy?"

"Yeah?"

"This thing with Sean . . ."

It felt as though a thorn had wedged in my throat.

"It's temporary. He cares about you. A lot."

"Thanks, Sam. Call me if you find anything."

As I lowered the screen on my laptop, I heard a car outside. Grendel heard it too. He was already at the door. Probably hoping it was Thoreau. Poor, lovestruck kitty.

Unfortunately, I knew how he felt.

I peeked through the drapes. Aiden was walking up my front steps. Quickly, I opened the door.

He wiped his feet before coming in. "I was thinking about what you said."

"What did I say?"

"About love at first sight."

He still looked like he hadn't slept in a week. Bloodshot eyes, unkempt hair. It just wasn't like him.

Aiden dutifully scratched Grendel's ears as he sat on the couch, stretched his long legs. He tipped his head, studying my crooked Christmas tree. He nodded to the stack of mail on the table. "Anything new?"

He was asking about the Handmaiden letters. "No."

"That's good."

"Is it?"

"Not escalating."

"Plotting instead?" I asked sarcastically. "Lulling me into a false sense of security?"

"You're being careful, right?"

I sighed. "Always. So what's this about love at first sight?"

"I do believe in it. Now are you going to tell me why you asked?"

"I told you. I was curious."

"And I'm a performer with Cirque du Soleil."

The image was so funny I couldn't help but laugh.

A smile cracked his serious face. "Spill it."

"I just think people should trust their instincts. Fight for what they want. Don't you?"

"Not necessarily. Not if someone you care for is going to get hurt in the process."

"But what if they're not? Going to be hurt, I mean. In the long run, at least?"

"Lucy."

"Aiden."

"What are you trying to tell me?"

A horn honked from outside. Preston was here.

I opened the door, made a be-right-out gesture.

Aiden stood. "You have plans."

I made a split-second decision. "You can come."

"Where?"

I hesitated for only a second before saying, "Well, Marisol and I are on a quest to prove that Joseph Betancourt is a no-good, lying, cheating sleazeball so Em will break up with him. Preston and I are going to Spar tonight because Joseph has reservations. The plan is that Preston is going to try to seduce him, I'll take some pictures, we'll show everything to Em, and bing, bang, boom, the wedding is off and maybe Em will live happily ever after with someone she truly loves."

He didn't so much as blink. "I'm in."

"I'll get my coat."

Spar was packed wall to wall with bodies. If I had any worries that Joseph might spot me and be suspicious, they were erased the minute I walked in the door. We were late, having run into traffic on the highway. The snow was affecting the roads, but not business at Spar. I could barely move between people.

"He's already here," I shouted to Preston after I spotted Joseph at the same table he sat at last night and with the same man.

"That's him?" she asked.

"Yeah, why?"

"He looks wormy."

Preston was growing on me.

People seemed to disperse, leaving a path for Aiden. He had that look about him, bloodshot eyes or no. The cop look. It was coming in handy as two men vacated stools at the bar.

"I'm going over," Preston yelled, slipping off her coat.

She'd dressed the role of hussy in a shiny halter top and microminiskirt. Though she was short, her legs were long, especially in the four-inch heels she wore. She was just the right amount of trashy to get any man's attention.

She gyrated over to Joseph's table, sidled in right next to him. The look on his face was priceless.

I noticed Aiden pull his pager from his hip. He frowned at the readout. "I have to make a call," he shouted.

I nodded. It was easier than yelling.

I watched him head for the door, the crowd parting. I turned my attention back to Preston. She was having an in-depth conversation with the man sitting with Joseph.

Great.

I felt a buzzing on my lap and realized my phone was ringing inside my purse. I pulled it out and saw that I had eight missed calls, all from Marisol. I headed for the door to call her back.

Outside, I found Aiden leaning against a lamppost, talking on his cell. Snow was falling more steadily as I dialed Marisol's number.

Marisol picked up on the second ring.

"Lucy! Thank goodness."

"What's wrong?"

"It's Em. She's lost it."

"Lost what?"

"It!" Marisol cried. "We were at the dress shop for her fitting and next thing I know, she's running out of the store leaving me behind in a cloud of satin and tulle."

"She ran out in her dress?"

"Drove off in a cab, her dress caught in the door, dragging down the street."

I gasped.

"I know! A twenty-thousand-dollar Reem Acra

mopping up Comm Ave. She's lost it. Completely and totally lost it. But I hope this means she's having second thoughts about marrying *him*. It has to be a good sign, right?"

I was too worried about Em to agree.

"How're things there?"

"The bait's been planted. So far, no biting."

"Shit. Well, I'm sure Em's on her way to you. Just wanted to give you a heads-up."

Em had a habit of turning to me in times of stress. Not long ago I found her camped out at my house after taking a hiatus from her life.

I hung up just as Preston came out, looking around. "There you are!"

"How'd it go?" I asked Preston.

"It didn't. He certainly wasn't interested in me. Or anyone but the man he's with."

My eyes widened.

"No, no! Not like that! The man—"

Aiden walked over. "I have to get back, Lucy. There's been a break in a case."

"Sarah's?" I asked.

"No," he said, glancing at Preston. "A different case; someone's been receiving threatening letters and we might finally be able to nail the guy who's been sending them."

"Some people are just sick," Preston said.

My blood ran cold as I stared at Aiden. He nodded. He was talking about the Handmaiden letters. They had a lead. I wanted to cry.

Aiden and I started walking toward the car.

"Hey!" said Preston.

We turned back and looked at her. "First," she said, "I have the keys. Second, the man who was with Joseph?"

"Yeah?" I asked, hesitant. There was something in her tone.

"He's a lawyer."

"So?" Aiden asked. "I'm sure he does lots of business with attorneys."

Preston shook her finger at him. "This one was *his* attorney. They were going over the prenup Joseph had asked to be drawn up."

18

As I stuck my key in the lock of my front door, I thought I heard the sound of the TV over the crashing waves.

As the door swung open, I blinked.

Em sat in a cloud of creamy white that swallowed my sofa. Layers and layers of silk were being weighted down by Grendel. It was completely dark inside except for the glow of the TV set.

Em pulled her sky-blue eyes from the screen. "I've got to get one of those! Blankets with arms! What a great invention."

Glancing at the TV, I set my things down by the door. "Why do you need a blanket with arms?"

"I get cold. Where's my cell phone?" she said, patting all around her dress. "Oh! That's right." She pulled it from her cleavage beneath a beautiful sweetheart neckline.

I strode over to her, snatched her phone out of her hand.

"Lucy!"

"Em! As your best friend, it's my duty to stop you.

Unless you want to wear a giant long-sleeved fleece muumuu. Because that's what it looks like."

"It looks cozy!" she argued, reaching for her phone.

Grendel had had enough. He rrrreowed and hopped off the couch, landing on his three legs without a wobble. Tail high, he stalked into the kitchen, sat by his bowl.

"No," I said, tucking the phone into my pocket.

"Lucy!" she whined.

I turned on some lights, plugged in the tree. "No. And why are you watching infomercials?"

"I'm not—this is just a commercial. I'm watching a rerun of *What Not to Wear*. Do you think I'm frumpy?"

"Frumpy? Never!"

"I think I might be. I mean, this lady on the show wears sweatpants and track jackets all the time and they're calling her frumpy."

"You never wear sweatpants."

"Sometimes I do. When no one's around. And didn't I almost just buy a fleece muumuu?"

I sat in my club chair that rocked and swiveled. "Em."

"What?"

"Have you been drinking?"

She shook her head. Her red hair had been twisted into a severe bun that looked nothing short of painful. "Not yet. But I'm thinking it's a good idea."

I couldn't argue with that. "What's going on?"

She stared at the TV screen.

"Em?"

Her fair complexion colored to a splotchy red.

Against the dress, her face looked like a cherry on top of vanilla ice cream. "There was this couple. Outside the dress shop. I was watching them. They were barely touching, but you could tell . . ."

"Tell what?"

"Their love just kind of surrounded them, wrapped them in this glow. A little lovely cocoon." Tears shimmered in her eyes. "It's the way you and Sean are too."

A painful lump wedged in my throat. I prodded her. "It's not how you and Joseph are?"

I knew it wasn't, but I wanted to hear it from her. Make her acknowledge it. I couldn't wrap my head around that prenup. Em was going to flip out when he presented it to her.

And it seemed vaguely ridiculous. After all, Em was the heir to millions and millions. Sure, she and her parents were on the outs right now, but eventually the rift would be mended. The Baumbachs were too close-knit to let anything come between them for long.

"No. And I think it should be, shouldn't it? If we're going to be married? Shouldn't there be that kind of, I don't know, silent passion? Is that too much to—"

A car door slammed, cutting her off.

I rose, peeked out the window. My heart thrummed. "It's Sean."

I cringed as Em wiped her eyes with a silk ruffle. The bottom of her dress was a mess, covered in dirt and grime.

"I can send him away," I offered.

"No, no. It's fine. I'm fine."

I pulled open the door. Thoreau raced up the front steps, zipped into the house, yipping and yapping. Grendel tore himself away from his food dish to pounce on the dog.

The two tumbled across the dining room. Em laughed. "They're adorable together."

Sean came up the walk carrying an overnight bag. Just one look into his eyes and my knees went all wobbly and little firecrackers of heat shot through my stomach.

"I hope you don't mind me coming over this late," he said, pulling me into his arms before I could say a word.

His fingers threaded through my hair as he lowered his lips to mine. He tasted of cinnamon and smelled like . . . Sean. The scent wasn't something I could identify by name, but my body, my heart, would know it anywhere.

It was like Em said. As if love surrounded us, wrapping us in a warm glow that kept out all the bad stuff. Cara, Cupid's Curse, Sean's health.

Even now, as his heart beat strongly against mine, I worried about it stopping. That the defibrillator implanted in Sean's chest might misfire and just like that he'd be gone . . . No good-byes, no I-love-yous, no forever after.

The thought alone made me tighten my arms around him, lean into the kiss. Our tongues caught, tangled, teased. The promise of more hung in the air.

We tumbled backward into the house. Sean kicked the door closed. As he lifted the hem of my sweater, the sound of the TV penetrated my happy fog.

I jumped back.

"What?" Sean said.

I glanced at the couch.

With folded arms, Em said, "That. That's what I want."

Sean looked at Em, then back at me, then at her again as though he thought he was seeing things.

I went over to the sofa, sat on the arm. "You can have it, Em."

"But not with Joseph."

It was hard, so hard, to keep from cheering. Maybe she'd break up with him on her own and Marisol and I would never have to say a word. "No?"

She stood up, layers of silk falling around her. With a yank, she pulled her hair loose. It fell in luxurious waves around her face, down her shoulders. Put a wand in her hand and she could almost be Glinda the Good Witch, but Em was so much prettier. Standing there, in that amazing dress, with that hair, and the pink in her cheeks, she took my breath away she was so lovely.

"I don't know," she said. "I just need some time to think. Can I stay here tonight?" She looked between Sean and me and said, "I'll take the couch."

My gaze shot to Sean. I didn't think I wanted my first time with him to be while Em was snoozing on my sofa. Yet, if we shared a bed, I didn't know if I could keep my hands to myself.

He looked like he knew exactly what I was thinking. His eyes danced.

"Wine," Em said. "I need alcohol."

I couldn't agree more.

* * *

It was late.

I'd given in to Em's adamant wish to wear a pair of my sweatpants as pajamas. She threw on my old Bridgewater State sweatshirt and a pair of gym socks to complete the outfit. Wine glass in hand, she was stretched out on the couch under a down comforter, watching another episode of *What Not to Wear* (it was a marathon), the sound blaring as if she were trying to block out the voices in her head.

The steady thump, thump, thump of Odysseus running on his wheel reverberated through the wall of my bedroom. I grabbed a strawberry from the fridge, popped half in my mouth and brought the other to him. I lifted the door of the cage, held out the remainder of the strawberry. Immediately he stopped running. His little hamster nose sniffed the air. He looked at me with his one and only eye and seemed to be waging a war within himself if I could be trusted. Slowly, he ventured to the door, took the strawberry from me with his teeth. He sat on his haunches, nibbling contentedly until I tried to pat his gray and white fur. At that, he shoved the strawberry into his cheek and ran to the far corner of the cage.

So much for trust.

Odysseus and Grendel had been "gifts" from Marisol. As a vet, she often tried to place strays with loving families. And strays with issues, like a one-eyed hamster and a three-legged cat, were harder than most to find a home. I've been known to complain when Marisol left a pet with me (usually while I wasn't home), but was secretly glad to have both my critters.

Back in the kitchen, I rinsed dishes, put them in the dishwasher, suddenly thinking of Faye Dodd. Sean and I had plans to return to Portsmouth in the morning to see if we could track down Jimmy, Shannon's boyfriend. We had to find out where he'd bought that bracelet.

I finished cleaning up, shoving the pizza box into the recycling bin. The L-shaped granite breakfast bar overlooked both the dining room and living room. I glanced at Sean as he moved about my bedroom, getting ready for bed. He'd showered and his bare chest glistened with wetness. I couldn't help but stare. And want.

Grendel and Thoreau had claimed the end of my bed and were wrapped together like Yin and Yang.

Sean crossed in front of the door again and caught my eye. He smiled. My heart crashed into my rib cage as heat slowly built inside me. I tore my gaze away before I self-combusted.

In the living room, Em refilled her wine glass, refocused on the TV. She glanced up, caught me staring. "I'm okay, really. I'll figure everything out."

Raising her glass to me in a silent toast, she turned back to the TV. I recognized the need to watch TV as an escape. Mindless filler to calm the thoughts racing through her head.

"Long day?" Sean asked, padding into the kitchen in bare feet and an old pair of gym shorts.

His pearl-gray eyes looked nearly opaque in the dim light. Stubble covered his superhero jaw, and the slightest hint of darkness caressed the skin under his concerned eyes.

"Pretty long," I said, leaning against the counter, my hands behind me so I'd keep them off him.

With the pad of his thumb, Sean traced my jawline. I pressed my cheek into his palm, let my eyes close.

His touch soothed the rough edges of my day. "But there were some good parts." I told him about Leo.

"And where were you tonight?" he asked.

I glanced at Em. "I'll tell you later."

He leaned in, pressed his forehead against mine. His hands slid down my arms and pulled them out from behind me. Skimming along my skin, he stopped just above my hands. I turned my palms over so they hovered just under his touch.

My fingers tingled with the electricity.

I couldn't explain the how or the why. I could just feel. The electricity. The magic.

We rarely allowed ourselves to touch hands. The experience was too powerful, and honestly, I was scared. Scared of what I might possibly see. I didn't want to risk seeing something I wouldn't like.

Slowly, I drew my hand away. "I think I'm ready for bed."

His eyes twinkled. "I was just thinking the same thing."

"Great minds," I teased.

I went over to Em, glanced at the TV. "I suggest staying away from QVC."

"Don't worry. The fleece muumuu was temporary insanity."

We said good night and ten minutes later I'd

brushed my teeth, washed my face, and had stalled long enough. I stepped out of the bathroom, wearing a tank top and lounge pants—my normal PJs.

I had bought something silky and sexy in hopes that someday I'd wear it for Sean, but tonight didn't feel right.

In the living room, the TV blared. I closed the door tight, listening for the click of the latch.

Sean had stripped to his boxer briefs and was standing in front of Odysseus' cage, letting the hamster sniff his fingers.

"He likes you," I said, sitting on the bed. "He doesn't trust easily."

"Few do." He closed the door on the cage, turned around.

"I'm surprised to see you here tonight," I said.

He sat down next to me and made a little twirl motion with his finger. I twisted, turning away from him. My breath hitched as his warm strong hands splayed against the small of my back, the heels pressing into my muscles.

"You don't mind, do you?"

"No." I tried not to moan as he massaged away aches and worries and inhibitions. "Just surprised. Is Cara okay?"

"She was discharged, and I took her home."

His right hand went under my shirt. His roughened palm slid up my spine.

Goose bumps rose on my arms while a fiery hot pool of desire spread in my stomach, lower.

"She asked me to stay the night with her, that she was scared."

I tensed.

"Now, now," he soothed, his left hand joining his right, under my shirt, working magic with my muscles, my skin, my longing.

"And although I had reservations, I was going to." His hands pressed, kneaded.

"Reservations?"

"She was so upset after fainting the doctor in the ER gave her a sedative, to calm her down. It made her chatty."

His fingers spread as his hands swooped up and down my back. His fingertips grazed the sides of my breasts. His hands slid away, to my lower back. I bit my lip to keep from crying out.

"What . . . did . . . she . . . say?" I managed to sputter.

"She talked a lot about us getting back together. That she didn't like living alone. That if she was sick I couldn't walk away from her."

I tensed again.

"Ah, ah," he admonished, pushing harder, leaning into the pressure. "When she asked me to stay the night, this little seed of doubt was planted."

"Oh?"

"Every test has come back negative. All her symptoms could be for diseases not easily proven, like MS. She's a nurse, she'd know how to get away with it."

"But," I said, melting under his touch, "what if she's not faking?"

"That's the million-dollar question, isn't it?"

"So why didn't you stay tonight, with her? You know, to watch over her?"

"I was going to, just because there is still that possibility she's not faking, but I had a savior."

I glanced over my shoulder at him. "A savior?"

"Sam's wife, Lizzie. She showed up on Cara's doorstep and said she'd stay the night with Cara. It wasn't an offer I was going to refuse."

Sam had to be behind this turn of events. I loved that Sam. "And how did Cara take it?"

He curled his hands into fists, massaged in delicious circles. "She didn't look too pleased, but she didn't argue."

"And you came here."

"And I came here."

His hands circled around my waist and swept upward, stopping just short of my breasts. Down they went, only to swing up again to stop short.

I let out a deep breath. "Why?"

Down, up.

Tease, tempt.

I leaned back. His lips were hot on my neck as he kissed little delicious pecks from my shoulder to just under my ear.

I could feel his heat, his hardness pulsing against my lower back. As much as I wanted to flip over and have my way with him, I was enjoying what we were doing, this give-and-take.

"When I was in the hospital room," he said, his hands going down and up, "I realized there wasn't a place I'd rather be than with you."

He moved from behind me, keeping his arms around me as he lowered me onto the bed. Rolling next to me, he propped himself on an elbow and looked down.

In his eyes there was a question.

Yes or no?

Do we finally give in to what was, frankly, inevitable, or do we keep on waiting? Torturing ourselves while trying to figure out how we felt about each other and if it was strong enough to withstand curses and exes and anything the Fates threw in for good measure.

I'd had enough torture. I rose up on my elbows and kissed him. We fell back onto the bed, earning a "rreow" from Grendel. I took it as encouragement rather than what it probably was—crankiness that we'd disturbed him.

My hands dove into Sean's hair. It was still slightly damp from his shower. He tore his mouth from mine, leaving me wanting, and dragged his lips down my neck, over my collarbone. He tugged down my tank top, and his lips seared a path downward.

I dropped my hands, let my fingertips roam, down his back, over each bump of his spine. I dragged up the edge of his boxer briefs and I felt a little whoosh of air as he exhaled.

"I'm thinking," I said, "that we have too many clothes on."

"I couldn't agree more, Ms. Valentine."

He stood and, before I could blink, stripped.

A knock sounded. "Sorry," Em said, "but I need to use the washroom."

Sean scrambled for cover as the door opened. Em had her eyes covered with one hand and was blindly feeling around with the other.

"I'm not looking," she said unnecessarily.

Sean grabbed a pillow. As soon as the bathroom door closed, he dove for his underwear. I tossed him his shorts.

"Sorry!" Em said again. "I hope I'm not interrupting."

I held in a groan. "Nope," I lied.

Sean slipped in between the covers. I crawled in next to him. When I glanced his way, he whispered, "I should have known something would stop us."

"It's just a delay," I said.

"You think so?"

"Of course."

"What have you been telling me about curses?"

"Who believes in curses?" I scoffed, wishing I didn't.

The bathroom door squeaked open. "Is it okay to look?" Em asked.

"Yes," I said.

Em stepped into the room, took one look at us cozied up in bed, and burst into tears.

As I jumped up to comfort her, I could have sworn I heard Sean mumble, "I told you so."

19

Jimmy Jasteziak lived three blocks from Shannon O'Meara's rundown duplex in a large subdivision of cookie-cutter Colonials. The teens were swaying on a porch swing as Sean and I pulled into the driveway.

Both of us had been quiet on the long drive up here, either too sleep- or sex-deprived to chat.

I'd been up with Em until the early hours of the morning, trying to comfort her as best I could. When I finally climbed back into bed, Sean was fast asleep.

A brisk breeze chilled the already frosty air. I turned up the collar on my coat and wished I'd grabbed a scarf on my way out the door today.

Em was still sleeping when we left, but I knew she planned to go home and have a long heart-to-heart with Joseph.

Jimmy rose and shook our hands (I didn't see anything) as we stepped onto the porch. Tall and lanky, he looked to be late teens. He still leaned toward a tendency for acne, and had yet to need a good shave, but would one day be a looker, with his piercing blue eyes and easy smile.

Shannon was obviously smitten, never taking her adoring gaze from him.

I had a feeling I looked at Sean the same way.

He and I both sat in wicker chairs.

"Thanks for meeting with us, Jimmy," I said.

"No problem. Shannon wouldn't really say what this was about though."

I glanced at Shannon, who had a possessive grasp on her bracelet.

"We need to talk to you about Shannon's birthday present," Sean said.

"Her present?"

"My bracelet," Shannon said, holding her wrist aloft. The small silver heart swung back and forth, the inscribed *S* seeming to mock me.

Color leached from Jimmy's face. "Oh, ah, right. What about it?"

"Where did you get it?" Sean asked, his voice firm.

I looked at him, at his silky black hair, his concerned eyes. In an instant, I saw him as I did last night, naked and wanting me, and just like that I yearned for him so badly I could barely breathe.

He looked my way, as if sensing a shift, and lifted an eyebrow. I didn't dare look him in the eye. I tried to focus on the conversation.

Jimmy's cheek pouched as he held his breath. "Where?"

Shannon laughed and elbowed him. "Go on, tell them." She gave an exasperated sigh and leaned in to us. "He got it at Tiffany in Boston."

Jimmy stared at the porch planks.

"Is that right, Jimmy?" I asked.

"Why do you want to know?" he said.

I glanced at Shannon. "Maybe we should take a walk around the block, Jimmy? Without Shannon?"

"What? No!" she cried. "What's going on? Jimmy, tell them where you got my bracelet."

His shoulders stiffened. "I still wanna know why they need to know."

Sean rubbed his hands together. White clouds puffed from his lips as he said, "The bracelet belongs to a missing woman. We're trying to find her."

Shannon gasped. "No way! Jimmy bought this for me!"

"Jimmy?" I pressed.

"Missing?" he said.

"For two years," Sean answered. "Her name is Sarah."

Shannon jumped to her feet. Her ponytail slashed through the air. "You two have it all wrong. All wrong! Right, Jimmy?"

He wouldn't look at her.

"Jimmy!"

"Well, I—"

Her eyes widened. "You didn't get this at Tiffany?" she asked, shaking her wrist. The heart bobbed accusingly.

Wincing, he shook his head.

"You lied to me?"

"Sorry, Shannon, but I—"

She painstakingly unlatched the bracelet and tossed it at him. Storming off the porch, she didn't look back.

"Shannon!" Jimmy shouted.

Acting as if she didn't hear him, she kept going.

"Look what you did," he said to us.

Sean said, "Us? You're the one who lied to her."

Thick eyebrows dipped in anger as he watched Shannon turn a corner and disappear.

"Give her time," I said.

"I need to go after her. Are you two done here?" he asked.

"Where did you get the bracelet?" Sean asked.

"Yard sale."

Good thing Shannon hadn't heard that. "Where?"

"Shannon's street. I was on my way to her house when I spotted the bracelet and bought it. Cost ten bucks."

He probably didn't want to know how much the real thing retailed.

"You remember which house specifically?"

He scrunched up his eyes. "If you're looking at Shannon's, three doors down on the left."

"You're sure?" Sean said.

"Positive."

I pulled out the picture of Sarah Loehman. "Have you ever seen her before?"

He cocked his head. "I don't think so. We done?"

"Yeah."

"Here," he said, handing me the bracelet. "I don't think she'll want it back."

I folded my fingers around the metal, wondering what happened to Sarah, how something so treasured had ended up in a yard sale. "Thanks."

Jimmy took off running.

We drove the three blocks to Shannon's street, parked in front of her house. "One, two, three," I said, counting houses. It was a small bungalow, the yellow paint cracking. Chunks of brown poked through the snow on the sidewalk.

I knocked on the door. No one answered.

By the time we got back into the car, Jimmy had caught up with Shannon and looked like nothing had been forgiven. "Young love," I said.

Sean threw a look my way that nearly melted my shoes to the floorboard. "It doesn't get easier as you get older."

Unfortunately, he was right about that.

"What now?" I asked.

Sean took out his BlackBerry. "We find out who the house belongs to."

As he logged on to the Internet, I leaned back in my seat and wondered why I hadn't heard from Aiden. Had he found out who sent the letters? Had his lead been a dead end?

I let my eyes close. Next thing I knew, the car was moving. I glanced at the clock. Three hours had gone by.

I jolted awake.

Sean said, "Hello, sleepyhead."

I smiled. "Why didn't you wake me up?"

"You needed the sleep."

"When did it start snowing?" Fat flakes fell from the sky, coating everything in sight. There was an inch on the ground already, maybe two.

"A couple hours ago."

I tried to shake myself awake. "What happened with the yellow house, the yard sale . . . ?"

"I thought we might as well take advantage of being up there."

I rubbed my gritty eyes. "I'm glad I could be of help."

He laughed. "The house is owned by a local LLC, and is rented to a man named Jerry White. He pays monthly, in cash. My search into his history went as well as could be expected. No one came or went the two hours I watched."

I tried to listen, to process, but my mind was still fuzzy with sleep—and not having enough of it.

"I talked to some neighbors. Most people in that area are hardworking blue-collars who don't want any trouble and keep to themselves. No one knew anything of much interest. Yes, a man named Jerry lives there and has for a couple of years. No, they don't know what he does for a living. He drives a Ford truck. He's quiet, doesn't go out much. I'm not ready to call it a dead end by any stretch, but we're going to need to call in some help if we want to do surveillance properly. Might want to check with Aiden, see if he'll okay the expense."

At the reminder, I checked my phone. Aiden hadn't called. "I'll ask. But I also think it's time to take the next step."

"Which is?"

"I need to contact Scott Loehman. I might be able to get a reading from Sarah's wedding band."

Snow crunched under the car's tires as Sean turned

into Aerie. It was early afternoon—if this snow kept up there could be a foot of it by tomorrow morning.

My cottage was aglow with Christmas cheer as Sean rolled to a stop. As I unbuckled my seat belt, Sean touched my arm. "I can't stay."

"No?"

"I had a call while you were asleep. Cara's back in the hospital. Another fainting spell."

How convenient, I wanted to say, but was immediately shamed. She might really be sick, and even I didn't hate her enough to wish that upon her. "Okay," I said.

"I don't know how long I'll be."

"I won't wait up." He had a key, knew the alarm code.

He leaned in and kissed me, deep and tender. "Wait up."

I smiled. "Okay."

Inside, I puttered around, doing some light cleaning. I finally stopped procrastinating and picked up the phone. I took a deep breath and dialed, while looking at Scott's photo from Sarah's file.

Scott Loehman answered on the second ring. I introduced myself, hoping I didn't sound as though I had already pronounced him guilty.

"Detective Holliday said you might call. I was hoping you would," he said.

"Oh?" I studied his eyes in the picture. The eyes of a killer?

"Ms. Valentine, there is no one on this earth who wants to find out what happened to Sarah more than I do. No one."

I tried to dissect his tone. Did I hear any deception? Any hesitation? I simply couldn't tell. "I'm glad to hear that."

"I'm desperate, Ms. Valentine. Do you think this will work?"

"I can try," I said, walking over to my mantel. Sarah's bracelet glimmered in front of thick pine garland. I ran my finger over the silver links. "No guarantees."

"Are you free now?"

I hesitated. Actually, I was. Cutter McCutchan's showing didn't start till seven. I had plenty of time. "I can be there in half an hour."

"There's a park near my house. The kids are dying to get out in the snow. It's a busy neighborhood. Plenty of people around."

"I, ah, thank you."

"I'm well aware of my reputation, Ms. Valentine. I don't want you to feel uncomfortable. Like I said, I'm desperate. I need your help. You might just be the only person who can prove I had nothing to do with Sarah's disappearance."

Or the only one who could prove his guilt. "I'll see you soon."

"I look forward to it."

20

Empty swings were mounded with fluffy snow as a pack of small children scampered from the merry-go-round to the jungle gym, bundled against the cold. Red cheeks glowed, laughter carried, and I watched with a smile from the warmth of my car.

There was nothing quite like the happiness of a child.

I opened the folder propped against the steering wheel. I'd read every sheet in it multiple times. If I had to make a snap judgment based on that information, I'd label Scott Loehman guilty. He had motive, opportunity, and the know-how to make someone disappear without a trace.

Yet . . . he agreed—he even seemed eager—to let me do a reading.

I decided to go into the meeting with an unbiased opinion. Let him talk, hear what he had to say. And of course, use my psychic abilities to try and find his wife.

I watched two small girls chase each other around a seesaw, giggling as pigtails bounced beneath knit caps. I guessed they were about three years old. The same age Maddie Loehman had been when she sustained a broken arm after falling down the stairs at her house on the morning of her first day of preschool.

And poor Jake. On his first birthday, he'd spent most of the day in the ER. Turned out he'd had a tear in his intestine—from falling into the corner of a table, Sarah had said.

If Scott had been abusing the children, it was easy to see why Sarah would cover for him. She was scared too. And now she was missing . . .

Not wanting to read any more, I closed the file. I hoped that after today I could close the file permanently.

My cell phone rang as I watched for Scott and the kids to show up. Was he calling to cancel? He was already late by five minutes, and I began to doubt that he would come. After all, if he was guilty I might be able to prove it. I might stand me up too, if I were him.

Or maybe it was Aiden with more information on the possible break in the Handmaiden case. I was almost afraid to hope that I could start living without fear again.

As I fished my phone out of my bag I saw it was neither. I smiled at the ID screen and answered. "Did you shave yet?"

Raphael laughed. "Not yet, but I'm beginning to itch. I don't know how much longer I can hold out."

"I'm sure Maggie will understand."

"I'm sure she wouldn't."

"Mmm-hmm."

"Don't mmm-hmm me, Uva. Spit it out."

"It's just that it's clear to me you know how much

Maggie likes the Grizzly Adams look, and you like Maggie, and you want her to keep liking you. But what you're not understanding is that Maggie will like you, furry or not."

"Mmm-hmm. It's clear, is it?"

"Crystal." My gaze scanned the park, across the playground to the far corners of the snow-covered fields, past the picnic shelters, naked maple trees, looking for Scott. No sign of him.

"Are you free tonight for dinner to discuss this theory further? If you get here soon, the roads won't be so bad."

Across the street I spotted a man walking hand in hand with two children. They were headed this way. "I can't. I'm going to Cutter McCutchan's showing at a fancy gallery downtown."

"I see. Actually, no I don't. Why? You don't even know Cutter McCutchan."

"I have a sudden interest in the arts?"

"Uva . . ."

"All right. I'm curious about him. Preston Bailey lied about knowing him. Dad added him to Dovie's party guest list . . . I just want to go. I feel like I'm being kept out of something and I don't like it."

"Mmm."

The man smiled as the little girl looked up at him, chattering a mile a minute. "No 'hmm' to go along with that?"

"I don't think this is a good idea," Raphael said sternly.

"Well, I do."

"Oscar's business is his own, Lucy."

I watched the man cross the street with the children. As soon as they were safely across, he released their hands and they took off running and laughing toward the slides. The father then glanced around as if looking for someone.

"Look, I've got to go, Pasa."

"Lucy, do not go tonight. Come here instead. I'll make your favorite. Belgian waffles . . ."

Scott Loehman turned in a slow circle, hands in his pockets. I pushed open my car door. A frosty gust of air cut right through my peacoat.

The waffles tempted, but I held firm. "I've got to go, Pasa."

Stepping into the cold, I hung up and tossed my cell on the passenger seat. I didn't want to fight with Raphael. After his reaction, I was more curious than ever about Cutter McCutchan.

Closing the door behind me, I glanced Scott's way. He wasn't as tall as I imagined. Around five ten or so and stocky. Wide across the shoulders, thinner through the hips. He wore a green windbreaker over a plain white button-down shirt, jeans, and sneakers.

"Lucy?" he asked as I approached, my boots sinking into the deepening snow.

I nodded.

"Scott Loehman," he said, holding out his hand.

"If you don't mind, I'd rather wait on touching your palm."

His outstretched fingers slowly curled into a fist and he drew his hand away, tucking it back into his pocket. "Would you like to sit?" He motioned to a bench and swiped it clean of snow.

"Sure."

Across the playground, I noticed a group of mothers had stopped what they were doing to stare at us. And I noticed that none of the other children played with the Loehman kids.

"As if they're little pariahs," Scott muttered, following my gaze.

My outrage on the children's behalf must have shown on my face. "Why?"

"Because their father killed their mother. Maybe their kids are at risk."

I snapped my head to look at him.

"It's not a confession, if that's what you're thinking. It's simply what everyone believes. I'd be a fool not to know it."

"Why do you stay here?" I asked, watching Maddie and Jake climb the ladder of the slide. Maddie, at five, carefully watched over her brother, following behind him to make sure he made his way safely.

"What if we move? Will Sarah be able to find us again?"

I held his gaze. It was as though his blue eyes dared me to see his pain, laid out raw and bare, pulsing behind cool, calm irises.

I didn't know what to say, how to react. Finally, I said, "How did the two of you meet?"

"I pulled her over for speeding. She batted her eyelashes at me, said she'd rather have a dinner date with me than a date in court. I let her go. With my phone number. We were inseparable after that. She found out she was pregnant with Maddie about a year later and we flew to Vegas and got married. Sure, the elopement was driven by the pregnancy, but it was the happiest day of my life. I couldn't believe how lucky I was."

The Loehman kids seemed used to playing by themselves. The monkey bars cleared of other children as they approached and started swinging bar to bar. "And your marriage? It was a happy one?"

"We had issues, like every other married couple."

"Such as?"

"Her family. They couldn't accept that she had wanted to marry me of her own free will. They thought I took advantage of her, then coerced her into marriage. Hardly. Sarah couldn't wait to get out of her house. Her mother practically kept her under lock and key, she was so controlling. Sarah tasted freedom with me, and liked it." His gaze veered from his kids, landed on me. "I suspect she got pregnant on purpose just so she had a reason to escape her mother."

His story was the complete opposite of Faye's. I felt myself believing him and gave myself a hard mental shake. What else was he going to say? He was an abusive husband who killed his wife? I hardly thought so. "Anything else?"

"Sarah had a lot of responsibility at home. I worked. A lot. I was often gone, pulling double shifts to make ends meet. We fought about it all the time. She wanted more help at home, and I wanted to be able to pay the bills and feed my family. She didn't understand that I hated every minute I missed of the kids' lives. That it broke my heart to miss first steps, first words, Jake's birthday, Halloween, Maddie's first day of school, Easter. She felt as though she'd lost her freedom all over again."

"Why won't you let the kids see Faye?"

"I've offered more than once for her to see them. She refused."

"That's not what I heard."

"I'm not surprised. She refused because I wouldn't let her see them without supervision, the kids' nanny. I don't trust Faye not to badmouth me or even to steal them."

"You think she'd go to that extreme?"

"Absolutely."

There was no question in my mind that Faye hated Scott. What remained was, did she have good reason?

"Daddy!" Maddie yelled, running across the grass. "Look what Jakey found!"

She reached our bench and launched herself into her father's arms. He easily scooped her up, holding her close. Jake barreled toward us, holding a feather in front of him as if it were a carrot and he was a rabbit.

Jake leaped at his father, who caught him and swung him onto his free knee. "It's a feather!" Jake yelled.

With reverence, Scott took the feather from his son's hand, examined it. "It's the most beautiful feather I've ever seen."

Jake's eyes glowed with pride. "You can have it."

"Thank you!"

Maddie wiggled free. "Let's go, Jake!"

"'Kay!"

They skipped off, heading for the seesaw. Scott's gaze never wavered from their small forms.

It was as if I weren't there. The three only had

eyes for each other. Hard to believe he'd hurt those kids. And they hadn't shown any fear of him at all.

Then I remembered what Aiden had said. That Scott was now playing father of the year. The kids were young—could they have simply forgotten that he'd hurt them?

Too many questions. "Did Lieutenant Holliday explain how I work?"

"My hands, right?"

"I'd like to try and get a reading from Sarah's wedding band. So I need you to think about it, okay?"

"All right."

I held out my hand. He cradled it gently.

I pressed my palm against his, closed my eyes.

Images zipped by, blurring together. In an instant I crossed the border into New Hampshire, took back roads through Portsmouth, saw a neighborhood of rundown duplexes, cracked sidewalks, towering trees. Inside Jerry White's small yellow house, through the living room, past a kitchen, into a back bedroom. Inside a dresser drawer, tucked into a pair of old gym socks, sat Sarah Loehman's wedding band.

I drew my hand away, kept my eyes closed. When I finally opened them again, I was surprised by the tears I saw glistening on Scott Loehman's lashes.

"Did you see her?" he asked.

I shook my head. "I saw the wedding band. It wasn't with her."

"Where was it?"

"I'll give that information to the state police."

He nodded, causing a tear to spill over.

"Are you okay?"

"I just couldn't help but think about our wedding, placing that ring on her finger. Pledging for better or worse. I just can't believe she'd do this."

Squeals of laughter pierced the air. "What do you mean? Do what? Wait a minute. You don't think she met with foul play, do you?"

"No, Ms. Valentine, I don't. I think she ran away. From me, our kids, her responsibilities. But no one would listen to me when I tried to tell them. Are you listening?" he asked, his voice cracking.

"You really love her."

"I always have. And I want her back. I thought she would have come home by now. Please find her, Lucy. Bring her back to us."

21

I couldn't go to New Hampshire tonight. Not with this weather. As it was, I questioned whether going to Cutter McCutchan's showing was a good idea. Only pure stubbornness had me driving north.

As for Sarah Loehman . . . I'd go tomorrow as soon as the snow stopped and the roads cleared.

I took precautions against the weather. I parked my car at my father's penthouse and would take the train home after meeting with Cutter McCutchan. I could walk home from the train station, something I was already looking forward to. I loved walking in the snow.

The only downside was that I'd have to skip and evade Raphael to avoid another lecture. I left a note for him on the kitchen countertop so he wouldn't wonder about my car and caught a cab to the gallery.

It was only a little after five, but I hoped the gallery would let me in. I had a ruse planned and everything in case I needed it. The only catch would be if Cutter wasn't there early, but I hardly knew an artist who wasn't prepping his work hours before an event. Hopefully Cutter was the same way.

The cab rolled slowly through the snowy streets. Total accumulation was at four inches at this point, with more to come in the overnight hours. The city was absolutely gorgeous covered in white. Like a scene from an old-fashioned Christmas card. Flakes clung to spindly trees, sat adrift on light posts and mailboxes.

The gallery was located on Newbury Street, sandwiched between two other swanky storefronts. Hoisting my tote bag onto my shoulder, I paid the cabbie and stepped into the snow. On an easel behind the glass of Fallon's Fine Arts an oil portrait of a Red Sox star shone under spotlights.

It wasn't until I realized I was shivering from the cold that I made a move for the door. I'd been captivated by the painting. Cutter would do well tonight, I was sure, despite the weather.

A delicate bell chimed when I entered the shop. A woman dressed impeccably in a black pencil skirt and pale blue cashmere sweater hurried toward me. "May I help you?"

"I hope so. I'm looking for a Christmas present for my father. He's a big Sox fan."

"You've come to the right place," she said with a smile. Her heels tapped on the polished stone floor as she showed me around. All Cutter's paintings were Red Sox players, and looked lifelike on canvas, yet ethereal at the same time. I couldn't quite figure out the technique, but it captivated me, and almost made me want to shell out the high four figures it would cost to bring a painting home.

I refrained.

"You're actually quite lucky," the woman said.

"How so?"

"These paintings will be gone in a few hours. We're having a showing tonight." Her face lit. "Would you care to meet the artist? He happens to be here."

"Oh, I don't know," I hedged, trying to play it cool.

"Nonsense. You must! Your name?" she asked.

"Lucy Valentine."

Her eyes widened. "Any relation to Oscar Valentine?"

"My father."

She practically cooed, probably seeing dollar signs. "I'll be right back. Look around," she offered. Heels tapped as she hurried away.

I stared at the painting before me, the face of the ballplayer blurring under my gaze. It was the colors, I realized. The background colors that fascinated me. Each player was surrounded by a glow of varying col—

"Lucy Valentine? I'm Cutter McCutchan."

I tore my gaze from the artwork and turned around.

My breath caught, and I staggered backward.

He took a step back from me as well, as if surprised.

My jaw went slack, my eyes widened.

His lips tightened, his eyes narrowed in a deep squint.

"I—ah—" I couldn't find words.

He was tall, with old-fashioned movie-star good looks. Dark brown eyes, dark hair. Strong chin, chiseled cheeks, full lips.

Cutter McCutchan was nothing short of drop-dead gorgeous.

And he was the spitting image of my father.

"I'm s-sorry," I stuttered. "I have to go."

It was too much for me to take in. The realization that my father had a son.

Bells chimed as I pushed into the snow. I stared blindly, unable to remember which way to turn.

"Uva! Uva!"

I lifted my head, focused blurry eyes.

Raphael.

I ran toward him, slipping and sliding through the snow.

I threw my arms around him. He wrapped me tightly in warmth and protection and love.

"Come," he said, opening the car door for me. "Let's get you out of the cold."

"He has a son, Raphael."

"I know, Uva. I know." He guided me into the car.

Before I knew it, we were sliding into traffic.

He patted my hand. "I came as soon as I saw your note."

"Does he know he has a son?" I asked. "Of course he knows. He has to know."

"He only found out a week ago."

"Does Cutter know about him?"

"No, Uva. Sabrina didn't want either to know."

I swallowed hard. "Has Dad told Mum?"

Raphael shook his head. The wipers swiped the window in soothing rhythm.

Thoughts raced, questions too.

A brother. I had a brother. Younger, by the look of him, but not by much. "How old is he?"

"Twenty-four."

Four years younger. I had a brother.

I'd always wanted siblings. For company, but also because of the Valentine legacy . . .

Gasping, I said, "Does he see auras?"

"I don't know."

"He does," I said adamantly, answering my own question.

"How do you know, Uva?"

"His paintings. I was fascinated by them—because he painted auras around his subjects."

"I hadn't noticed."

I leaned back in the seat, closed my eyes.

Thoughts jumbled together, some knotting, some unraveling, as I tried to piece together how I'd gotten to this place.

It had all started with my father's strange behavior lately, then Preston Bailey and that Christmas invitation. Then there was the lie that she didn't know Cutter when she had the flyer for the opening . . .

My eyes popped open. "Preston knows Cutter is a Valentine."

I could see this. It was why she'd acted so strangely when I told Leo I was an only child—not because she might be my sister (I can't believe I ever entertained that notion) but because she knew I had a brother.

"Yes. She requested your father's help to get her a job with one of the bigger papers. If not, then Preston would bring Cutter to Dovie's Christmas party."

I could see this. She knew Dad had contacts at the

Globe . . . She was desperate to leave the *Beacon* and move on to bigger opportunities.

"Your father is complying, but he fears she will write a tell-all article. She insists she will not. He doesn't know whether to believe her."

Oddly, I did. Though she was desperate enough to use Cutter, I didn't think her so immoral as to reveal the truth in an exposé. Just a smidge immoral. After all, blackmail was blackmail.

"But how did she know about Cutter in the first place?"

"Something about old photos. Your father will have to explain."

"If he ever tears himself away from Sabrina."

"They have been getting together, trying to figure out what to do."

"What do you mean? Figure what out?"

"How to keep it all quiet. They don't understand."

"What?" I asked, not sure I agreed with keeping Cutter a secret. Though I was shocked and ran out, I knew immediately I wanted him in my life, that I already cared for him.

"Objects set in motion tend to stay in motion."

Surprisingly, traffic was congested, but not nightmarish. "You aren't about to launch into a physics lesson now, are you?"

"Would I do such a thing?"

"Yes."

"You're right. But I won't. My point is that Preston Bailey set the ball rolling. Your father found out. You. That ball will keep rolling."

"Unless someone stops it."

He beamed. "You were paying attention to your laws of motion."

"You're a good teacher."

He patted the top of my hand. "You're a lousy student."

"Pasa!"

"It's the truth."

"Doesn't make it any easier to hear."

"It never is," he said solemnly. "And now, will you tell your mother?"

I wanted to. And she deserved to know. "No, I don't think so." I said softly, echoing Raphael's words to me yesterday, "Dad's secrets are not mine to tell."

22

As soon as I came in my front door, I dropped into my favorite chair. Raphael and I had driven around for a while in silence until I realized I just wanted to go home.

I skipped the train idea and braved the ride home. The drive had been slow but not too bad. Plows were working hard, pushing snow, dumping sand. By first light all the streets would be clear. And I would be free to follow my vision right back to Sarah Loehman's house.

Grendel was lying atop Em's wedding dress, which was balled in a corner. That she left it here told me more about her state of mind than anything.

Maybe Marisol and I wouldn't have to become (more) involved at all. And maybe the prenup Joseph was filing would never come to light and break Em's heart.

Grendel hopped into my lap, stared at me with his big golden eyes. "I have a brother," I said aloud.

He tipped his head, swished his tail.

"I know. I'm kind of shocked too."

I wanted to pick up the phone, call my mother, more for comfort than anything. But I knew myself too well. The minute she suspected I was upset, the news would spill from me, and I couldn't let that happen. Dad needed to be the one to explain about Cutter.

My second thought was to call Sean. I glanced at the clock. He should be here soon enough. I'd just wait him out.

I checked my phone for messages from Aiden. Nothing. I dialed, hoping he had news about the case. He didn't answer.

Dropping my head on the back of the chair, I closed my eyes. When I opened them again, it was two hours later and my phone was ringing. I jumped up, stubbed my toe on a kitchen stool, and answered it. "Ow, ow, ow!"

"Lucy, are you okay?"

"Stubbed my toe." I blinked, the pain momentarily forgotten. "Dad?"

"Who else?"

My heart squeezed a little too tight.

Raphael mumbled something in the background.

"That's enough out of you, Raphael. Such harassment. I should fire him. I should for the beard alone. Hideous."

"What did Pasa say?" I asked, not worried about Raphael's job in the least.

"Nothing your tender ears should hear."

He'd have himself another heart attack if he knew what I had planned with Sean later.

I grabbed a piece of cheese from the fridge. Grendel

came running when he heard the crinkle. I needed to start weaning him to every other day . . . starting tomorrow. "He told you I knew."

"He told me."

"You should have told me."

"I didn't know how. I'm—I'm still trying to deal with it myself."

I sank onto the couch, pulled my legs up. Grendel circled the leg of the coffee table. I tossed a section of cheese and Grendel pounced on it, dragging it around.

"Is this why you've been acting so strangely? And have you rekindled your relationship with Cutter's mother?"

"Yes," he said. "Threw me for quite a loop. And as for the second half of your question, that's none of your concern."

"I beg to differ."

"Our relationship is none of your concern. Perhaps Oliver is. I'm sorry you had to find out about him the way you did. Does your mother know?"

Oliver "Cutter" McCutchan. My brother. Love filled my heart. But how would Mum feel?

"No. Are you going to tell Cutter?"

"When the time is right."

Grendel was back, licking his lips. I tossed another piece of cheese in the opposite direction. "And when might that time be?"

"I don't know."

I didn't like that answer. "It doesn't seem fair that he's been left in the dark. You too. Did Sabrina have any explanation?"

"Oliver has had a good life, Lucy. Not lacking for anything," he said, not really answering me.

"Except for me. And you. And Dovie."

He didn't say anything.

"How did Preston know about him?"

"While researching our family for her articles, she kept coming across photos of Sabrina and me together at various events taken years and years ago. She put two and two together that we had had a relationship. Then she came across a photo of Sabrina with Oliver when he was younger. The resemblance was striking even then."

"And you never guessed?"

"I never met the boy. Oliver was raised primarily in Vermont with his father. He's only returned to Boston in the last year."

"You're his father."

"Semantics, Lucy."

"Not really."

He had nothing to say, not anything about sass or impertinence. I dropped the last piece of cheese square on the coffee table, and Grendel vaulted up, speared it with his fangs, and dove for the floor, sending mail and folders flying in the opposite direction.

Kneeling, I swept the papers into one big pile. Most had spilled out of Sarah Loehman's and Leo Epperson's files.

Sifting through the stack, I fished out the mail and set it aside. Picking up a sheet of paper, I scanned it. Leo's. I dropped it back into his folder.

"The sooner you tell Cutter the better."

"Stop calling him by that ridiculous nickname."

"I like it."

"I forbid it. Are you laughing at me?" my father asked.

"Yes."

"I forbid that too."

"When are you going to talk to Mum?"

"Is this interrogation over?"

"Dad."

"Lucy."

"You need to talk to her. You don't want her finding out on her own."

"Lucy?" my father said.

"Yeah?"

"I'm sorry I didn't tell you sooner."

"You're forgiven. Consider it a Christmas gift."

"I suppose it's better than the cactus you got me last year."

"Hey, I thought you liked the cactus."

He laughed. "It's the thought."

Smiling, I hung up. Glancing out the window, I noticed Dovie's house, all aglow. It was late, but I knew she wouldn't mind. I threw on a coat and headed out the door.

I trudged through the snow up to Aerie. It was closing in on midnight, and I thought Sean would have showed by now. He wasn't answering his phone either, which caused a pit in my stomach I could fall into.

The lights blazed in Dovie's sitting room as I climbed the steps to the deck, opened the back door. I peeked in. Dovie was asleep, curled in one corner of a cozy couch, a cashmere throw tucked all around her. Papers were strewn across her chest, lap, and couch. The TV was turned down low. On the screen Iron Chefs sliced and diced.

The floor creaked as I took a step back. My hopes of not waking her vanished as she lifted her head. "Lucy?"

"Sorry. Didn't mean to wake you. I thought you were up. The lights were on."

She quickly gathered a handful of papers, shoved them into a box. One fell to the floor and I crouched down, picked it up. It was an old letter, the writing long, sloping, masculine. The paper was yellowed with age, creased from wear. "What's this?"

"Nothing at all. Just a foolish old woman spending too much time in the past."

I noted the signature on the letter. *Yours with much love, Henry.*

In all the busyness of late, I'd forgotten about Dovie's penchant for melancholy this time of year. I sat down next to her, handed her the letter. She shoved it in the box.

"It's silly," she said.

"It's not."

"I hated him."

"I doubt that."

"I wanted to hate him."

"That I believe."

She cracked a smile, set the box of old love letters on the floor. "He was an amazing man. A stubborn, headstrong, foolish, amazing man. But enough. I don't want to talk about it anymore. I've had my night of woe. Now, what brings you up here?"

I sat down next to her. I couldn't tell her about Cutter. I just couldn't.

"I don't know. Lonely, I guess."

"Where's Sean?"

I picked at the edge of her cashmere throw. My bottom lip quivered. "I don't know."

Between Cutter and Em and the letters and Sean . . . my chest hurt with all I was holding in.

"LucyD? Are you crying?"

I backhanded the tears from my eyes. "No."

"Lucy, darling, what's wrong?"

"I'm going to lose him."

"Don't you worry about that curse. I'm convinced he's the one to break it for good. You need a drink." She patted my leg and rose. "Martini?"

I nodded. "It's not the curse."

"Then what is it?" she asked, pouring gin into a tumbler.

"His ex."

"She's got nothing on you. I'm sure she's an ugly, warty, big-nosed rhinoceros of a girl with a mean streak as wide as her ass."

"Dovie!"

"What?" she asked innocently as she shook the tumbler. "I'm just supposing."

"She's not any of those things." I tried hard to keep the tears at bay. "But she might be sick." I explained the whole situation. "She's having all these tests done, and begging Sean to be by her side the whole time. He can't say no."

"I suppose not. He's a good man, that one." She opened the tumbler, poured in more gin, started shaking again. So vigorously I was afraid if the tumbler slipped and hit the wall, it would leave a hole.

She poured the martinis. "What are you going to do?"

Softly, I said, "I don't know. What can I do?"

"But he and you, you and him . . . belong together."

"Dovie, if she's sick, really sick . . ."

"It's the curse for sure." She handed me a drink.

I pulled a face. "I thought he was the one to break the curse?"

"You shouldn't listen to me."

I nodded, watching the olive bob in my cone-shaped glass.

Dovie said, "I see the way that boy looks at you, LucyD. He's head over heels."

I nudged the box of letters. "We both know sometimes love isn't enough."

"But sometimes it is."

"How are we supposed to figure out which is which?"

"Damned if I know."

I drained my glass, smiled at her wry tone.

My phone vibrated. Dovie raised an eyebrow.

"It's Sean," I said, checking the screen.

"Answer," she urged.

"Hi," I said, my cell phone warm against my cheek.

"Hey."

"I'm waiting up."

There was a stretch of silence before he said, "Lucy . . ."

"Don't tell me."

"Lucy, I don't like this any better than you. Just

remember that Cara's mother is flying in tomorrow night."

Then what? I wondered. Would he still feel the need to stick around? Or would he be able to walk away—for good?

"Are you going to be at work tomorrow?" I asked.

"I'm going to try, but the MRI is scheduled for noon."

"Okay."

"That's all you have to say, *okay*?"

"It's all I have right now."

He swore under his breath and hung up.

Dovie was perched on the edge of the sofa, the box of letters in her lap. "The ex?"

I nodded.

"The battle begins."

Why did I suddenly feel like surrendering?

23

The next morning, the ringing phone jarred me awake. I reached over Grendel and grabbed the handset. I mumbled a groggy hello.

"LucyD, your father is on his way over here. He wants to talk. Do you know what this is regarding? He said he's already spoken to you."

"Hello, Mum."

"Don't hello me. He sounded serious. You know stress isn't good for his heart. What's this all about?"

"What time is it?" I rubbed my eyes.

"Eight."

Eight! I'd overslept. I wanted to get an early start to the day. I needed to follow up with my vision in Portsmouth, find a way to see Leo, and after seeing Dovie last night, I had a plan to help take her mind off Grandpa Henry.

"Is he sick? Dying? Was his heart attack a symptom of something bigger?"

I pressed my fingertips into my temples. "You're giving me a headache."

"It might be from drinking with Dovie last night."

"You've already talked to her?"

"Of course! Dovie mentioned you called *her* your favorite felon. Where's the love, LucyD? Where's the love?"

"Sorry. I wasn't thinking straight."

"Why? Are you worried about your father too? Because I'm worried."

"Nothing to worry about."

"How can you be so sure?"

"Because I am."

"You're not going to tell me."

"Not my place to tell."

"You used to be my favorite child."

"I'm your only child." Not something I could say any longer with my father.

"Easily remedied. I can adopt one of those big-eyed adorable orphans from India that the guy from *Trapper John, M.D.* is always talking about on TV."

"Isn't that Africa?"

"Lucy!"

"What time is your court appearance?" I asked, changing the subject.

"Eleven."

I winced as I said, "Do you want me to come with you?" I didn't really have the time and was hoping she'd say no.

"Not necessary, LucyD. It's not like it's the first time."

"Don't I know it."

"Sass!"

"Genetic."

"Are you sure he's not sick?" she asked.

"Mum."

"Lucy! Tell me!"

"I've got to go, Mum. If you want to talk later, call me."

"Argh!"

I made kissy noises into the phone, hung up, and wandered into the kitchen. As I ground coffee beans my phone rang again. It was Em.

"Why is Marisol inviting Aiden to Dovie's party? Are they dating?"

I nearly dropped the phone. "She's what?"

"She told me she's bringing Aiden to Dovie's party, as her guest. Do you know why? Did she tell you?"

"No, I don't know." Though I had a good idea. Jealousy was a powerful motivator. "How're things with you? You okay?"

Grendel skulked to his food bowl, stared at me.

"I don't know."

"Did you talk to Joseph?"

I'd almost said "him." Too much time with Marisol.

"He wasn't home when I came back, then I must have fallen asleep. When I woke up I lost my nerve because he was acting so weird."

"How so?" Probably he was wondering the best way to broach a prenup conversation.

"Paranoid. Thinks people might be following him."

I choked on my coffee. "Why would he think that?"

"How the hell should I know?"

"Grumpy."

She exhaled. "I really am. I'll talk to you later."

I fed Grendel and was pouring a second cup of coffee when someone knocked on my door.

I peeked out the window and half expected it to be Sean. It wasn't.

Aiden smiled. "I brought doughnuts."

"You've come bearing gifts. Should I be scared?"

"Only if you're terrified of crullers."

I poured him a mug of coffee and sat in my favorite chair. "You're out early."

"Thought I'd bring bad news to you in person."

"Bad news?"

"The lead on the Handmaiden letters didn't pan out. We had a partial fingerprint."

"Whose?"

"A man who works at Milton Hospital in registration. His prints happened to be in the network for a long-ago shoplifting conviction. He took a lie detector test of his own volition—he's never even heard of you, Lucy. We'll find out who's behind those letters. I promise." He reached for a cruller, glanced at the Christmas tree. Automatically tipped his head to the side.

I was beginning to believe we'd never find out who was behind the letters, that I was always going to live in fear, one eye in the rearview mirror, my house alarm always set.

"I met with Scott Loehman yesterday."

Aiden coughed. A piece of cruller went flying across the room. Grendel made a dash for it and dragged it away. "You what?"

"I met with Scott Loehman."

"Alone?"

"In a public park. Very busy. Lots of kids to defend me if necessary."

"It's not funny."

"I was fine. I did a reading on Sarah's wedding ring."

"And?"

"I saw it in Portsmouth. I'm going up there today to check it out."

"Damn it. I have a meeting today. Can you hold off until this afternoon?"

I shook my head. "I just heard on the news another storm is blowing in. I'm afraid if I don't go today, then it'll be days."

"That might not be a bad thing."

"I'll be fine, Aiden."

"You're bringing Sean, right?"

I shook my head. "He has other plans."

"Jesus." He swiped a hand over his face. "Don't go alone."

"Okay."

"Lucy . . ." he warned.

"You're cranky when you don't get enough sleep."

He growled. It reminded me of the first time I'd met him, when he thought I was a crackpot and he'd been nothing but rough and tough, a mean old cop.

"Tell me what you saw."

I went through the reading I'd had with Scott Loehman. "The bracelet I could see being a fluke. Maybe Jerry White picked it up at a pawnshop, a different yard sale, something. But to have her bracelet *and* her wedding band?"

"And what are you planning to do, Lucy? Barge in and get a confession?"

"Hardly. Sean was running into trouble getting

anything on Jerry White. I thought I'd get his license plate number, maybe try to talk to him. The neighbors mentioned he comes home for lunch everyday. I'm going to stop at an office store and get a clipboard and pretend I'm getting a petition together. I'll make up something on the fly. That way when I hand him the clipboard, I'll get his fingerprints. I figured you would know what to do with them."

He let out a long string of curse words. "Tell me Sean didn't teach you these tactics."

I tried not to take offense. I thought it was a good plan.

"As soon as my meeting is over, I'll head up there. I'll try to cut things short. I can probably be up there by noon. Do not approach the house on your own, Lucy."

"I'm not stupid."

"Good to know. And as a friend, I'm asking you not to go alone."

Inwardly, I groaned. He'd played the friend card. No way could I betray that. "All right."

"Who're you taking?"

Sean was out. Mum and Dovie too, since they were due in court. Aiden couldn't make it. My father was busy, Raphael too. Marisol was working. Em was having a crisis. It really only left one person. Someone I wanted to have a word with anyway.

"Lucy?"

"I'm taking Preston Bailey."

24

Preston's voice was clear over the phone line despite background noise; she was at work. "You're going where?"

"To Portsmouth. I thought you might want to come since it involves Sarah Loehman."

She said, "I'll go."

"I'll pick you up in ten minutes."

"Twenty?"

"Eight minutes."

"Fine." She hung up.

I took side roads into Scituate. In front of the paper, I set the parking brake so I didn't slide down the hill into the harbor. A bright swath of teal Atlantic stretched, broken only by moored sailboats, rocky jetties, and the lovely white column of the Scituate lighthouse.

Preston dashed out of the building, slid into the passenger seat, took one look at me, and her face fell.

I released the parking brake, swung the car around. "I know about Cutter."

I glanced her way. Her forehead was crumpled, her lips twisted, her eyes in a tight wince.

"And," I said, "I know you were blackmailing my father."

"Blackmail," she squeaked, "is such a harsh word."

"Is that one of your shades of gray?"

"It was a favor for a favor, that's all."

Slushy snow piled along the sides of the road the color of charcoal. Gritty sand covered black pavement, scraped smooth by the plows overnight.

"And threatening to bring Cutter to Dovie's party?"

Her chin went up a notch. "Insurance."

"Blackmail."

"I never would have gone through with it, you know. It was all a bluff."

"How am I supposed to believe that?"

She shrugged. "Because I'm telling you it's the truth."

"And you never lie."

"There's a difference."

"How so?"

"It's another of those shades of gray. I might lie once in a while, but when I say I'm telling the truth, I'm telling the truth." She adjusted the heater vent, turning it away from her flushed face.

I arched an eyebrow. "Once in a while?"

She cracked a smile. "Hardly ever."

I merged onto the highway. "Right."

We sat in silence for a few minutes. Finally, Preston said, "Why did you bring me along today? Why are you still even talking to me?"

"I figured I'd swap you one big story for another. You forget everything you know about Cutter, and

I'll give you the exclusive on Sarah Loehman's disappearance."

"You already promised me the exclusive."

"No, I agreed to let you in on the story."

"So much for black-and-white."

I smiled. "You must be rubbing off on me."

"I'm not reading that as a compliment."

"How intuitive of you."

"You know, just for the record, I was feeling really bad about asking your father for a favor."

"Blackmailing him?"

"Whatever. I tried to contact him a few times, call it all off, but he's been avoiding me."

He'd been avoiding everyone but Sabrina McCutchan. And though I liked to think they were solely discussing Cutter's best interests, I had my doubts. My father didn't go to L'Espalier without having something else in mind.

"Why would you do that?" I asked. "It's the story of a lifetime."

She frowned and fussed with the fringe on her scarf. "I don't know, really. It just didn't feel right. Not after I got to know you."

I looked her way—she seemed serious.

I thought about how I'd suspected she might be my sister—and my father's reaction to the subject. I couldn't help but laugh.

"What's so funny?"

"Did you know that for a while I suspected you might be my sister? With all your questions about siblings, and your strange reaction that day Leo asked if we were related. I see now why, but at the time you had me worried."

She wasn't laughing with me. "Would it have been so bad?"

I stole a look and noted the hurt in her eyes. It took only a second for me to remember that Preston had no family left. I tried to lighten the mood. "We're all too nutty for the likes of you."

"Yeah, 'cause I'm the pillar of sanity."

"There's a saying: 'In the land of the blind, the one-eyed man is king.'"

Her eyebrows dipped. "Are you calling me a one-eyed man?"

"I think so."

"Again, not feeling the compliment." But she smiled and said, "Now tell me what we're doing."

I filled her in on the reading I'd had with Scott Loehman, the little yellow house, and my plan to get more information.

"Even I realize how stupid this is," she said.

"And you complain about my compliments?"

Traffic was surprisingly light as I headed into the city. "Do you have a better idea?"

"Yeah. How about you leave this to the professionals?"

"Excuse me, but we are the professionals. You're an investigative reporter and I'm . . ."

"What?"

"A locater."

She laughed her tinkly laugh. "I'm really much better at human interest pieces, and I don't think a locater will be much good if this guy comes after us.

Unless you're a fast relocater." She chuckled at her own joke.

"We're not going to do anything stupid. We're just surveilling, that's all. Gathering information."

"Is surveilling a word?"

"Not sure but it sounds good, doesn't it?"

She nodded. "Speaking of surveillance, what's happening with the guy from the bar?"

Joseph. "Not much."

"Does Em know about the prenup yet?"

"No." And when she did—she was going to flip. I should probably think about getting a sleeper sofa, because I had a feeling she'd be camped out at my house for a good long while.

"Well, I hope she dumps his ass."

I couldn't help but laugh and say, "You and me both."

"And how about Leo? Have you reached him yet? I've been calling, but he's still not answering."

"I haven't had any luck either. I thought maybe we could swing by his house on our way home. It's on the way."

"And Lea? Any news?"

"Let's check." I grabbed my cell phone, dialed Sam.

"Sam Donahue."

"It's Lucy," I said.

"Hey." I heard his chair creak and could imagine him leaning back in it. "Sean's not in."

My heart double-clutched. "I—I know." I snapped to. "Did you find anything on Lea Epperson?"

"Actually, yeah. I was going to call you later this afternoon, after I heard back from a few sources."

Hope buoyed. "What did you find?"

"Her birth certificate. Leo was listed as her father. And her marriage certificate. She was married in the sixties. Her new last name is Czo. C-Z-O. Currently she and her husband are living on a sailboat in the Bahamas. They could be sailing in the open waters, or docked on one of the many islands and cays down there. At this point it's a needle in a haystack. I've got some feelers out to try to get an exact location. If that fails, you might have to schedule a trip down there if your client is willing to pay for it."

"I'll pay for it myself if I have to." For Leo's sake. "Thanks, Sam. That's the best news I've heard all day. By the way, have you talked to Rosalinda yet?"

"I—uh, not yet."

"You're going to be sorry." I hung up.

"Who's Rosalinda?" Preston asked.

"Former receptionist."

"The Santería one? They want to hire her back?"

"Not quite."

"Is this about the curse?"

"Something like that."

"I sense a story there."

"You sense a story everywhere."

"Very true."

A while later we pulled off the highway just north of the city. At a big-box office-supplies store, I picked up a clipboard, and quickly drew up a phony petition letter, a blundering paragraph on rezoning. Maybe Marisol wasn't the only one who used *Magnum, PI* tactics. But what worked, worked. And my plan had to work.

Half an hour later, we were parked across the street from Jerry White's Portsmouth house. The wind blew, rocking my car with the gusts. Dark clouds crowded the blue out of the sky. I checked my watch—it was close to twelve-thirty. Aiden was taking longer than I thought.

Not that it mattered. Jerry White wasn't home. His pickup was nowhere to be seen. Where did he work? Had Sean told me? Maybe I could go there, check things out.

"Surveilling isn't much fun," Preston said, fighting a yawn.

It was pretty close to torture. Now I knew why Marisol had been so miserable the other night.

"Maybe we should just go?" Preston asked.

"Not yet. At least not until Detective Holliday gets here."

I picked up the phone.

"Are you calling replacements for us? I can barely feel my toes."

"Leo. Thought I'd try again."

"I like the idea of replacements better."

I rolled my eyes and dialed. On the fifth ring he answered. I let out a breath of relief. "Leo! It's Lucy. I've been trying to reach you."

"You have news?"

"I have news." It might not be what he expected to hear, but I had news. "Can Preston and I come by this afternoon?"

We set a time and as we waited for Aiden, I wondered how I was going to break the news to Leo.

A tabby cat prowled around the outside of the

house, hunting through the bushes. It was the only movement I'd seen in the neighborhood. It was like a ghost town.

My gaze wandered to Maggie O'Meara's house. I couldn't help but feel sorry for her, raising a daughter on her own while dealing with a serious illness. How much could Shannon possibly earn working at McDonald's? Enough to pay the rent every month? I remembered what Maggie had said about needing a job, and I suddenly had a thought.

It couldn't hurt to try . . .

I opened my phone, clicked through old calls.

"Who are you calling now?" she asked, sounding hopeful.

"Not someone to take your place."

"Just when I was starting to like you."

I found the number I was looking for.

"John McGill," he answered.

"It's Lucy Valentine," I said. "Do you remember me?"

"You're not easy to forget, young lady."

I smiled. "I'm calling about that job. Did you find someone yet?"

"No, are you interested?"

Preston sat straighter, stared at me.

"Not for me, but I might know of someone . . ." I told him all about Maggie O'Meara. "Is it possibly a job where someone could work from home?"

"It's not what I had in mind, but you've cut to the heart of me, young lady. If she's willing to give it a try, so am I."

"Really?"

"Really."

"I'll go talk to her right now. Thank you so much."

He laughed. "Just don't tell anyone what a sappy old man I am."

"I promise."

Preston was giving me a funny look.

"What?" I asked.

"You. Are you always so . . ."

"I hope you're not waiting for me to fill in that blank."

"Nice?" she said.

"No," I answered. "I'll be right back, okay?" I shoved the clipboard into her hand. "If anyone comes, call my cell."

"Can't I come with you? Maggie's story could be big . . ."

"Preston."

"But—"

I thought about the outpouring of support Maggie would receive if a good, well-written article were published about her plight.

"I'll ask her. She seems the private type, though, so don't get your hopes up."

Preston turned her hundred-watt smile on me, and I could kind of, sort of, see her charm.

"Aye, aye."

Jumping out of my car, I hurried down the cracked sidewalks to Maggie's house. I pulled open the screen door, knocked loudly.

"Who is it?" she yelled through the door.

"Lucy Valentine."

Slowly, the door opened. Maggie looked cozy,

wrapped in a fuzzy robe. A pink bandana covered her bald head. "Is there something wrong?" she asked, motioning me inside.

"Not at all."

It was chilly in the house. A fire sputtered in the fireplace, and I wondered if that was the only heat source.

On the kitchen table sat stacks of bills, a calculator, and a checkbook.

"What's that saying?" she asked me. "Robbing Peter . . ."

"To pay Paul?"

"Yeah. But I don't think Peter has enough for me to steal." She slumped into a kitchen chair.

I sat opposite her and noticed most of the bills were medical in nature. Then there were the usual utilities, credit cards, cable, and phone. PAST DUE was stamped on the top of most of them.

"We'll get by," she said. "We always do. What brings you by? It's not Shannon, is it?"

"No, I—"

"Good. She's been moping most of the week."

"Over her breakup with Jimmy?"

"Nah. They're back together, and she finally told me all about him. She's missing that bracelet." Maggie shook her head. "It meant a lot to her that she had something so nice. Something all her own. I'm not a materialistic sort, so I don't completely understand, but I hate seeing her so upset." She shrugged. "We deal with what we're dealt. Try to make the best of it." She smiled. "Jimmy is working extra hours at the supermarket. I think he's trying to earn enough to get her another bracelet. He's a keeper, that one."

"I think so too."

"They're young, but the way I look at it, love doesn't know any better. Those kinds of feelings are rare. You need to hold on to love when you can. And if it lasts, it lasts. And if it doesn't, you deal with it."

I thought of Sean. Was I holding? Or was I dealing? "I came for two reasons."

"What's that?"

"One, if you're still interested, I think I may have a job for you." I told her about it.

"You're serious?"

"Absolutely."

Caution crept into her eyes. "Why?"

"Because I want to help."

"Why?"

I smiled. "Why not?"

"You don't want anything in return?"

"Maybe just for you to do a good job. Mr. McGill is a good man."

"And he's willing to take a chance on me?"

"Yes," I said, laughing.

"Why?"

"Are you always like this?"

"It's just not often I get handed something for nothing."

"It's not for nothing. You're willing to work hard. He needs the help. Though I have to tell you, I've seen his handwriting and you've got your work cut out for you."

She laughed. "You're serious? About the job?"

"Yes!"

"Thank you," she said, her eyes filling with tears.

"You're welcome." I wrote down his phone number, slid it past the stack of bills.

"And, I know a reporter. She wants to write a piece on you, your story. If you're interested."

A blush crept up her neck. "Oh, I don't know about that."

"I'm sure the article will tug a lot of heartstrings. People will want to help." I eyed her bills.

"I don't think—I mean, I don't know."

"Just think about it, okay?"

She nodded.

I met her eyes. "The other reason I came by . . . I'm still looking into the disappearance of Sarah Loehman."

"And it brings you back here?"

"Three doors down, actually. A man lives there. Jerry White? Do you know him?"

"Not really. You know how sometimes you just know to steer clear of someone? That instinct? I have it with him. I told Shannon to stay away from him too. Something's just off. The way he looks at you kind of thing. You think he had something to do with the woman you're looking for?"

"Jimmy bought Sarah's bracelet at a yard sale at his house."

"Really? I never would have thought that guy was the type to have a yard sale. Was Jimmy sure?"

"He seemed to be." I rose. "Thanks for everything, Maggie. Thank Shannon for me too."

"We should be the ones thanking you."

"Not at all. I'm glad I could help." And I knew, just knew, that if Preston didn't write the article on Maggie, I'd be dipping into my trust fund to help her out. It didn't seem right having all that money sitting there with Maggie suffering. Helping pay those bills definitely qualified as something important.

Outside, the wind took hold of my hair, lifted it into the air. Tendrils crisscrossed my face as I made my way back to my car. My empty car.

Frantically, I scanned the area and finally spotted Preston talking to a woman outside Jerry White's house, clipboard in hand.

As I hurried down the sidewalk, I noticed the woman carried a bag of groceries, wore no coat, no hat, no gloves. She had to be freezing in jeans, sneakers, and an oversized sweatshirt. The wind was doing a number on her platinum-blond hair, lashing it against her face. Shoulders squared, she was listening to Preston blab on about zoning issues.

"I'm sorry," the woman was saying as I neared. "I don't know anything about that."

She turned and her hand shook as she tried to get the key into the lock. Her fingers were white with cold. The key ring fell out of her grasp, clinked on the stoop. She shifted her bag of groceries, bent down, but I reached out and snatched up the keys before she could.

I held them out.

The woman turned around. The first thing I noticed was her black eye. The second was that I was looking at Sarah Loehman.

25

My fist closed around the keys and drew them back to my chest. "Sarah?"

I was surprised I recognized her. Beyond the new hair color and the black eye, she'd changed. Aged. She'd lost a lot of the sparkle from her picture.

The bag of groceries slipped from her hands, fell with a thud to the ground. A bag of apples spilled out, dropping down the steps one by one. Her brown eyes widened and immediately filled with tears.

Preston gasped. "You mean—" She looked at me, and I nodded. She quickly pulled out her recorder. Her hands were shaking.

Behind me, I heard a car door slam. Aiden, at last.

"H-how?" Sarah asked me, tears streaming. She fell to her knees, bent over and sobbed.

Aiden rushed to my side, looked at me, his eyebrows drawn together in question.

I sat down on the step next to Sarah, not sure what to do. The anguish in her sobs tore at me. I reached out and rubbed her back.

"Lucy?" Aiden asked.

I shimmied out of my coat, draped it over Sarah's shoulders. "It's going to be okay."

"He'll kill me, he'll kill me."

"Who, Sarah?" Preston asked. "Scott?"

Sarah swiped her eyes, blinked. "No. Scott would never hurt anyone. Jerry. He'll kill me if he finds me with you. And he'll be here soon. For lunch. He comes home every day for lunch. You have to go. You have to. Now. Right now."

Aiden's jaw dropped. "Sarah *Loehman*?"

"Did Jerry do this to you?" Preston asked, examining her black eye.

She keened, a wail that told of more pain than I could imagine. "You need to go. Please. All of you."

I took hold of her shoulders, made her look at me. "Sarah, do you really want to stay?"

Sadness radiated from her eyes. She shook her head. "But I can't go with you."

"The hell you can't," Preston said, looking at Aiden. "Right?"

Aiden took hold of Sarah's elbow, helped her stand. "Right. Sarah, you come with me. Lucy, you can follow us."

"What! No, no! I can't go. He'll hurt them!"

Aiden said, "Hurt who?"

"My kids. Jerry knows where they are. He'll kill them. I know he will. Please just go! Leave me alone. They've been hurt enough." She wiggled. "Please, please just leave me alone."

Aiden held tight. "Stop it, Sarah! We can help you. You just have to come with us."

"No!" She struggled against him.

Firmly, he said, "Look at me! Sarah, look at me!"

Slowly, she raised her chin.

"We won't let anything happen to the kids. Or to you. Do you hear me?" When she didn't answer, he repeated, "Do you hear me?"

She nodded.

Aiden moved fast. "If he's going to be home soon, we need to leave."

I stood to the side, let Aiden do what he did best. When in crisis, he was the go-to man. Strong and sure, he led Sarah to his car, deposited her in the front seat.

Preston, I noticed, was still shaking.

And so was I. A full body tremble that didn't subside as I blasted the heat. Sarah Loehman was alive . . .

I hadn't thought so. Not even after Scott begged me to believe that she'd run away. I thought he'd been holding on to a pipe dream, or perhaps trying to cover his tracks.

Now this. She was alive. She'd clearly been abused. For how long? How did she end up with Jerry White?

As I pulled away from the curb, I looked back at the house, at the apples spilled across the stoop. A tear slipped from my eye.

Preston handed me a tissue. We silently drove, following Aiden to the McDonald's where Shannon O'Meara worked. It wasn't exactly where I thought he'd take Sarah.

Pulling in next to him, I rolled down my window. "Shouldn't we be going to the police station?"

"I don't know where the hell we are. Can you take

her inside?" he asked. "I need to make some phone calls."

Preston helped Sarah into a booth. She gripped my coat with both hands, pulling it tightly around her. I kept an eye on her as I stood in line. I ordered four coffees and brought them to the table. Sarah rocked back and forth.

"He'll kill them," she said.

Preston patted her arm. "Detective Holliday will make sure that doesn't happen."

"You have to promise me," she said to us.

We promised.

Through the plate-glass window, I saw Aiden on the phone. His arms swung as he spoke, gesturing madly. I could almost imagine the conversation he was having.

"How did you find me?" Sarah asked suddenly.

"Your bracelet," I said.

Confusion furrowed her brow.

"Your anklet," I clarified.

"I didn't want to sell it, but I needed some money. Jerry didn't ever give me any, and I was hungry. So hungry," she said, sipping her coffee. Her eyelids drifted closed and I saw the moisture perched along the edges of her lashes. "When he was at work one day, I snuck out and had a little yard sale. I had to."

"Did he . . . kidnap you?" I asked, wondering if I shouldn't. If I should wait for Aiden to question her formally.

Preston didn't reach for her recorder, only listened.

"I was stupid," Sarah said. "I met him at the park.

He said all the right things to me, all the things I was stupid enough to fall for. I thought he was what I wanted. Freedom. Ha." Her laugh held no humor. "We were supposed to go away for the night. One night. I haven't been home since. He locked me in his house." Her eyes fluttered closed, stayed that way for a long time. "He did terrible things to me."

"I'm so sorry." My voice cracked. I sipped my coffee, wishing my chest didn't feel so tight.

"Me too," Preston said in a small voice.

"When I tried to escape, he threatened to hurt my kids. I couldn't leave. I couldn't put them at risk."

"They're going to be fine," I reassured her.

"My kids . . . are you sure they'll be okay? They don't deserve to be hurt. Maybe I did. For being so selfish, so spoiled. But they don't. Never did."

"No one deserves to be hurt. No matter what." I reached across the table, rested my hand on top of hers. "I'm not sure if you know, but Scott has been under suspicion for your murder for the past two years. Everyone's been convinced you were dead and that he did it."

Her eyes grew wide. "Oh my God, oh my God. Poor Scotty. Oh no. Jerry told me Scott hated me, that he filed for divorce. Why would anyone think he'd hurt me?"

"Circumstantial reasons," I said softly. "You disappeared without a trace."

"I didn't know. Jerry wouldn't let me watch TV or read papers for more than a year. He only let me out of the house in the last couple of months. He'd always threaten me. He had pictures of Maddie and Jake. Recent ones. I didn't dare disobey him. I didn't know! Oh God," she cried, her face mottled with emotion.

Preston stared into her coffee cup.

"Scott never believed you were dead. He thought you ran away. That you'd come home one day. He's refused to move so you'd know where to find him."

She crumpled, tears flooding her eyes. "I never realized just what I had until it was too late. I never knew." Resting her head on her arms, she cried silently.

I kept hold of her hand, not knowing what to say or how to comfort her.

I didn't even notice Aiden had come in until he slid into the booth next to me.

"We're going to have to leave, Mrs. Loehman," he said. "Head over to the Portsmouth police department. You and Preston can head on home, Lucy. There's no point in sticking around all day. Your statements can be given later."

He was right, but I didn't want to leave her. "Do you want me to call your mother, Sarah?"

Her head snapped up. "Not my mother. I can't deal with her right now."

In that instant, I knew Scott had been telling me the truth about Sarah's relationship with her mother. "All right. Is there someone?"

She sniffled. "Can you call Scott?"

I glanced at Aiden. He nodded. "Yeah," I said. "I can do that."

As Preston and I settled into the car, she let out a deep whoosh of breath. "You know what this means, don't you?"

"What?"

"All hell is about to break loose for that family.
Those poor kids."

"I was sure you were going to tell me what a big
story this was, how it was going to make your career."

She glanced out the window. "Some things are
more important."

I backed out of the parking space. "Don't tell me
I'm rubbing off on you."

With a sigh of disgust, she said, "It's not a compliment or anything, so you can stop that ridiculous
smiling."

26

Boston's skyline rose up, the skyscrapers outlined against the dark gray sky. Fat snowflakes fell lazily.

Preston and I were headed south, on our way to Leo Epperson's house.

Somewhere in the northbound lanes, Scott Loehman was going to see his wife.

I wanted to believe in happily ever after for them. Right now there were slivers of light cutting through the darkness they'd lived in for two years, but I had the feeling they'd be dealing with shadows for a long time to come.

Aiden had called a few minutes ago with the news that Jerry White, aka Jerry Whitehead, aka Josiah Whitcomb, had been taken into custody. He had a string of outstanding warrants that included assault, rape, and attempted murder on top of what he was facing now.

There was no doubt in my mind that Sarah had been living a nightmare.

And that Maggie O'Meara had excellent instincts.

Bumper-to-bumper cars wedged into the lanes stretching across the Southeast Expressway, south of the city. I turned on the radio, listened as forecasters warned everyone to go home early. The doozy of a storm was finally on its way.

Preston had a legal pad on her lap and was sketching ideas for a story.

I was fidgety, at odds with myself.

I was missing Sean.

Picking up my phone, I let it rest in the palm of my hand. Willed it to ring.

It lay heavy.

As did my heart.

Should I hold or should I deal?

It was well past two o'clock now. Plenty of time for Cara's test to be over and done with.

"You waiting for a call?" Preston asked.

I shook my head.

"Just call him," she said.

"Call who?"

"Whom."

"This from the double negative user?"

She ignored me. "Look, okay, so you've thrown me for a few loops over the past couple of days, made me think I didn't really know you at all. But I know you well enough to know how you feel about Sean. And it's easy to see how he feels about you."

"Oh?"

"Don't act so coy. You two . . . well, you belong together. My God," she said. "I can't believe I just said that. So sappy and sentimental. Maybe I have been spending too much time with you."

"We can fix that."

"I'm hurt. Wounded."

"Dramatic."

"Call him."

I smiled. The thought of dealing *was* almost too much to bear. Biting the inside of my lip, I dialed. The call went immediately to voice mail. His voice asked me to leave a message. I contemplated hanging up, but finally said, "I hope you're okay. I miss you, Mr. Donahue."

Preston made gagging noises. I ignored her.

Traffic crawled along. Preston went back to her notepad.

My wipers slid across my windshield, removing the snow. Ahead I could see a break in the traffic, just beyond flashing red and blue lights. A fender bender.

The snow fell harder as my GPS instructed me to exit the highway near the South Shore Plaza. The voice, a sultry-sounding female, then guided me along back roads into Braintree and often implored me to stay to the right. Leo lived in a small ranch house that didn't look any bigger than Dovie's garage. Pale green aluminum siding, newer roof, big picture window, and a carport that protected Leo's Buick LeSabre from the weather.

"Somehow I knew he'd drive a Buick," Preston said.

"Really? I'd been thinking more of a town car."

"Cars are like underwear, Lucy. Personality. Leo is not a town car." She glanced over her shoulder at my Prius, arched an eyebrow, and didn't say a word.

Which was fine by me.

I shuffled through two inches of snow. Leo's sidewalk had already been shoveled once, but was now skimmed with a top layer of fluffy flakes.

He opened his front door before Preston could knock.

I stomped my feet on the welcome mat and followed her inside.

"Did you find Joanne?" He motioned for me to sit on the sofa. The house was cozy, with dark woods, cool neutrals, and an inviting scent of coffee hanging in the air.

Preston bounced like a kid on Christmas morning, sitting in front of a pile of opened presents. She was obviously dying to blurt out why we were here.

"Not yet," I said. "But I hope soon. I tracked your class ring to an antiques shop in Falmouth. The jar of buttons it was in had been bought by the store owner from David Winston's estate."

His brow furrowed. "Joanne's son?"

"Right. He passed two years ago." I glanced around the room, at the oil prints of old ships hanging on the walls. There were no photographs. "Long story short, I contacted the attorney who handled David's estate. I went and met with him."

"We," Preston corrected, still jiggling.

I sighed. "*We* contacted the attorney. *We* met with him."

"Joanne is alive?"

"As far as anyone knows. The lawyer knew the family quite well. He lost touch with Joanne after David died. She was living in Florida."

"The same dead end your Mr. Donahue hit?"

Your Mr. Donahue. I liked that.

"Not quite. The lawyer suggested I ask Joanne's daughter where she might be."

His brow wrinkled. "Daughter? But she only had the son."

"She only had a son with Charles Winston. She had a daughter," I said softly, "with a man who died in the war before the baby was born."

His mouth opened, then closed.

"Leo," Preston shouted, "you have a daughter!"

He stared at me, eyes wide, then at Preston, as if he were trying to wrap his brain around what we'd both said. "A daughter?"

I nodded.

And he crumpled.

"Are you crying?" I asked my mother. "Please don't cry."

"I'm not crying for me. I'm crying for you."

I'd just dropped Preston off at the *Beacon* and was heading home when Mum called. Snow fell faster than my blades could wipe it away. I was in a good mood, thanks to Leo. He'd been in a daze when we left. A happy delirium that had him bubbling with excitement and more enthusiasm than ever to find Joanne . . . and his daughter. He was ready to pack his belongings and head to the Bahamas to find Lea himself, but I managed to talk him out of it—for now.

"That's even worse. I'm fine!" I insisted.

"How can you be? How could your father do this to you?"

"I'm thinking it had nothing to do with me at the time. Mum, really. I'm actually kind of happy to have a brother. Well, I will be when I can acknowledge him as my brother. Have you Googled him yet?"

"What's a Google?"

I smiled. "Do you ever use your computer?"

"For accounting."

"Hmm. Too bad. If you had actually paid attention when I taught you how to use the Internet, you could go on right now and see a picture of Cutter McCutchan. He looks just like Dad."

"Oh! I have to see him."

"Go to Dovie's. She'll show you, and you can tell her all about Cutter."

"Dovie knows how to Google?"

"She paid attention."

"Well, you're a fine one to talk to your mum like that. Exactly how many piano scales do you know?"

"That would be none."

"My point precisely. After three years of lessons."

"All right, all right." I laughed. "Truce! Are you really okay?"

"I have to say the news came as quite a shock. Though why it was, I don't know. Your father has been far from celibate all these years. I confess to being a little blue," Mum said. "I guess I liked knowing I was the only one your father chose to have a child with."

"You're the only one he chose to marry."

She laughed. "I'm not so sure that's a good thing, LucyD."

"Did Dad say if he was going to meet with him?"

"No. Not a word. I think he's waiting on Sabrina to make the introduction. And I think he should be the one to tell Dovie, don't you?"

"Probably, but you're lousy at keeping secrets."

"Maybe I'll go away for a few days."

"Good luck getting out of the city tonight."

She sighed. "Maybe I'll be snowed in."

Being snowed in sounded wonderful to me. "How'd the court case go?"

"Five-hundred-dollar fine, community service, blah, blah, blah."

I turned onto Atlantic Avenue. The snow was deep. "Would any of those blahs be a warning about getting arrested again?"

"I don't know. I tuned him out after the community service. But have no worries, LucyD."

"You know, telling me not to worry only makes me worry."

"Genetic."

"Let me guess—on Dad's side?"

"Of course!"

We hung up as I parked my car in Dovie's garage. I trudged through the snow to my cottage, glad to see none of it had been trampled. No lurkers, no peeping Toms.

Grendel met me at the door with a forcible *mreow*, and I scooped him up. "A diet," I told him. "Soon."

His ears twitched as though he were saying he wasn't listening.

I nearly jumped out of my skin when my phone rang. I let go of Grendel and answered.

Aiden said, "I thought you might like an update on Sarah Loehman."

I heard voices in the background. "Are you still in Portsmouth?"

"Yeah. I'll be here a while."

"Is Sarah doing okay?"

"Seems to be holding up. The media caught wind. It's all over the news."

"Has Sarah seen her mother yet?"

"Earlier. It was a lukewarm reception on Sarah's part."

"And the kids?"

"They haven't seen her yet. Sarah's at Deaconess now, staying the night there. They're running some tests, checking to make sure she's truly okay. Scott's with her. And yeah, I'm man enough to apologize for judging him wrongly."

I smiled. "That hurt to admit, didn't it?"

"I think I'm bleeding. Hey," he said. "I got a call from Marisol tonight. Something about a party? You know what that's about?"

It was about Phase 2 of the Get Rid of Joseph plan. I lied. "Not a clue. Maybe something about Butch?"

"I'm not getting in the middle of that relationship," he said firmly. "No, thanks."

"One way to find out. Call her back."

"Can't you just ask her?"

"What is this, high school?"

He laughed. "Fine. I'll call her first thing tomorrow. It's late."

"She's working. Third shift at the animal hospital."

"I still think I'll call tomorrow."

"Chicken."

"You're not funny."

Laughing, I hung up.

I gathered up the courage to let go of my fear for a while and left my drapes open. I dimmed the indoor lamps and turned on the porch lights, watching the snow fall in the glow.

An hour later, I'd checked e-mail, Googled Cutter, watered the Christmas tree, turned on the fireplace, cleaned Grendel's litter box, and whipped up a bowl of Lucky Charms for dinner. I gathered all my wrapping supplies, a cup of tea, and cleared a space in front of the fire to wrap presents.

Grendel attacked the bag of Christmas bows with gusto, catching one between his front paws. He flopped backward onto the paper I'd laid out on the floor.

"Scoot," I said, pushing him off. I scissored off the perfect paper size to wrap Sean's book.

The fire flickered. Fiery shadows leaped across the floors, the walls, blending in with the colorful dots of light cast from the Christmas tree. The snow kept falling outside. Carols hummed from my CD player, and I sipped my tea as I picked up Sean's present.

It was getting late, and I should probably be tucked into bed with visions of sugarplums dancing in my head. But although it had been a long, exhausting day I wasn't tired.

I couldn't stop thinking about my father, my brother, Leo and Lea, Sarah and Scott. And about Preston Bailey and how she'd worked herself into my life—and the fact that I didn't mind all that much, despite some very big character flaws.

I gently covered Sean's book in tissue paper, then carefully wrapped it in colorful snowman paper. Grendel pounced on the ribbon as I curled the edges with scissors.

Odysseus watched us from his wheel. He had a Popeye look to him, complete with perpetual squint.

My gaze wandered to the coffee table. I'd printed out a picture of Cutter I found online. It amazed me how much he resembled my father, not just in looks but in traits too. The quirk of his lip, the glint in his eyes. I settled Dovie's tea caddy into a cardboard box. I tried to focus on what I was doing, but was distracted by the picture. So much so that I finally turned it upside down. The last thing I wanted to do was break Dovie's present before I'd even paid off my credit card bill.

Grendel had settled into my lap, purring contentedly. I gave up on pushing him away and worked around him. I tied a piece of ribbon into a bow and pushed the box under the tree. I sipped my tea and nearly dropped the mug as someone knocked on my door.

My pulse jumped in my neck as I set Grendel on the sofa. "Who is it?"

"It's Sean."

27

My heart thrummed. I flipped the dead bolt, slid the chain back. I barely noticed the cold and the foot of snow outside. Thoreau barked and pranced and dashed into the house.

Over my shoulder, I saw Grendel pounce on Thoreau. Both rolled together in a furry ball across my wrapping paper and trimmings. I turned back to Sean, my throat tight and thick.

Dark circles hung beneath his eyes, and his ashen skin blended with the snowy backdrop. I was unsure what to say. Unsure if I had any words at all.

The ocean crashed against the bluff as snow fell, thick and heavy.

Sean drew in a breath. "I miss you too, Ms. Valentine."

With that I was in his arms. He held me tight, my head buried in the curve of his neck as tears trickled down my face, seeping into his shirt.

He gently nudged my chin so he could look me in the eye. "Can I come in?"

I stepped inside, held open the door. He brushed

by me, kicking off his snowy shoes onto the floor next to the door as I closed it and used the dead bolt.

Though he was wearing only a long-sleeved T-shirt and jeans, I could feel the heat of his body from a foot away. His gray eyes were pools of warm liquid silver in the dim light, and I couldn't look away, so mesmerized by what I saw in the depths. The want. The need. The hunger. The desire.

For me.

"Hi," I said lamely.

"You can talk," he said in a whisper, a smile curling the ends of his lips. "I was beginning to have my doubts."

My heart free-fell to my toes. It was the first thing he'd said to me when we met, the day I wondered if love at first sight was possible. I now knew it was.

"Y-you want some tea?" I asked, even as my body fairly purred under his intense gaze.

"No."

"You want to sit down?" I asked.

"No."

I knew what he wanted.

I wanted it too.

But there were so many reasons not to, to keep holding back. To not give in to the passion, the desire, the love.

With everything I've ever wanted in my whole life standing before me, I couldn't help but hear Maggie O'Meara's voice in my head, rhapsodizing about holding and dealing.

I didn't know what was to come of his and Cara's relationship. I didn't know when Cupid's Curse would strike. I didn't know what would happen with his health . . .

All I knew was that I'd lost my heart to him the minute we'd met. And I was sick of taking our relationship slowly out of fear. I wanted more. I wanted it all. And I was going to take it. Eventually I would have to deal with my decision, but for now . . . I was going to reach out, grab hold, and not let go for a long, long while.

"How about helping me wrap presents?" I ventured playfully.

His eyes flashed, darkened. "No, thanks."

I smiled, bent down and picked up a bow from the floor. I set it atop my head. "How about helping me unwrap presents?"

I took a step forward, pulled the bottom of his shirt up, revealing a thin trail of hair stretching from his belly button down beneath the button of his jeans. I ran my fingers along the hard planes of his stomach. Muscles quivered beneath my touch. Boldly, I grasped the hem of the shirt, pulled it up over his head. I tossed it on the floor. "I'll go first. So far, Mr. Donahue, I'm quite happy with my gift."

When I glanced at him, I was taken aback to see moisture shimmering in his eyes. But before I could question my decision or what I saw, he cupped my face with his hands and brought his lips to mine.

My breath caught. Or maybe my heart had stopped out of sheer pleasure. I wasn't sure. I wrapped my arms around his neck, plunged my fingers into his hair as we touched, tasted, tempted each other.

Reaching down, I unbuttoned his jeans. He groaned,

which made me all that much bolder. I slowly drew down his zipper.

His lips slid down to my neck as his hands found the buttons on my shirt, undoing each one, slowly, carefully, methodically, his fingers grazing the sensitive skin of my breasts.

Sean gently pulled my shirt from my shoulders. It fluttered to the ground.

Skin to skin, heart to heart.

We didn't bother with the bedroom, just sank to the rug in front of the fireplace. Snow swirled outside, and the colorful lights of the tree glowed on our skin. I took it all in, his breaths, his kisses, his gentle touches. My heart nearly bursting, my sighs, my body thrumming with happiness.

Déjà vu. I smiled as I recalled having already seen us doing just this. I would die a happy woman if I kept having visions like those. Or if he kept touching me like that . . .

I cracked open an eye early Wednesday morning. Light spilled in from the kitchen and I realized it had been the coffee grinder that had roused me from a deep, wonderful sleep.

Rolling onto my back, I bit back a contented sigh.

Tuesday had passed in pure bliss.

It had been a day of snow angels, hot chocolate, warm fires, tender lovemaking, hot sex. Of playing, laughing, exploring, loving.

Yesterday had not been a day of doubt, of deep thoughts, of thinking about anything other than each other.

Sean and I had not answered our phones, watched TV, checked e-mail, or ventured farther than the yard. We neither saw nor spoke to anyone other than our furry friends. Even Dovie had kept her distance, a miracle in itself. No doubt she'd figured out what was going on here and was futilely hoping a great-grandchild was in her future.

But now, as the scent of coffee tickled my nose, teased my senses, it was time to come back to reality. As much as I longed to stay this way, life had to go on. The roads had been cleared of two feet of snow, and even the walkways and paths at Aerie had been shoveled.

It was time to face all the things Sean and I had been avoiding.

I threw the covers off, grabbed my robe. In the living room, Sean had the fire going, and Thoreau and Grendel were curled together in front of it.

"He's not going to want to leave," Sean said, motioning to the Yorkie with his mug.

I sat on a kitchen stool and measured my words carefully. "He's welcome to stay here as long as he wants."

Sean glanced at me. "He might take you up on that."

"I hope he does."

"Coffee?"

"Definitely."

He poured me some. "Your phone almost shimmied off the counter."

It had been recharging, set on vibrate. I checked it for messages. I had three voice mails waiting.

Everyone was back to work after yesterday's reprieve. "Life calling."

Sean leaned against the sink, hooked his thumbs in his pockets. "I suppose we can't ignore it forever."

Coffee scorched the back of my throat, a welcome burn. It took away from the sting in my nose, the lump in my throat, the twisted mess in my stomach. I didn't want this, my time with Sean, to end. "No."

"I talked to Sam this morning. Still no news on the current whereabouts of Leo's daughter."

I was determined to find her. "We might need to take a trip to the Bahamas."

"The horror."

I noticed Cutter's picture on the fridge, the edges frayed from claw and teeth marks. I pointed to it. "Grendel's handiwork?"

"Caught him tearing it apart this morning." His forehead wrinkled as he studied the image. "Is this your dad when he was younger?"

I shook my head.

"Wow. Dead ringer. Who is it?"

"My brother."

Sean sputtered. "Your what?"

"I just found out on Sunday, and my father only found out about him a week before that."

His eyes widened, the gray lightening to a soft pearl color as my words sank in. "Whoa. Wow."

"I know. His name is Cutter. Well, Oliver. Mc-Cutchan."

"How did you find out?"

I shared the whole story, starting with the invitation and ending at the gallery and my father's phone call.

"I'm sorry," he said.

I tipped my head. "For what?"

"Not being around for you."

Ah, well. I couldn't deny I'd wanted him with me. "It's okay," I said, wishing it were true.

Sean's phone rang. He checked the ID, silenced the phone, and set it back on the counter. I didn't need to ask who was calling. It was clear from the tortured look that had crept into his eyes.

Setting my mug on the granite island, I slipped off the stool, padded to the windows. Bright sunlight bounced off the snow, spilled into the living room. Sparkling snow stretched to the edge of the bluff. Beyond, rough surf surged and ebbed, giving and taking, holding and dealing.

I gathered what little courage I possessed and asked, "Any news on Cara's condition?"

"No."

"But her mother is with her now, right?"

"Should be. I left before she arrived."

I straightened magazines on the coffee table, plumped pillows.

His voice was tight as he said, "Cara's going to take a medical leave of absence from her nursing job until all this is figured out."

I checked the moisture on the Christmas tree. It was okay. My ornaments hung askew, thanks to the crooked trunk. I fussed with the silver garland and strands of cranberries.

"Is her mother going to move in with her?"

17×3 is 51.

"Her mother goes back to Arizona on Saturday."

"Is Cara going with her?"

"No."

I shook out the drapes, trying to achieve the puddle effect the designer pulled off so well. My attempt only caused dust particles to launch into the air. I gave up on the drapes, moved on to Sean's shoes by the door. I straightened them, rubbing at water spots with the hem of my robe.

I noticed a piece of paper sticking out from beneath the couch and pulled it out—I scanned the page. It was from Sarah Loehman's file; I must have missed it the other night when Grendel knocked the files over. I set it on the table.

"Who's going to look after her?" Because it had become clear over the past week that Cara needed extra care.

I was holding my breath, waiting for his answer. An answer that would inevitably change my life forever. I drew in a deep breath, spun around.

"I know what you're wanting to hear," he said. "But I can't say it."

My heart slowly sank.

"I just can't leave her alone. It's not right."

I bit back my reply. She had been more than willing to walk away from him, from his illness, from all the changes he'd had to make in his life after nearly dying.

But I couldn't really hold his stance against him. One of the things I loved most about him was his devotion, his dependability, his compassion. Of course, I liked it more when those qualities were aimed my way.

Not something to be proud of, but the truth was the truth.

Black-and-white.

He came up behind me, kissed the curve of my neck, put his strong arms around me. "I'm trying not to say anything too sappy."

"I'm okay with sappy."

"Men aren't supposed to get sappy."

I drew my arms back, placing my hands on his rear, pulling him ever closer to me.

"If you keep doing that," he said, his hands skimming down my arms, raising goose bumps. "I might get a little sappy."

"Like I said, I'm good with sappy."

He untied my robe, turned me around. I looked into his eyes, those gray milky eyes I loved so much. I could see how torn he was, between what he felt was right and what he really wanted.

Taking a deep breath, he said, "Just know, Ms. Valentine, that even when I'm not here, my heart is."

A painful, welcome knot formed in my chest. It hurt how much I loved him. "That's pretty sappy."

He laughed as he slipped my robe from my shoulders. As I leaned up to kiss him, a kiss so full of passion, of heat, of love, that I could barely breathe, I knew one thing for certain.

I had to fight for him.

I just had to figure out how.

28

Later that afternoon, I stopped into the Porcupine.
Raphael was just finishing a takeout order when he
spotted me.

"You shaved!" I squealed.

He rubbed his jaw. "Oddly, I feel naked."

"You look much younger, Pasa," I said, trying to
placate him.

He arched an eyebrow. "I'm not falling for that."

"How's Maggie?"

"I can't explain it, but she's happy with this old
man."

"Can you ask for anything more?" I asked.

"You were supposed to argue that I'm not old,
Uva."

"Can I tell you you're crazy instead?"

He tipped his hands like scales. "Okay."

I kissed his bare cheek. "I'll see you Saturday
night?"

He shook his head. "Maggie and I are heading out
of town, a little place in Maine."

My heart warmed for him. "Can I start pestering
about a wedding date?"

"Only if you want me to start prying into your love life."

"You know, weddings are rather personal. I think I'll just wait for an announcement," I said, headed for the door.

"Smart girl, Uva."

Upstairs, I took the steps to the third floor to SD Investigations to check on Andrew. He was back at work and smiled shyly when he saw me.

"Feeling better?" I asked.

"Much."

"Good."

"Sean's not in," he said. "Had an emergency call."

I knew. He'd left Thoreau at my place and was headed to Cara's apartment. Apparently, her mother had never arrived Monday night because of the storm and decided to stay home. Cara was in desperate need of Sean's help for something or other.

I was beginning to have my doubts Cara had ever called her mother. I knew Mum would have found a way to move heaven and earth to be with me if I was sick. But my suspicions might have something to do with doubts about how sick Cara really was.

Sam appeared in the doorway. "Thought I heard voices. You need something, Lucy?"

"Just checking on Andrew."

Sam smiled rather smugly. "Come on back, have some coffee."

"All right." I owed him a thank-you.

I followed him down the hall to the kitchen. He filled two mugs and motioned me into his office.

"Andrew looks well," I said.

"Told you so. He's completely healed without so much as a phone call to Rosalinda."

"Actually," I began, "you might want to know that you sent Rosalinda a big bouquet of imported flowers and a very generous severance check on Monday. She was quite grateful when I made my follow-up call ensure the office juju would return to normal."

"Juju?"

"You owe me five hundred dollars, by the way, and you can thank me later."

He snorted. "I don't know about that."

"Why?"

"Andrew's a really lousy receptionist."

I laughed. A picture of Sam's twin girls sat on his desk. They were adorable, with dark pigtails and blue eyes. "I wanted to thank you," I said.

"For?"

"For having Lizzie stay with Cara the other night."

"You're welcome." He shook his head. "What a mess all of that is. I can't believe Cara called Sean this morning to help her clear her locker at Milton Hospital. Did you know she's taking a leave of absence? And she's taking advantage, if you ask me."

"I know," I murmured. She'd be home all day, every day, just thinking of ways to keep Sean at her beck and c— "Wait. Did you say Milton Hospital?"

"Yeah. She's worked there for years. Why?"

My hands started shaking. I set my mug on his desk.

"Lucy? Are you okay?"

Milton Hospital. The Handmaiden letters. And

with that I knew. I *knew*. Cara had been sending me the letters—probably pinching the paper from the registration desk. This explained why the letters had dropped off in the past week. Her focus was currently on Sean and digging her claws into him.

This was just the ammunition I needed to stay in this fight.

"Lucy?"

"Hmm?"

"Your face is flushed."

"I'm okay."

"You sure?"

I jumped up. "I have a battle to win." And I knew just how I was going to do it.

His eyes widened. "Um, good luck?"

"Thanks. Gotta go. I have a meeting."

I hurried downstairs, Cara weighing heavily on my mind. I tried to let that go for a while because I had other pressing issues. Em had called an hour ago, asking to meet with Marisol and me. I suggested my office because it was central to all of us. Something was up, and I only hoped it was the news Marisol and I were wishing for.

Suz was on the phone and waved as I passed through to my office. My father's office door was closed, but I could hear the rumble of voices from within. He was booked solid with clients until March. It was a wonder he could even find time for his own love life—yet he managed. Again. And again. And again.

I was surprised to find Marisol already in my

office, spinning in my office chair, her black hair flying out like a six-year-old's on a merry-go-round. "So what's this about?"

"Em didn't tell you either?"

"Not a word. Just asked me to meet her here. Do you think . . ."

"I'm hoping."

"I'm trying not to get *my* hopes up."

"You're making me dizzy." I set my things on the coat rack and added, "Do you think he told her about the prenup?"

She stopped spinning. "Something big must have happened, right? It's not like her to call spontaneous meetings in the middle of the day."

My intercom buzzed. Suz said, "Em and Joseph are here."

Marisol's eyes went wide. "She brought *him*?"

I pressed the intercom button. "Please send them back, Suz."

"Why?" Marisol asked.

I didn't know, but suddenly I had a gaping pit in the hollow of my stomach.

Marisol stood as Joseph marched into the room, Em behind him.

I crept up next to Marisol, linked our arms. We were in this together.

"Em?" I asked.

She looked like hell. Her hair was frizzy, she wore no makeup, there were bags under her eyes.

"Hi," she said lamely.

Marisol said, "What's this all about?"

"Just what I wanted to know," Joseph snapped.

Em winced. "I'm sure there's a good explanation."

He glared at her. She wouldn't look him in the eye. "What's *what* about?"

Joseph pulled a compact disc from his briefcase, tossed it on the table.

I swallowed hard. "What's that?"

"Just a little home movie," Joseph said with a sneer.

Preston was right—he did look wormy.

"Thought you might be interested, since you both star in it."

"We what?" I said.

Em's eyes drifted closed, then opened. "Our apartment is under video surveillance."

He said to her, "And you thought I was being paranoid, thinking someone had been in the place, that someone was following me. You were following me, weren't you?"

Marisol hedged. "A little."

"And you broke into our loft?" he pressed.

"We had a key," I said feebly.

"Why?" Em asked.

I cleared my throat. "It's like this," I started.

"Well, you see," Marisol said.

Joseph tapped his foot. He actually tapped his foot. The jackass. "What?" he demanded.

"We don't like you," I said.

"Not a bit," added Marisol.

Em gasped. Joseph's face hardened. He said, "The feeling is mutual."

Em gasped again.

"You didn't find anything, did you?" Joseph snapped up the disc and put it back into his briefcase.

"Condoms," Marisol said bravely. "Care to explain those?"

Em said, sounding as though she were in pain, "Joseph likes to be extra safe."

His cheeks flared red. "You do not need to be explaining our lives to them."

"But—"

"There are no buts, Emerson."

"We have to tell her," Marisol said to me.

I nodded. We did.

"Tell me what?" Em asked.

"Well, the other night at Spar," I began.

"You followed me to Spar?" Joseph sputtered.

"On Friday," Marisol said.

"And Saturday night," I added.

"We had this idea, you see." Marisol's hands flew as she spoke. "About using bait."

"A decoy," I corrected.

"A decoy," Marisol said, "to, you know, see if Joseph was faithful."

"Entrapment?" Em asked.

"That sounds so harsh," I said, realizing Preston might be right about shades of gray.

"Doesn't matter, does it?" Joseph asked. "Because I am faithful. I'd never cheat."

"Is that true?" Em asked us.

Joseph stomped his foot. "Why are you asking them? I'm the one who just told you I don't cheat."

Em's cheeks began glowing a soft pink.

I wanted to reach out and slap Joseph's forehead.

"Yeah, it's true," Marisol grumbled.

"But at Spar, we did learn something," I started, but was interrupted by Em.

"Friday night? Wasn't that the night you had dinner with your parents?" she asked him evenly.

The red spread to his ears. "I, ah, just dropped in for drinks. After."

"Ah, ah, ah," Marisol said, wagging a finger.

"What?" Em asked. "What's going on?"

"He was clearly uninterested in the decoy," I said, "but that might have been because he was so focused on the documents he was signing."

"Documents?" Em asked.

"For a prenup." Marisol winced.

Em's eyes widened.

"I can explain," Joseph said.

"I'm sure you can," Em murmured.

From the doorway, someone cleared his throat. "Is everything okay in here?" my father asked, his eyebrows drawn together in agitation.

"Depends on who you ask," Marisol said.

"Explain, Lucy," he said.

"Well, you see, Marisol and I are convinced that Joseph isn't the right man for Em, and, well, we had questions about his character, so we kind of, you know, followed him around—"

"It was all my idea," Marisol piped in.

"I'm not surprised," Joseph said.

"That's not true," I said to Marisol. "You can't take all the blame."

"Ahem." My father never had much patience for this sort of thing.

"We got caught," I filled in. "And now the worm is trying to wriggle off the hook."

"The worm?" Joseph looked ready to explode.

Marisol flipped her hair. "If the slime fits."

"That's it. That's just it. The last straw. It's either them or me, Emerson," he said in a raised voice.

Her mouth fell open. "You're kidding."

"I'm not."

My father raised an eyebrow and spoke as if he were bored. "I believe that's an easy choice, seeing as how you two don't match at all. Em, he's not your true love."

"And just how do you know that?" Joseph demanded.

Dad's eyes darkened. "Do not question me."

Joseph shrank, then quickly recovered. "I'm leaving." He headed for the door. "Em."

She looked at him for a long minute, then stepped next to me, linking to my free arm. And just like that, we were seven years old on a beach with red and blue lips. We'd come a long way from not having a care in the world, but right here, right now, it still felt as though we were never going to let go.

Joseph stormed out.

Dad said, "Good riddance."

I folded Em into a hug. Marisol joined in. "We're sorry," I mumbled.

"I'm not," Marisol said.

Em sniffled. "I think it's rather sweet, actually. I always want the two of you to look after me."

Dad cleared his throat again. "All is well now?"

I nodded.

Em walked up to my father and said, "Not yet. How do you know Joseph's not my true love? You sounded so sure."

He chucked her on the chin. "Experience." He nodded and smiled at me, giving silent permission to tell Em and Marisol the truth.

I let out my breath. I hadn't liked keeping secrets from them, and couldn't wait to fill them in on the auras, on Cupid, on everything.

Dad said, a twinkle in his eye much like Santa's, "Good day, ladies."

Em flopped into a chair. "What now?"

Marisol crouched next to Em. I sat on the edge of the table. "Anything you want," I said to her.

"My parents aren't talking to me. My wedding is off. I don't have a job. I don't have a place to live. I can't even hock my wedding dress because I went and ruined it."

"You're such a loser," Marisol drawled out.

Em's jaw dropped. Then she started laughing. Next thing I knew the three of us were hugging again.

"You can stay with me as long as you want," I offered.

"Or me," Marisol said.

Em sniffed. "First I should probably go pack my things. I only have a suitcase worth, maybe two. The rest of my stuff is in storage. Joseph doesn't like clutter."

Talk about a loser.

"All right," I said, slipping into my coat. Cara could wait. Em came first. And this little detour was just the time I needed to explain everything to them.

"But please tell me you're not taking the painting over the sofa."

"No way, it's hideous," Em said.

Marisol wrapped a scarf around her neck. "Really? I kind of liked it."

29

Em and Marisol had been stunned by the aura news. They hadn't asked many questions, but I knew they would come.

As soon as Dovie heard about Em being homeless, she insisted Em come stay with her. She would love the company, she had the room, and she pointed out that the minute Em's mother heard about it (which Dovie would make sure of) that rift would be well on the road to repair.

I watched Thoreau bounce around outside. The sun was setting, turning the snow a beautiful orange red.

Lights were blazing in Aerie's downstairs windows, and I'd been invited up for Dovie's (in)famous stew. After that, I had plans to see Cara Frankin.

"Thoreau," I called, slapping my thighs. "Come on."

Thoreau pranced into the house, shaking his fur. Grendel pounced as soon as he had an opening, and the pair tumbled across the living room, bumping against the coffee table.

The paper I'd found lodged under the sofa that morning fluttered down. I grabbed it before Grendel could make confetti, and was about to tuck it in my tote bag when I started reading.

I stared at the paper from Sarah's file and was trying to figure out what was bothering me.

I read and reread the paragraph about Jake's injury—the one that sent him into emergency surgery on his first birthday—an intestinal bleed that was almost always caused by blunt force, physical abuse. The injury Scott was supposedly responsible for.

Then it hit me. Jake had been hurt on his first birthday.

What had Scott said to me at the park? That he'd been working double shifts . . . and had missed Jake's birthday. Jake was one when Sarah went missing, so there had only been one birthday Scott could have been referring to.

Scott couldn't possibly be responsible for Jake's injury . . . he hadn't even been home. And he'd also missed Maddie's first day of preschool—the day she'd broken her arm.

Which left only one person who could have hurt the children.

Sarah.

A half hour later, I'd scarfed down a bowl of stew, endured a guilt trip from Dovie about working so hard, and was on my way to Rockland, driving with one hand, punching numbers into my cell phone with the other. I hoped I wasn't making a huge mistake.

I was pretty sure the only reason Em agreed to stay with Dovie was because she knew how hard this

time of year was for my grandmother. And it gave
me warm fuzzies that Em would be trying to help
Dovie at a time like this.

And it also reminded me that I'd never followed
up on my plan to help Dovie through this season.

The phone rang and rang. I almost chickened out
and thought about hanging up, but remembered all
the blind dates Dovie had set me up on. There was no
way she could get mad at me for doing the same.

Finally the phone was picked up. "John McGill."

"Hi, Mr. McGill, it's Lucy Valentine."

"Well, young lady, I didn't think I'd hear from you
so soon. I'm fresh out of jobs."

I smiled as the snow-covered landscape zipped by.
The road had been caked with salt and sand, dirtying
the edges at the curbs. "Good thing I don't need one.
It's last-minute, but I was wondering if you'd be interested in attending a party Saturday night at my grandmother's home in Cohasset."

"Your grandmother, you say?"

"She's quite lovely."

I could hear the smile in his voice as he said, "And
single, I take it?"

"Very."

He laughed. "And what does she say about this?"

"She doesn't know. You see, Mr. McGill, matchmaking is in my blood."

"It doesn't mean you're any good at it."

How very true. "Only one way to find out."

"Did you inherit her smile?"

"As a matter of fact . . ."

"What time should I arrive?"

I turned on to the Loehmans' street as I finished giving him directions to Dovie's and said good-bye.

I didn't want to see Dovie go through another Christmas crying over an old box of letters. That she had kept them this long was something in itself. Though I had to laugh, because I had most of my old love letters too, from boyfriends past. Those sorts of mementos were hard to throw away, no matter how the relationship ended.

Those sorts of mementos . . .

I nearly ran off the road. My tire bumped over the curb before I regained control.

Quickly, I pulled over and my GPS woman snottily told me I still had three tenths of a mile to go before reaching my destination. Grabbing my cell phone, I dialed Leo Epperson. His phone rang once, twice, three times. *Please answer, please answer . . .* Four, five, six . . . *Come on, Leo!* Seven, eight, ni—

"Hello?" Winded, he added, "I'm here. Hello?"

"Leo! It's Lucy."

"Darling, hold on." A second later he was back. "All right. I had to take off my boots. Dripping all over the house. I was out on the back porch and thought I heard the phone ring. Any news for me?"

"I'm hoping you have some for me."

"How so?"

"Did you ever write Joanne letters? Like a love letter?"

"Of course."

"Women most always keep love letters, Leo."

"What are you saying?"

"I'm saying I think I may be able to get a reading. Can I come over? About an hour?"

"Sure thing!"

Hanging up, I continued down the street. My good mood evaporated as I pulled to the curb under a street lamp in front of the Loehmans' house. I took in the white split-level with black shutters with dismay.

A wintry breeze nipped my ears as I climbed the front steps. Snow covered the lawn, hung from the evergreen shrubs. The red front door bore a cheerful wreath of cranberries and jingle bells.

I knocked.

I heard soft footsteps. The door opened. Sarah Loehman was almost unrecognizable—again. Gone was the platinum hair, replaced now with a pretty auburn brown. Her haggard face had been softened by makeup that artfully hid what was left of her bruise, but couldn't quite conceal the pain lingering in her eyes.

"Lucy! I'm so glad you're here. I've been wanting to call you. Come in." She held open the door.

Inside, the scent of baking cookies filled the air. She led me to the back of the house. To my left in the family room, a tall Christmas tree twinkled in a corner, and a small fire crackled in a marble fireplace. She turned right, into the kitchen.

"I thought I would get some baking done while Scott took the kids Christmas shopping. They've been a little uncertain about having me home. Scott thought having them help choose my Christmas presents might help in the transition. They don't realize that *they* are my presents."

Spread out on the kitchen table were dozens of sugar cookies in varying shapes and sizes. Gingerbread men, bells, stars, Christmas trees, reindeer, stockings. All waiting to be frosted and sprinkled with colored sugars.

"That's a lot of cookies," I said.

She laughed. "I know I went overboard, but I've missed Christmastime with them. Please sit down."

I sat, my heart heavy. "You look happy."

Tears welled in her eyes. "I'm trying to come to terms that I deserve a second chance. Scott insists everyone does, but . . . I know I've made a lot of mistakes."

I nodded to the cookies. "Is this part of making up for them?"

"I guess. In a way."

"Have you spent much time with your mother?" I asked.

"Only briefly." Sarah poked at a cookie. "At the hospital."

I pressed. "She admitted to me she's made a lot of mistakes too. With you."

Her eyes flashed. "She said that?"

I nodded.

"She's right."

I thought of Faye Dodd and the love I'd seen in her eyes when she spoke of Sarah. And the love I'd seen in Sarah's eyes when she spoke of Maddie and Jake.

"I came across something in your file today."

"Oh?"

"About Jake's first birthday. And Maddie's first day of preschool."

I didn't need to say more. Splotches of red formed on her cheeks. A tear rolled out of the corner of her eye.

"I'm trying to make it up to them. I love them. Back then I didn't have the patience to be a mother. A good mother. I was angry all the time, so unhappy. I thought life was all about me, me, me."

"What happened?"

"On Jake's first birthday, I was rushing around, trying to get everything right. I was mad that Scott had to work, that he didn't seem to realize how much I had to do on my own. I accidentally knocked into Jake. He fell into the coffee table. He cried and cried, and I only got angrier. I finally put him in his crib. After a while I realized he was still crying. I went in, fit to burst, but one look at his face and I knew it was bad. I took him straight to the ER. I told them he fell into the table. And they told me it had to have been with some force to tear his intestine. I didn't tell them the truth and no one really pushed for it."

"Did Scott know?"

She shook her head. "I never told him."

"And with Maddie?"

"We were running late for her first day of pre-school. She was dancing around, laughing, giggling. Jake was fussy. It was just one of those mornings. On our way out the door, I had Jake in one arm and was trying to hurry Maddie along with the other hand on her back to keep her moving. I thought she had hold of the handrail but she didn't. She fell down the steps and broke her arm. If I hadn't been pushing her . . ."

She shook her head. "I didn't purposely hurt them,

but I was a terrible mother. No patience at all. Always losing my temper, always wishing I were somewhere else."

"And Scott didn't see any of this?"

"He worked so much. I resented him for that. Blamed him. Somehow convinced myself it was Scott's fault I was like I was. I was stupid, thinking a different man would make me happy, which is when I met Jerry. It took a long time for me to realize I was the only one in control of my happiness. I had a lot of time to soul-search while I was . . . away. I'm a different person now. I really am."

"I believe that, Sarah. I really do. I see it in your eyes." Slowly, I stood. "I came because I wanted to tell you that I have to turn this information over to the police. I didn't want the news to blindside you."

Her face paled. "But I thought you understood! I didn't hurt them on purpose! I've changed! Don't you think I've been punished enough?"

This was hard. So hard. "I think what you've been through is more than one person should ever bear. But for Maddie's and Jake's sake I need to make sure that you've really changed. I doubt after what you've been through the prosecutor will seek neglect charges, Sarah. They'll probably assign a social worker to monitor the kids. You have every chance to prove not only to the kids—but to you too—that you're going to be a different mother. A good mother. But here's the thing. You have a lot of hard work in front of you. Work that goes a little deeper than making cookies. You're going to need a lot of support from people who love you despite the mistakes you made. And perhaps the mistakes they've made."

She followed me to the front door. "You're talking about my mother."

I turned the doorknob. "You want your kids to forgive you. Don't you think you should set the example? Second chances *are* a precious gift."

"Maybe you're right," she said softly as a car pulled into the driveway.

I stepped outside as Scott unbuckled the kids from their car seats. He smiled when he saw me, waved. The kids came running forward calling out, "Mommy, Mommy!"

I looked at Sarah, saw the determination in her eyes, and hoped I wasn't wrong.

Leo had been watching for me. As soon as I pulled into his driveway, he opened his front door and waved me inside.

"I'm afraid to get my hopes up," he said once we were sitting in his living room.

"Even if this doesn't work, we'll find her. It's just a matter of time. Okay," I said, wishing Preston had answered her phone. She was going to be hopping mad she missed this. I held out my hand. "Think of one of the letters you wrote her."

A small smile played on his face.

I blushed. "You don't need to tell me what's in the letter."

"Darling, you're too young to hear such things." He placed his hand in mine. Images whirred by, taking me south, along the coast, across turquoise waters. To an island and a small waterfront house. Inside the house the letters sat in an old shoebox inside a closet.

I pulled my hand back. Waiting for the dizziness to pass, I said, "Do you have a pen? Paper?"

Leo dashed off.

The vertigo had faded by the time he came back, thrusting the pen and a notepad at me. I wrote down the landmarks I'd seen, including the island's name.

I picked up my phone and called Sean. A few rings later, his voice mail kicked on. I hadn't heard from him all day, not since that morning. I tried not to read too much into it, but I couldn't help the flash of jealousy. But soon . . . soon, Cara and I would be on even ground.

"Sean's not answering. I'll just call his brother, Sam."

"Something going on with that young man of yours?" Leo asked.

"Nothing we can't work out."

He nodded, his white eyebrows dipped in concern.

I dialed Sam and he answered on the fourth ring. "I think I know where she is," I said, watching the smile bloom across Leo's face.

"Lucy?"

"Sorry. Yeah, it's Lucy."

"You're talking about Joanne Winston?"

"I did a reading with Leo, using old love letters. I saw the letters in a house on an island in the Abacos." I described everything I'd seen.

"This is great, Lucy. I'll get my contact right on it. It shouldn't take long."

"It won't take long," I repeated to Leo. "Thanks, Sam."

Leo was looking at me as I hung up, a softness in his eyes. "Love can be complicated."

He was still talking about Sean. I smiled. "You know that better than anyone."

"I surely do. My best wishes to you."

"Thanks, Leo."

He kissed both my cheeks. "Call as soon as you hear anything."

"I promise."

"If you need me to talk some sense into that young man of yours, you let me know."

Laughing, I agreed to take him up on that offer if need be.

But if my plan worked, there would be no need. No need at all.

30

My GPS smugly told me that I'd reached my destination. I glanced up at the stucco apartment building. Despite my side trips to the Loehmans' house and to Leo's, I was right on time.

"Who is that with you?" my mother asked. "And why is Em living with Dovie?"

"Long story about Em, and it's my GPS, which I really need to give a name."

"Is that why you called me? To name your thingy-mahoo?"

"Is that a technical term?"

"Sassy!"

"Do I need a reason to call?"

"You're after something. I can tell with your tone. How about Judie for the thingy? And where are you?"

"I'd like to stick with my literary theme so Judie is out, and I'm at Cara Franklin's apartment."

"Judie *is* literary. 'Judy in Disguise With Glasses' is one of the best songs ever written. Who's this Cara? And you avoided my reference to you wanting something, so now I know you want something. You have my undying love. I'm not sure what else you want from me."

"And you call me sassy? And a bespectacled Judy is not quite the literary reference I was going for."

"Snob. John Fred and His Playboy Band would be crushed."

I smiled, purposely avoiding answering her query about Cara. "I'm thinking along the lines of Rebecca, or Jo from *Little Women*."

"How about Scarlett from *Gone with the Wind*? Oh, oh, or Scout from *To Kill a Mockingbird*. One of your favorite novels, as I recall."

This was why I loved my mother so very much. I suddenly wondered if Sarah Loehman had contacted Faye yet. Or if she ever would. I hoped so. I truly believed that relationship could be rebuilt over time.

"My GPS woman sounds too old to be Scout, so Scarlett it is. It fits. She definitely has a superiority attitude."

"And?"

"And what?"

"Why'd you call me, LucyD? Spit it out."

I drew in a deep breath. "I know you've had a few shocks this week, but can you handle another one?"

"I took a Xanax earlier, so I should be good."

I rolled my eyes, shut off the car. "I might need to use some of my trust fund."

Not for Maggie O'Meara—not yet. But for something equally important.

My mother gasped. "Lucy, why now?"

I looked at the apartment building. "I have a war to win. I have to go."

"War? What war?"

"Bye, Mum!" I snapped my phone closed.

I tamped down any reservations, checked my watch to make sure I was still on time, and climbed the steps to the second floor. Scrounging up my faltering nerves, I quickly knocked on the door. I knew Sean wasn't here—he'd returned my earlier call. He was done with Cara for the day and on his way to my place. *To be with me.* It bolstered courage.

84–6 is . . .

The door opened. Cara's jaw dropped.

"Hi," I said. "Should you be answering the door? Shouldn't you be in bed? Resting? Since you're so sick and all?"

"I—ah—no one else is here to answer it."

I barged right in. "Well, I'm here now." I linked arms with her. "Let's get you back to bed."

She wiggled free. "What's this about? What are you doing here?" she demanded with a gravelly, sultry voice I immediately envied.

"I came to see you, of course. Here." I thrust a bag at her. "I brought presents."

Pretty blue eyes blinked rapidly at me as if not quite believing I was standing in front of her. She sat down on the couch, slowly opened the bag. "Magazines? Books?"

"Keep digging." I sat next to her. "The good stuff is at the bottom. Junk food. You know, to keep you busy during your leave of absence."

I glanced around, wished I hadn't. Everywhere I looked were pictures of Sean and Cara together.

She followed my gaze. "We've been together since senior year of college."

"Long time," I said, not correcting her tense.

"Yes."

"Why didn't you get married?" I asked, knowing full well why. She'd all but deserted Sean as soon as he was well enough to care for himself after almost dying.

"I, ah, he, ah, we . . . That's none of your business."

"I think you're wrong about that."

"Sean and I were fine until you came along." She shook her head and her black hair shimmered in the light. "You just need to go away again."

"We both know that's not true."

"Things change." Her soulful eyes challenged me. "He seems to be spending a lot of time with me now."

"I'm not just walking away, Cara. I love him."

She snorted. "You can't compete with me. And definitely not now that I'm sick. Sean's going to be moving back in here soon enough."

"Why would he?"

"To take care of me. It's only a matter of time before he's back in my bed again for good."

My jaw clenched. "I don't think that's going to happen."

"You can't do anything about it. He'd never leave me here alone, not with all I have going on."

The doorbell rang. Right on time.

"I'll get that." I jumped up. In the hallway, I smiled

at the woman standing there. "Can you give us just another minute?" I left the door ajar.

"Who's that?" Cara asked.

"Your nurse. There will be two of them, splitting staying with you around the clock to make sure your every need is met until you have a firm diagnosis, and if you are seriously ill, they'll be staying on to help you out. If there's something the nurses can't provide, please let me know. I'll see you get it."

"Oh no! No way. I don't want a nurse."

"You don't have a choice."

"The hell I don't."

I opened my bag, dropped copies of the Handmaiden letters on the table. "No, you really don't."

She slowly sank down into the couch. "H-how did you know I sent them?"

"I'm psychic, remember?"

"There's no such thing."

"Then how did I know?"

Her eyebrows dipped, she looked at me, opened her mouth, closed it again. I sat down, trying to be cool and calm. I'd never been good at bluffing. Or calling them, for that matter. "Personally, I don't believe you're sick. It was smart to pick a disease that's nearly impossible to prove. But the letters . . . they were your big mistake. Because only another woman can truly understand why you mailed them. To hurt me, because you're jealous. And because you're so jealous I know you must want Sean back. But I have to wonder if your big ploy to get him back is worth going to jail?"

"Jail! For what?"

"Those letters fall under the stalking law, Cara." I stood. "I just wanted to warn you before I went to the police. The investigation might take some time, which is why I hired the nurses, but I'm sure you'll be proven guilty in the end."

She jumped up. "Wait!"

"What?"

"I'm sure we can work this out."

I picked up my bag. "I don't think so."

She rocked on her heels. "You can send the nurse home. I'm not sick."

Sick might be in the eye of the beholder. "I'm glad to hear that."

"And if you don't go to the police, I'll leave Sean alone."

"You must really love him," I said sarcastically.

"The hospital cut my hours. It's expensive living on my own. Not that you'd know about expensive. He's a decent guy," she said, shrugging. "He'll take care of me."

I stared at her, in shock. "You mean to tell me you put Sean and me through this because of money?"

"A girl's got to do what a girl's got to do."

"You're right about that." I headed to the door.

"So you won't go? To the police?" she asked, following after me.

"I haven't decided."

Her eyes narrowed. "But we had a deal. I can easily call off my end." She put a hand to her forehead, pretended to swoon. "I might have to call Sean. I don't feel so well."

"That's because you're not well," I said. "And I

think you're only allowed one call from jail, so you might want to think about calling a lawyer instead."

"Sean won't like that you threw his sick girlfriend in jail."

"We'll see about that."

Furious eyes rested on me. "You won't be able to prove a thing. I made sure my prints weren't on the notes. There's no DNA, no nothing."

I pulled open the door. "Did you get all that?"

"Every word." Marisol, dressed in scrubs, stood in the hallway with one of the thingy-mahoos (my mother would be proud) from Sean's toy bag. She rewound and played back Cara's confession.

Cara let out a small scream and slammed the door on us.

"She's mad," Marisol said.

A crash came from inside the apartment. And another as Cara threw things around. "Only a little. Thanks for helping me out."

We walked down the steps. "I had a blast. Now I can see why people do this for a living."

"Don't you remember being freezing in the car?"

"Everyone has to suffer for their art."

I laughed. "You're not planning to quit your job, are you?"

"Never. But it's been a nice side job. What would you have done if Cara hadn't confessed? If she was really sick after all?"

I appreciated that Marisol didn't lecture me about keeping the letters secret. "Tap into my trust fund and call in some nurses."

Marisol whistled. "Are you going to let the police know?"

"Probably not. I think I'll let her worry about it for a while though. Stew. She deserves some sleepless nights. Payback."

"You're going to have to tell Sean."

"Yeah." I wasn't looking forward to that conversation.

"I don't know what he saw in her anyway."

The cold stole my breath for a second. "Why? Because she's self-absorbed, malicious, crazy, and did I mention crazy?"

"No." She unlocked her car door. "Because she's nowhere near as pretty as you."

I smiled. Leave it to Marisol to tell me exactly what I wanted to hear.

31

Saturday afternoon the waiting area outside the security checkpoint at Logan was full of eager faces, waiting to be reunited with loved ones.

"Staring at it won't help," I said to Leo as he watched the arrivals and departures board with an eagle eye.

It was closing in on four o'clock. Joanne and Lea's flight had been delayed three times already. If this kept up, I was going to be late for Dovie's party. If I could get out of it without a year of guilt trips, I would. I yawned. I'd been up early, on a mission.

Preston checked her watch for the fifth time in a minute.

"They'll hold the deadline for you," I said.

"Yeah, but I still have to write the piece."

"Of course. Because this is all about you."

"Go away," she grumped.

The past two days had passed in a bit of a blur. I already had a new client for Lost Loves, my Christmas shopping was now all but done, and Sean and I had been spending a lot of time together. As much as we could manage with our crazy schedules. It wasn't until late yesterday afternoon when Cara called Sean to tell him she was moving to Arizona to live with her mother and stepfather that I told him about the Handmaiden letters and Cara's confession that she wasn't really sick.

"You took quite a risk," he said.

I shrugged. "All's fair in love and war, remember?"

"Love?"

"Love."

He took me in his arms, held me close. "You could have told me about the letters."

"You would have smothered me."

"If you want to call twenty-four-hour, never-leave-my-sight, glued-to-your-side protection smothering."

"Well, put that way, it sounds more like a fantasy come true."

And from that point on, all had been forgiven, and Cara had all but been forgotten.

It was sometime in the middle of last night when I realized that battle I had been waging had not been with Cara. It had been within me. Whether I'd been ready to make that leap into a full, long-term commitment, to voice what I truly wanted from Sean, what I truly wanted from *us*.

I should thank Cara, really, for provoking what I'd been trying so hard to deny—that I loved Sean Donahue. Deeply. Desperately. And knowing so, without a doubt, would help me fight anything that stood in our way. Stalkers, exes, curses, fates.

Leo paced a two-foot square. "What if she doesn't like me?"

He was referring to Lea. We'd already had this

conversation ten times today. I smiled. "She'll like you."

Sam had called last night with the news that Joanne and Lea were on their way to Boston. Leo had been beside himself since. Preston wasn't much better. She was alternately giddy and nervous.

"How can you be so sure?" he asked.

"Leo?"

"What?"

"Hush."

Using the information I provided, Sam's contact found Lea Czo yesterday afternoon. She and her husband lived on their sailboat months at a time but also rented a house on a small cay in the Abacos. The house, however, was where Lea's mother lived year-round. Both were home when Sam's contact found them.

And three hours later both were on a seaplane headed back to the States.

From Florida, they had a connection through Cincinnati before landing in Boston. Stormy weather had delayed their flight, making Leo a nervous wreck.

"There," Preston said, pointing to the board. "It's landed. It's landed," she squealed.

He went pale. "I can't do this."

I put my arm around him. "Come on. You lived for years as a prisoner of war and you're afraid of two women?"

"This is worse."

"I doubt that."

"It feels like it."

"Will you recognize Joanne?" I asked.

"I'd know her anywhere," he said, his voice thick.

Preston looked down, studying her shoes, but I saw the moisture in her eyes. She'd do just fine writing human interest stories.

Being taller, I spotted the pair of women first. There was no mistaking the genetic link between the two, mother and daughter.

Lea was a little slip of a woman, suntanned to a dark almond brown. She had her father's eyes, and the same face shape as her mother.

Joanne, I noticed, looked as nervous as Leo. With short white hair, deep tan, and a quick step, she didn't look anywhere near her eighty-plus years. She kept standing on tiptoe, obviously trying to see over the crowd of passengers leaving the terminal.

"You ready?" I whispered to Leo.

"For years I've been ready, Ms. Valentine."

I slowly spun him as Lea and Joanne emerged from the crowd. They both stopped still when they spotted us. Other passengers shot them dirty looks as they swerved around the teary-eyed obstacles.

Joanne stepped forward. Trembling hands covered her mouth. She was shaking her head as if in disbelief.

"Go," I said to Leo, nudging him.

He stepped forward. Stopped. Then in a burst, he rushed forward at the same time as Joanne, and he caught her, pulling her close.

Preston's lower lip quivered. I went to stand beside her.

Tears swelled in my eyes, blurring everything around me. I tried to stay strong and not cry like a baby. Then Joanne took a step back, and opened her arm to include her daughter.

Ah, hell. I let the tears fall.

Dovie's party was in full swing by the time I made it home. I took a quick nap, changed, and pulled my hair into a knot. I took a few minutes to let Thoreau out and play with Grendel, who stared at the fridge longingly.

"We're cutting back on the cheese," I said.

His tail shot up.

"Sorry."

I handed him a salmon kitty treat, which he sniffed, then dismissed.

"Suit yourself," I said as I picked up my handbag, checked to make sure I had everything, and drove up to Dovie's so I wouldn't ruin my shoes.

A valet driver insisted on taking my car, but it was Dovie who opened the door.

"Look at you, all dolled up. Beautiful," Dovie said, air-kissing my cheeks.

"Thanks."

She cornered me in the foyer. "LucyD, there is a very handsome man here saying you invited him. True?"

"Who? Mr. McGill?"

"Yes, I believe that's his name."

A uniformed woman appeared out of nowhere to take my coat. "Then yes, I invited him."

Dovie grabbed my arm. "What's this about? Who is he?"

A waiter passed by with a tray of champagne. I

snagged a glass. "A very nice gentleman. I suggest you get to know him."

She smiled, fluffed her hair. "You have good taste in men, Lucy. Speaking of which, is Sean here yet?"

"Not yet. He said he had something important to do and that it might take a while."

"Something with *her*?"

"I don't know. I'm not too worried about that." I filled her in on Cara's move to Arizona.

Dovie laughed. "A sure white flag on her part."

I smiled, enjoying my new love-can-conquer-all outlook. It had to be true. I refused to believe otherwise.

I caught sight of Em and Aiden standing near the piano. "Is Marisol here yet?"

"Canceled about an hour ago. Emergency call at the clinic."

Emergency call, my foot. It was all part of the plan—which seemed to be working. Maybe Raphael was right. *They know. They feel.* "Have you spoken to Dad lately, by the way?"

"Not a peep. Why?"

Now probably wasn't the best time to tell her about Cutter. "No reason."

She raised an eyebrow, turned, and disappeared into the crowd.

I wandered into the living room, glanced around. My mother and father were bent head to head, sharing a deep conversation. I left them alone. Suz and her husband Teddy were cuddled by the fire. They only had eyes for each other.

Preston appeared at my elbow and nodded toward my parents. "Inseparable since they arrived."

"They're fond of each other."

"The separate houses probably help."

I snapped my head to look at her.

"Don't worry. My lips are sealed."

"Why do I feel like you have an unspoken 'for now' at the end of that sentence?"

She shrugged. "You need to learn to be more trusting."

I scoffed. "You need to learn to be more trustworthy."

She smiled as she sipped her drink. "I heard from Maggie O'Meara. We're going to do an article."

"I'm glad. I think she needs all the help she can get."

"And"—she sipped—"Santa left a present on my doorstep this afternoon, all wrapped in pretty paper with a bow and everything."

"Oh?"

She blinked. "Thank you."

"You're welcome," I said. "But don't go thinking this means I like you or anything."

I didn't quite know what possessed me to wake up early this morning to make the long drive to Falmouth to buy the Little House book Preston had loved so much, but I found I wanted to do something nice for her, to let her know that she wasn't as alone in this world as she thought.

"Don't worry. I know you only went down there to see that table again."

"It was sold." I'd been heartbroken to see the huge red tag.

"Really? Someone bought that hunk of junk?"

"You better watch it, or I'll take your present back."

Happiness glowed in her blue eyes. "No takesies back. I have something for you too." She pulled an envelope from her handbag.

"This isn't going to be a gift certificate for Fruit of the Looms, is it?"

"Nah. That's coming in the mail."

I smiled as I lifted the flap. I studied the sheet of paper and oddly felt like crying again.

Preston said, "I talked to Oscar and turned down his offer to connect me with someone at the *Globe*."

The paper in my hand was a photocopy of an admission form for the journalism program at a local community college.

"I'll take some classes locally, then maybe transfer to somewhere bigger once I prove I can do it."

"Prove to who?"

"Whom. And myself."

"Can I keep this?" I asked, blinking hard.

She nodded.

"Thank you," I said with meaning. "It's a really great present."

She waved it off. "I'll definitely be busy. Between work and school and the articles for Lost Loves."

"You know, you don't have to keep writing those."

"Ah, ah, ah." She wagged a finger. "I'm not so easy to get rid of."

I cracked a smile. "I know. Trust me, I've tried."

She rolled her eyes.

"What are you doing here anyway?" I asked. "Don't you have a deadline to meet?"

"Met. The story just flowed. My editor loved it. You're stuck with me the whole night long."

"Then I definitely need another drink."

She was laughing as I walked away, headed for the kitchen. On my way, the bell rang in the foyer and I waved off the uniformed maid, and pulled open the door. My throat tight, I squeezed out a hello.

"Sorry I'm late," he said.

"What are you doing here?" I asked.

$45 + 9$ is 54.

He waved an invitation. "Someone named Raphael sent me an invitation. Was that okay?" he asked. "Wrote something about stopping a rolling ball?"

Looked like Raphael wasn't done with his physics lesson quite yet. He'd always been the best of teachers.

"It's absolutely all right. Come on in."

He waited, stared at me. "Ms. Valentine?" he said as he stepped into the house.

"Please call me Lucy."

"I want to ask you something." Cutter McCutchan looked dashing in a dark suit, silver tie. His hair had been combed back off his forehead, James Dean style, and he looked so handsome I could see why Mum had fallen for Dad all those years ago.

My heart throbbed in my ears. "Anything."

"I need to know."

"What?"

"Why can't I see your color?"

My color? Oh . . . "My aura?"

"You know what I'm talking about?"

I nodded. And I knew why he couldn't see my

aura. Because no Valentine could see another Valentine's colors. Blood relations, at least.

"How? Why? It's been bothering me for days. You're the only person I've ever met who doesn't have a color around them."

"Your mother hasn't spoken to you yet, has she?"

"My mother? What's she have to do with this?"

I squeezed my eyes closed, not sure what to do. Slowly, I opened them. Enough was enough. I grabbed his wrist, pulled him into Dovie's study. I flipped on the light, closed the door.

He raked his hand through his hair. "Don't think I'm coming on to you, but I get this funny feeling when I look at you."

It was no wonder. We shared the same heart-shaped face, the same nose, the dimple in our right cheeks.

"There's a lot you need to learn, but I don't think I'm the person to tell you."

"Like what? What do I need to learn?"

I held up a finger. I opened the door, flagged down a server, passed him twenty dollars to find my father.

Stepping back into the study, I closed the door behind me, locked it, so no one would barge in. I smiled at him. "I'm not a crazy woman."

"That's good to know."

"I want you to understand that before I say what I'm about to say."

"Is there a reason you locked the door?"

It had taken him no time at all to start acting like a pesky little brother. "Before all hell breaks loose, and yeah, it's about to break loose, I want you to know"—I swallowed hard—"that I'm really happy to know you."

I nearly laughed at the look on his face.

"Okay," he mumbled, eyes wide as he edged toward the door.

The door shook as someone tried to open it. "Lucy! What's going on?" my father demanded.

I glanced back at Cutter. "You need to meet someone."

"Who?"

"My father. Who also happens to be . . ." I pulled open the door, grabbed my father's sleeve.

"Lucy, this is highly unorthod—"

". . . your father," I finished.

Both took a step back from each other.

After a good minute, I walked over, stood between them. Looking at my father, I said, "No more secrets. He wants to know why he can't see my aura. Tell him. Tell him everything."

My father cupped my face. Moisture shimmered in his eyes. "I will, Lucy Juliet. Go on now."

I couldn't help myself. I rushed over and hugged Cutter. Much to my surprise, he hugged me back.

Reluctantly, I let go, hurried out of the room.

My mother stood in the hallway. "What's going on?"

"Cutter came to the party."

She gasped.

Dovie came over. "What are you two doing? Who's in the study? I thought I closed it off."

"Dad and Cutter."

"Who? Wait. Cutter McCutchan?"

"Your grandson," my mother said, not taking her eyes from the door.

Dovie's hand went to her heart. "My what?"

I smiled at her. "It's a boy! Congratulations!"

"I need to sit down, I need a drink, and someone needs to tell me what the hell is going on." She dropped onto the bottom step of the stairs.

Preston quickly stepped in and handed Dovie a champagne glass. "I saw him come in," she said when I raised my eyebrow in question. "I thought alcohol might be needed."

"I'm waiting," Dovie snapped.

I quickly explained to her what had been going on.

She was still soaking it in when Preston tapped my arm. "What did Cutter mean, about the colors? I heard him when he came in."

I was saved from answering by the doorbell. I rushed over, pulled open the door, smiled when I saw Sean standing there.

"What's going on?" he asked, watching my mother press her ear to the study's door.

"Dad's in there with Cutter."

"He knows?"

I nodded. "I think it's going to be okay."

Dovie fanned herself. "How can you say that? This is—" She broke off. "Wait! Does he have kids yet? Am I a great-grandmamma?"

I glanced at Preston. She would know better than any of us.

"Sorry, Dovie," she said. "No kids. Now about those colors—"

Dovie jumped up. "Now I've got two of you to nag. What are they saying?" she asked my mother.

"I don't know!" Mum said in a harsh whisper. "If you'd stop your yammering!"

"Hey, now." Dovie bumped Mum out of the way. "Move over."

Sean laughed. "This probably isn't a good time to steal you for a second, is it?"

I glanced at Preston. "It's the perfect time. Where are you stealing me to?"

"Your house."

"I don't think that's so much stealing as returning me, Mr. Donahue."

"Either way."

I tried not to think about my shoes as we tromped through the snow, his arm around me. "Is that a U-haul in front of my house?"

"Don't worry, I'm not moving in."

"Did I say I was worried?"

He stopped, turned to me, and kissed me. His arms wrapped me in heat, his kisses warmed me from the inside out. I wanted desperately to tell him I loved him, to yell it, but I held it in, not wanting to tempt Cupid's Curse.

Only the Christmas tree was lit as we stepped into my house. Grendel and Thoreau welcomed us home, purring and yapping.

"I have your Christmas present," Sean said.

I pressed in close to him. "Was that kiss in the yard a preview? Because that's a present I could really love."

His eyes glowed. "No."

"How disappointing."

"I have a feeling that won't last." He flipped on the light, spun me around.

"Oh! Oh!" I waved at my eyes so I wouldn't cry. I'd shed enough tears lately. "It's . . . How did you know?"

"I was on the phone with you, remember?"

I could barely move as I stared at my new dining room table. A small burl-elm and fruitwood dining table, magnificently crafted, early nineteenth century. With an inlay of acorn and oak leaf circling the edge.

"It took some doing. First I had to call Preston, find out what antiques shop you'd gone to. Then this feisty old lady haggles with me for an hour. I finally buy it and then the shop doesn't have delivery! I had to drag Sam down there today to pick it up. Do you like it?"

I looked deep into his eyes. "I love it. But you shouldn't have spent so much on me!"

"All's fair in love and war," he said simply.

"Love?" I asked.

"Love."

I jumped into his arms. He caught me and spun me around, kissing me so deeply and thoroughly I never wanted him to let me go.

Grendel rreowed. Thoreau barked and bounced around Sean's feet, tripping him. "Whoa!"

Sean put a hand out to break our fall onto the couch. Somehow, he ended up on the floor. Laughing, I held out a hand to help him up.

The visions came slowly. Of me in a white dress,

of him in a dark tux. Unexpectedly, tears filled my eyes.

"I've got a present for you too," I said. Shaky, I dropped in front of the tree, reached for Sean's book.

He saw my tears. "Is everything okay?"

I shoved away thoughts of curses ruining this moment. I thought about my family, my friends, of him and me. "More than okay. It's everything I could ever wish for."

Read on for an excerpt from Heather Webber's

next book

Absolutely, Positively

A Lucy Valentine Novel

Coming in February 2011 from St. Martin's Paperbacks

1

Suzannah Ruggieri blew into Valentine, Inc., like a Category Five hurricane. The antique mahogany door slammed into its stopper, rattling the beveled glass panes. Her eyes were wild, her hair disheveled, her round high cheekbones flaming. Winded, she huffed, "Hurry! The Lone Ranger's back!"

Spinning, she rushed out the way she came, her heavy footsteps thudding on the cherrywood stairs leading down to Beacon Street.

Preston Bailey, roving reporter, didn't need to be told twice. She jumped up from the russet-colored loveseat in the reception area, sending notes flying in all directions. She barely paused at the door to see if I was following. "Lucy, come on!"

I jumped up and hesitated. I had been manning Suz's desk while she was at lunch. If I left, no one would be here to answer the phones. I had a responsibility to the company—after all, my name was on the door. Valentine, Inc., the country's most successful matchmaking firm, had been in the family for generations. And though I wasn't a true matchmaker like my father, I managed to have a great success rate with clients in my division of the company, Lost Loves. My father and I used our psychic gifts in very different ways.

"Lucy!" Preston bellowed up the stairs. The sound echoed up to the third floor and back down to me. "The. Lone. Ranger. Move your ass!"

Ah, hell. I grabbed my coat and followed Preston down the steps and out the thick metal door into a typical gunmetal gray February afternoon of a Boston winter.

We dodged through stopped traffic and sprinted toward the mob gathered at Boston Common. A piece of paper fluttered across the crunchy, dormant grass, and I stomped on it.

"You got one!" Preston cried.

I picked up the twenty-dollar bill. Others floated by, people chasing after them, pushing and shoving.

"Do you see him?" Preston stood on tiptoes, but even in heeled boots she was vertically challenged.

Standing a good five inches taller, I scanned the throbbing crowd for any sign of a masked man. "No."

"He has to be here somewhere!" She threaded her way through the masses, throwing bony elbows and hips to get people to move aside. There was no stopping a reporter on the hunt of a huge story.

The Lone Ranger had struck again.

It was the fourth time in as many weeks. No one knew where he came from or who he was. By all accounts, he simply appeared in a mask and cowboy hat and started throwing money.

Last week, the unofficial tally hit two thousand dollars. By the look of the loot still skittering across the ground, this week's total was going to be even higher. Preston, a reporter for the *South Shore Beacon*, a daily paper that mostly covered areas south of the city, had taken to trolling the Common during the day, even though she was *supposed* to be writing feature stories on my Lost Loves clients. She was dying to find the man the media had labeled The Lone Ranger and crack the reasoning behind such outlandish behavior.

A WHDH news crew arrived on the scene, and a reporter tottered across the grass to interview people clutching fistfuls of money.

As I tucked the twenty into my pocket and leaned against a tree, waiting for the crowd to thin, I glanced to my left and found a homeless man watching me intently from a nearby bench. Caught, he looked down and started fussing with a plastic garbage bag filled with his worldly goods. He held a Thermos of what I hoped was coffee.

Sudden guilt flooded me. I didn't need the money, yet here I was eager to catch a few flying twenties. I tried to justify that I'd been caught up in the moment, but that excuse didn't pass muster as I'd caught three twenties last week and had used them to buy myself a cute scarf from a shop in Harvard Square.

Feeling slightly sick with shame, I pulled the twenty from my pocket, walked over, and handed it to him.

He looked up at me with a wary, faded blue gaze before reaching out with gloved fingers for the cash. A holey knit cap covered his head and an oversized black Michelin Man–type coat sheltered him from icy gusts. Dirt smudges darkened pale, yellow-tinted skin. White stubble covered his chin.

"Mind if I sit?" I asked.

He nodded to the bench.

This, I thought, was the real story. This man and all the other homeless who called the Common home, even in the midst of a brutal winter.

"You didn't want in on the action?" I asked, nodding to the crowd. I spotted Preston weaving in and out, still searching. Suz was headed my way.

"Legs don't work so well anymore," he shouted, his voice becoming louder with each word. "Can't fight off those young'uns like I used to, and it's not so bad being poor."

I jumped a bit before I adjusted to the volume. I only had vague memories of my Grandpa Henry, who died when I was five, but I remembered he used to shout, too. He'd needed a hearing aid and had been stubborn about getting one. Vanity at its finest.

"Did you see the guy who was throwing the money?" I asked loudly, doubting this man's lack of a hearing aid had anything to do with how it would look.

He took a draw from his Thermos. "Masked. Hat. No horse. Tossing money this way and that."

That about summed it up. Then I smiled when I realized he was speaking (well, shouting) in rhyme.

Suz counted twenties, her eyes glowing, as she walked toward us. It just went to show that anyone could get caught up in a situation. Valentine, Inc., paid her well. Not only because she was a valued employee, but because she was practically family. And being so, we had entrusted her with all the family secrets. A good salary ensured she'd keep them.

"One hundred forty! Woo-ha! I'll be treating myself to some nice wine while eating a nice big steak at The Hilltop tonight."

I jerked my head toward the guy next to me, silently asking her to make a donation.

Suz frowned as she followed the motion.

I widened my eyes and continued twitching.

She huffed, peeled off two twenties, and handed them to him. "Oh, fine." She gave him the rest of the cash. "You need it more than I do."

He quickly tucked the money inside his glove and stood up.

"Ladies, I'll be on my way," he shouted, tipping an imaginary cap. "Have yourselves a wonderful day." He winked, turned, and hobbled off.

"For the love of Dr. Seuss, Lucy. You know he's probably just going to drink the money away," Suz said in an are-you-crazy kind of whisper.

"So were you."

She flipped her dark hair. "Touché."

I stood and searched for Preston's spiky platinum

hair in the thinning crowd. "Besides, you don't know that he'll spend the money on alcohol. Maybe he's hungry. Maybe *he* wants a nice steak."

Soulful eyes narrowed. "You don't know he *won't* drink it away."

"You don't know he *will*."

"You can't be that naïve, Lucy."

I'd lost a lot of my naiveté over the last six months when I'd started freelancing as a consultant for the Massachusetts State Police, using my psychic ability to find lost objects to help locate missing persons. Often the cases didn't come with happily ever afters.

"I just want to believe that in every person there's a little decency. Is that wrong?" My breath formed little white clouds as I spoke. It was twenty freezing degrees, and I questioned why I'd left the warmth of the office.

Oh, right. Greed.

Now I felt really queasy.

Her eyes softened. "It's dangerous to only see the good in people. You, of all people, should know that."

I tossed a look over my shoulder. The homeless man had only made it ten feet or so, shuffling along at a snail's pace. It was because I'd seen firsthand the evils of the world that I searched for the good. I had to.

"We should head back," I said.

"What about Preston?"

"I'll leave a trail of bread crumbs."

The cold was starting to seep under my skin as we climbed the steps to the second-floor office. The door to Valentine, Inc., was ajar. I cautiously peeked inside and found my grandmother, Dovie, sitting in Suz's desk chair, flipping through client files. She harbored dreams of matchmaking, but she'd married into the family. Therefore, she didn't possess the ability to read auras, genetic only to bloodline Valentines—a gift, legend declared, bestowed on my family by Cupid himself.

"What are you doing here?" I asked Dovie. My father would have another heart attack if he found her rifling through his files. Was she trying to make matches or looking for love herself? Her last relationship, with a man I'd set her up with, had only lasted three fun-filled weekends. Dovie, like all Valentines, was as commitment-phobic as George Clooney. That being said, she might change her mind if *he* came walking through the door.

My mother came in from the back hallway, carrying two mugs of coffee. She handed one to Dovie and air-kissed my cheek, then Suz's. Mum was fairly glowing. Her hazel eyes danced, the gold specks glittering, and a smile flirted playfully at the corners of her lips.

"What's up with you?" I asked. She looked truly lovely in a purple cowl-necked sweater, dark jeans, and ballet slippers. Her pixie-style hair had just been cut and colored a golden blond. She looked younger. Happier.

"Me?" Mum waved a hand in dismissal as she sat on the loveseat. "Nothing. Nothing at all."

"Something," Suz said, shooing Dovie from her desk chair. "You look great."

Mum shrugged coyly. "Been on a little diet, that's all."

"Diet?" Mum didn't diet. Ever.

"I'm getting older," Mum said. "I need to be more

careful about my weight. I'm taking a Zumba class, too." Her eyes brightened. "You should come with me, LucyD!"

"A zoo what?" I asked.

Dovie laughed and launched into a cha-cha, her long legs lithe and graceful. When she was younger, she danced burlesque at a club in Manhattan—it was where she'd met my grandfather. After they married, and secretly divorced, she continued her dance training and eventually became a choreographer. These days she mostly used her talents for local musical theater and social events, but it didn't take much for her to randomly break into dance. "Zumba. It's an exercise program featuring dancing."

"Fun!" Suz squealed. "When and where? Count me in!"

Diet *and* exercise? I stared at Mum. Who was this woman? Certainly not *my* mother. "What's going on? I mean, what's *really* going on? You're not sick, are you?" She didn't look sick, but it would take something as monumentally life-changing as a chronic illness to get her to break a lifetime of (bad) habits.

"Do I need a reason to better myself?" Her nose twitched.

Aha! She'd stumbled on the word *better*. She wasn't as keen on all this diet and exercise as she let on. The nose twitch was a dead giveaway she was hiding something.

Dovie was still cha-cha-ing. "Oh go on, Judie. Tell her. It's past time."

Mum shot her an evil look. Good thing the two of them were the best of friends, a relationship Dad absolutely hated. His mother. His somewhat-ex wife (technically they were still married). It was a nightmare for him when they ganged up.

"What? What-what?" I pleaded.

Dovie dragged Suz into her dance. The two held hands as Dovie counted aloud, "One two three, cha cha cha." She thrust a hip and sing-songed in the same cadence, "Judie has a boyfriend, cha cha cha."

I gasped. "You do? Who?"

"Just someone," Mum said.

"Spill!" I urged. Though my parents were happily separated, it had been years since Mum had had anyone serious in her life. Her little on and off flings with my father hardly counted.

"Where's Sean today?" Mum asked.

She was referring to Sean Donahue, the super sexy PI who worked upstairs and partnered with me in Lost Loves. We were partnered in other ways, too. Just thinking about him made me go all warm and gooey inside.

"Don't change the subject," I said.

"I was simply asking a question, LucyD," she said.

The door crashed open. Startled, I jumped as Preston stormed in, limping.

"How can he just vanish?" she asked, throwing her hands in the air. "Poof. Gone. How? You'd think that a man who was tossing twenties like rice at a wedding wouldn't escape unnoticed."

"The Lone Ranger?" Dovie asked.

"Struck again," Suz said, setting her desk to rights. She was fussy about what went where and Dovie had obviously been rifling for a while before we caught her. "I had a hundred and forty dollars before Lucy made me give it all away to a homeless guy."

"He'll probably just drink it away." Mum sipped her coffee.

"That's what I said!" Suz shot me a look.

I sat on the edge of the couch. I could argue, but I was outnumbered.

"Well, I didn't get anything." Preston sighed. "Not any money, not a story, not anything. And I broke my heel." She sat next to Mum and peeled off her boot. The heel dangled sadly. "Someone had to have seen something."

"Doubtful." Dovie patted her hair to make sure it was still in place. Her stunning signature white locks had been loosely twisted into a knot at the base of her neck. "Once money starts flying, no one's going to notice anything but the green."

"I suppose you're right," Preston said, leaning back. "But there has to be a way to catch him." There was a look in her eyes I was coming to recognize. She was hatching a plan.

I checked my watch. Preston and I were meeting with a new client soon. The whole new-boyfriend conversation with Mum would have to wait until I had more time for a more prepared inquisition. "Are you two in town for a little shopping?" I asked Dovie.

"Actually, no," she answered.

"We came to see Sean."

"Sean? Why?" I scanned the headline.

LOCAL MAN STILL MISSING.

"I'm hoping you won't mind sharing," Dovie said, "because I want to hire him."